PENGUIN CANADA

RED SNOW

Criminal lawyer MICHAEL SLADE has acted in over one hundred murder cases. His specialty is the law of insanity. He argued the last death penalty case in the highest court. Backed by his experience, the fourteen Slade thrillers fuse the genres of police and legal procedure, whodunit, impossible crime, history, suspense, and horror. For the real-life story behind each novel, visit the Morgue at Slade's website, **www.specialx.net**.

MICHAEL SLADE

RED SNOW

PENGUIN
CANADA

PENGUIN CANADA

Published by the Penguin Group

Penguin Group (Canada), 90 Eglinton Avenue East, Suite 700, Toronto, Ontario, Canada
M4P 2Y3 (a division of Pearson Canada Inc.)
Penguin Group (USA) Inc., 375 Hudson Street, New York, New York 10014, U.S.A.
Penguin Books Ltd, 80 Strand, London WC2R 0RL, England
Penguin Ireland, 25 St Stephen's Green, Dublin 2, Ireland
(a division of Penguin Books Ltd)
Penguin Group (Australia), 250 Camberwell Road, Camberwell, Victoria 3124, Australia
(a division of Pearson Australia Group Pty Ltd)
Penguin Books India Pvt Ltd, 11 Community Centre, Panchsheel Park,
New Delhi – 110 017, India
Penguin Group (NZ), 67 Apollo Drive, Rosedale, North Shore 0745, Auckland,
New Zealand (a division of Pearson New Zealand Ltd)
Penguin Books (South Africa) (Pty) Ltd, 24 Sturdee Avenue, Rosebank, Johannesburg 2196,
South Africa

Penguin Books Ltd, Registered Offices: 80 Strand, London WC2R 0RL, England

First published 2010

1 2 3 4 5 6 7 8 9 10 (WEB)

Manufactured in Canada.

LIBRARY AND ARCHIVES CANADA CATALOGUING IN PUBLICATION

Slade, Michael
Red snow / Michael Slade.

ISBN 978-0-14-316779-2

I. Title.

PS8587.L35R42 2010   C813'.54   C2009-906009-4

Visit the Penguin Group (Canada) website at **www.penguin.ca**
Special and corporate bulk purchase rates available; please see
www.penguin.ca/corporatesales or call 1-800-810-3104, ext. 2477 or 2474

For Steve Pohl and Slade Art

And, as his strength
Failed him at length,
He met a pilgrim shadow—
"Shadow," said he,
"Where can it be—
This land of Eldorado?"

"Over the Mountains
Of the Moon,
Down the Valley of the Shadow,
Ride, boldly ride,"
The shade replied,—
"If you seek for Eldorado!"

—EDGAR ALLAN POE, "ELDORADO"

WHITE GOLD

WHISTLER, BRITISH COLUMBIA
December 2009

"*Yippie kay-yah!* Powder super G!"

It had puked the night before, so white gold sprayed behind him in a big rooster tail as he rode his board down four thousand vertical feet of virgin snow. "Puking" was snow hound slang for a hard snowfall, and all those Olympic hopefuls who'd been lured to Whistler for the upcoming weekend's trial runs were currently snapping on skis or boards to schralp both mountains. "Schralp" as in laying down tracks till the fat conditions were gone. Call it OCD, but what the hell. For Boomer, the thrill of boarding was in going where no one had boarded before, just him and a landscape of untracked powder, free from the affront of some yahoo's name peed in the snow.

"*Yee-hah!* Ride 'em, cowboy!"

Boomer had spearheaded the throng, taking the first lift up to the summit that morning. From there, he'd had his pick of over eight thousand skiable acres, including three glaciers, twelve alpine bowls, two hundred trails, and forty lifts. As any boarder will tell you, "Friends don't have friends on powder days." It's every man for himself in a post-snowfall feeding frenzy. The Olympic herd had complicated things, however, for they were *all* top-notch, and each one yearned to conquer a virgin run. As the day progressed, the white gold had begun to mine out.

Time for poaching.

A poacher was a boarder who cruised the backcountry, that fabled realm beyond the boundary ropes, where only the laws of nature applied. The ski patrol had closed this face because wind-whipped snow deposited on the lee side of its ridges had formed unstable tongues of ice. What looked like meringue was really a time bomb set to collapse on those below. But Boomer knew a run that bypassed the cornice hazards, and he felt compelled to shred that chute after every big dump.

"Yabba dabba doo! Tarzan doesn't pay taxes!"

So here he came, riding the run as free as a dude can be, a poacher ripping through "pow" on waves of white. His weight on his back foot and leaning into lazy turns, Boomer carved wide arcs down to the glades. Wisps of snow whipped his boots and lassoed his bent knees. Small avalanches of slough followed him into the trees. The only noise was the sound of snow flattening under his board. Then the trees closed in and the run plunged steeply, forcing Boomer to slash across the fall line with air between his turns.

Swoosh ...

Cold, crisp wind rushed past his ears, the snow parting before him like the Red Sea before Moses. All board runs weren't created equal, and as this run went from eighties rad to *über* cool, his speed increased.

Whap! Whap!

A switch or two revved things up, then ...

Shwwt!

"Hi-ho, Silver!"

Boomer rode his ribbon of white gold down the crook of the gully. Ahead, the chute ended in a sudden cliff drop. There, this poacher would abruptly transform into a huckster, a boarder with a penchant for hurling himself off bone-breaking precipices.

High noon. The sun overhead beamed into the gully, and Boomer chased his shadow down the chute. In a second, he would launch off the lip of the gully like a ballistic missile, hanging for long, effortless moments in thin air. Reaching down to grab his board, he'd drop, drop, drop, until he landed steep, smooth, and soft at the bottom of the jump.

Pulling himself into a tuck as he approached the lip, Boomer saw his shadow vanish over the cliff face. Then his board soared into the bright blue yonder, his feet sliced off cleanly above the ankles. Propelled as far as momentum could carry it, his headless body spewed blood across the powder. He, however, lagged behind, hanging in midair until gravity yanked his severed head face down into red snow.

BUSHWHACKED

Corporal Nick Craven had no trouble tracking the path of contamination to the crime scene. Normally, most bodies were found sprawled on a patch of floor or ground. The killer's route to and from the corpse was a potential gold mine of clues, so the Mounties would cool their spurs until the Ident techs had created a clean corridor for them to follow.

But no need here.

This case had opened with two lovers having an adulterous nooner. A premature climax resulted when a snowboard smashed through the window and knocked the man unconscious in mid hump. The woman started screaming and scrambled from the tangled sheets to call 911. The medics who responded took one look at the severed feet riding the wayward board and concluded there was a man uphill with no way down.

Thus, the ski patrol was called to the rescue.

There was always some fool running into trouble, a back-country maverick who thought hazard signs didn't apply to him. A boarder could trip over a buried tree branch at a thousand miles an hour and break a leg or two. Or veer off course and tumble headfirst into a tree well, suffocating himself.

This, however, was new. A tale to tell at happy hour in Whistler's après-ski bars. What could slice a snowboarder off at the shins?

The ski patrol found out.

That's why the Mounties had been called.

And since Nick was the best skier among the cops currently posted to Security at Whistler, he was the one now shadowing the path of contamination to the crime scene.

For once, there was no need for Ident to mark the route. The Mountie was free to take any path untouched by the tracks of Boomer's board.

No tracks meant no forensic clues.

With his blond hair and prosthetic ear tucked under his black toque, the corporal followed the line a snowball would travel if it rolled down through the glades to the gully. At the chute, where both flanks were thick with trees, he snowplowed over the swath the ski patrol had churned up. Luckily, he knew this wasn't the route the killer had taken, for the ski patrol had already found snowshoe tracks leading down one side of the chute to where the trap was set.

Ski tips together and heels spread, Nick plowed down to the body, which had come to rest just this side of the ledge that would have launched the boarder into the air.

The ski patrollers guarding the corpse were known as Moe and Curly. Moe was Moe's real name, and Curly, of course, had curly hair. There was a Larry, too, but he was sick with the flu. The fourth member of the patrol, off on another rescue, was named Gene. The Stooges, however, had dubbed him Iggy.

"Stop!" Curly shouted as Nick approached. Waving one arm of his ski patrol jacket, red with white crosses on the chest and upper sleeve, he stood uphill from the body, which was sprawled in a drift of bloody snow. "Want to lose your head?"

Nick dug in his edges. "Fill me in," he replied.

"Boomer got bushwhacked."

"Boomer?" said Nick. His breath billowed out like a dialogue bubble in a cartoon.

"Dominick Ricci. Everyone called him Boomer. His dad was one of the Crazy Canucks."

Young and wild, with a kamikaze flair, the Crazy Canucks had burst upon the European ski scene in the 1970s. With a fearlessness that knew no bounds, the Canadians raced downhill as fast as they could, scoring fifteen World Cup wins, and even laying claim to the downhill title that Europe had never lost. A witness to their antics—which included as many spectacular falls as it did spectacular wins—had once muttered about those "crazy Canucks," and the name stuck.

"You sure it's Boomer?"

"Yep," Curly said. Ice was caked to the curls hanging stiffly to his shoulders. "On powder days, Boomer always rides this run. The season's pass clipped to his jacket says it's him. We tracked his bleeper and found *this*."

Worn by off-piste snow hounds, a bleeper transmits a high-pitched signal that can be used to rescue mavericks lost in the backcountry or buried beneath avalanches. A radio transceiver homes in on the beacon and calculates its location.

"Show me what happened," said Nick.

Releasing the skis from his boots, he swapped them for snowshoes and tailed Curly down the gully to where Moe stood beside a warning barrier fashioned from crossed skis. Although his face was browned by a tanning parlor, Moe looked exhausted from what Nick suspected were too many nights entertaining snow bunnies.

Ah yes, Whistler!

Sex, drugs, and white gold.

"The killer descended from there," said Curly, pointing up through the trees. "You can see the line of snowshoe tracks leading down from the ridge to the trap."

"How do you get to the ridge?"

"Ski down from the peak till the treeline becomes a dead end. It's dangerous because the route passes under one of the cornice hazards that has closed this face permanently."

"A poor run for a trap," said Nick.

"Not if you knew that Boomer poached. On powder days, he'd invariably shred this run."

"Who knew that?"

"Regulars at the Gilded Man. Those who haunt the pub call this Boomer's Run."

"And the ski patrol?"

"Sure. Boomer wasn't a fool. We don't sweep closed slopes when the sun goes down, so he always carried a bleeper and notified us before boarding here. If we didn't hear from him within a few hours, two of us would ski Boomer's Run."

"Sounds dangerous."

"Nah. This run has no cornice hazards. The slope's closed because the surrounding runs do."

"I meant that *you* could have run into the trap, too. Maybe Boomer was bait for the ski patrol."

Curly frowned. "Why?"

"Who knows? Motives for murder vary as much as the personalities of the killers."

"You think we were the intended victims?"

"Most likely not. But I want your input into who might have done this. Let's assume the killer knows that Boomer chutes this run. He—or she—skis to the ridge above the gully, then snowshoes down through the trees. Show me the trap."

Curly ushered the Mountie around the makeshift barrier of crossed skis to a pair of trees flanking the lip that would launch a poacher into space. The sun no longer shone into the depths of the gully, but despite the rising shadow line, Nick easily spotted the two blades strung across the chute. The lower was a cutlass wedged into the tree trunks just above the surface of the bloody snow. The upper, no wider than a tape measure, crossed the path at what would have been the throat level of a boarder pulling himself into a tuck to shoot off the ledge.

Shewww …

Nick imagined he was Boomer roaring down the gully. Ahead, he saw the blue sky and a momentary glint of sunlight off steel. The upper blade slipped under his chin and slit through his neck like a knife through butter. The cutlass below thwacked his shins. The snowboard, with both feet still attached, soared off the ledge and kept on skidding until it shattered the cabin window below. The headless, footless body vanished into scarlet mist. The human brain can remain conscious after beheading for up to a minute. The last thing Boomer would have seen as his head somersaulted to the snow was a dark figure emerging from the trees.

"Where's the head?" Nick asked.

"It landed there," said Curly. He pointed to an indent in the snow. "See where the snowshoes switch back to skis? The killer took the head and skied off the ledge."

EL DORADO

They, too, had come for the gold.

The conquistadors.

Drawn to the Amazon rainforest by Christopher Columbus, who said: "Gold is the most exquisite of all things. Whoever possesses gold can acquire all that he desires in the world. Truly, for with gold he can gain entrance for his soul into paradise."

Cortez conquered the Aztecs, taking gold from Montezuma, their chief, in Tenochtitlan, now Mexico City. Pizarro subjugated the Incas, forcing their ruler, Atahualpa, to buy his own life with a room filled with gold. Then he executed him anyway. From these South American natives, the Spaniards heard the legend of *el hombre dorado*, "the gilded man." El Dorado. They were told that in a ceremony at Lake Guatavita, near Bogota, the Muisca had smeared the naked body of their chief with pitch and covered him with gold dust until he shone from head to foot. On a raft made of rushes, the gilded man and several masked shamans drifted across the blue waters to the center of the lake. There, El Dorado offered the heap of gold at his feet to the lake god, then plunged into the icy water himself to rinse the gilt from his skin.

But that was fifty years before the conquistadors arrived. And since there were no gold mines in the land of the Muisca natives, the Spaniards concluded that their wealth had to come from those with whom they traded.

El Dorado wasn't a gilded man. It was a *city* of gold.

Manoa del Dorado!

The gilded *place*!

So the Spaniards plundered their way inland, egged on by natives who wished to expel them to other realms. Venezuela, Colombia, Ecuador, Peru. The fabled city of El Dorado could have been anywhere. Some thought it was in the mountains, just beyond the next range. Others heard it was deep in the unexplored part of the jungle. The myth became more elaborate as each expedition met with grief. Emaciated, fever-stricken men crawled back from disaster, having eaten their horses and dogs to escape alive. Others got shot with arrows poisoned with curare. In 1595, Sir Walter Raleigh sailed up the Orinoco River in search of El Dorado, then wrote in his *Discovery of Guiana* that somewhere in the Amazon jungle were "more rich and beautiful cities than either Cortez found in Mexico or Pizarro in Peru."

Gold.

Greed.

Gold!

It was greed that drew the conquistadors to the tropical rainforest of Ecuador and Peru, where the eastern foothills of the Andes meet the headwaters of the Amazon River. They didn't find El Dorado, but they did find plenty of gold, so the invaders established five towns and forced the local Jivaro to labor in the mines, thereby riling the New World's fiercest headhunting tribe. When the Spanish governor levied a grasping tax on the gold trade in 1599, twenty thousand warriors crept from the jungle in the dead of night and, led by their chief, Anirula, attacked the sleeping conquistadors in the town of Logrono.

"Jíbaro!"

Shouts of warning crescendoed into a chorus of screams as headhunters burst into bedrooms and hauled the Spaniards from their sleep, dragging them into the moonlight so fearsome warriors could hack at their necks with stone axes, bamboo knives, wooden machetes, and clamshells honed as sharp as razors. Those breaking free were brought down by poisoned darts puffed through blowguns. Twelve thousand men, women, and children were among the dying and dead.

To the Spaniards, the jungle was a green hell, and they were being mauled by demons. Roofs were torched to set the haciendas ablaze. Burnished by the firelight, monsters with long flowing hair and woven headbands crowned with toucan feathers moved from corpse to corpse to string the heads of the slain along ropes of bark. The cords went in through the mouths and came out through the dripping necks.

Hellish men with designs painted on their faces and skeletons drawn on their naked chests herded the governor from his home out into the chaos. There, several Jivaro melted gold in a pot heated by an angry fire. The conquistador shrieked as they poured the liquefied metal down his throat.

"Have you had your fill of gold now?" the Jivaro taunted as billows of steam rose from his lips.

The governor's bowels burst.

For centuries to come, the Jivaro would be the only savages to thwart the Spanish empire. With the town of Logrono burnt to the ground and all but a handful of sex slaves slaughtered, the headhunters vanished into the mists of the primeval rainforest, leaving nothing behind but the stench of charred human flesh.

The conquistadors had come for gold.

The Jivaro had come for *tsantsas*.

———·•·———

With the head of this gold-seeker in his hand, the headhunter worked diligently to peel the skin from the skull. The only light came from a flickering candle and the fire under the pot, but in his imagination he could see the festering jungle around him. Enormous trees soared overhead, their branches dark with every hue of green. Purple orchids hung from the tangled limbs, and poisonous fruits dropped into the undergrowth to rot. Up there, coveys of vampire bats slept in the foliage, their furry bellies bloated with blood. Down here, in the musky odor of damp and decay, tarantulas with fuzzy legs watched anacondas slither through the gloom, the jaws of their spade-shaped heads lined with teeth.

Parting the hair of the severed head from the crown to the hack line at the base of the neck, the headhunter slit the skin by pressing the tip of his knife against the bone. Carefully, he peeled the flesh back on both sides. Cutting was required at the ears, the eyes, and the nose, but soon the skull was naked except for the eyeballs and the lipless teeth.

Had he been close to a river, the headhunter would have tossed the skull in as an offering to the anaconda god, feared for its strength and its supernatural powers. But instead, he mounted the flayed skull on a candlestick.

The bulging, bloodshot whites stared at him.

The teeth flashed an ivory grin.

Pushing back from the table, the man who had bushwhacked Boomer carried the snowboarder's head across to the pot boiling on the stove and turned the gas flame down to a simmer. Holding the trophy by its long locks, he lowered Boomer's face into the spaghetti pot and watched it sink slowly into the bubbling water. Then, with half an hour to wait before the next step, he left the kitchen for the main room.

As he crossed the threshold, he morphed from a bronze-skinned Jivaro with long hair into that which he'd seen in the bathroom mirror before setting out to trap the poacher that morning.

"El Dorado," he prophesied.

The window of the mountainside chalet looked down on the village sprawled at the base of the snow-covered peaks. Twilight stained the slopes an iridescent blue as gold lights below lured Olympic hopefuls to nightlife in the bars. Along the windowsill were several carnivorous plants, their deadly maws yawning for their evening meal. With long tweezers, the headhunter plucked bugs from an aerated jar and dropped them into the hairy funnels. As he did, he smiled down at the skiers, snowboarders, and other athletes converging on the pub in the El Dorado Resort.

"Have you had your fill of gold now?" he asked rhetorically.

If not, they soon would.

SO THIS COP WALKS INTO A BAR ...

"What'll it be?" the bartender asked.

"Whisky," said Nick.

"Whisky with or without the 'e'?"

"Single malt."

"Brand?"

"Surprise me," said Nick.

"One *uisge beatha* coming up," the bartender said, turning her back on the Mountie to choose from the line of bottles ranked along the wall. The brunette poured a dram of Glenmorangie into a glass, held it up to the light to admire the amber color, and set it down in front of Nick with a flash of cleavage that convinced him to increase her tip.

"What's that mean?"

"What?"

"'You ski' whatever."

"*Uisge beatha?*" She threw him a bright, white grin. "The same as *uisce beatha*. Both mean 'water of life.' The first is Scots Gaelic, the second Irish Gaelic. Scotsmen drink whisky without an 'e,' and Irishmen drink whiskey with an extra letter."

"I didn't know that."

"You learn something new every day," she said, giving him a wink like a starlet from a 1940s movie.

"Whisky or whiskey—does it matter? They'll both take you where you want to go."

"Shh!" shushed the bartender, raising a finger to her candy apple lips. "If a Scotsman hears that, the two of you'll be busting up the pub."

"You think?"

"'Whisky or Whiskey?'" the brunette said as if standing in front of a mike:

A Scotsman who spells
Whisky with an "e"
should be handcuffed
and thrown headfirst in the Dee.

In the U.S.A. and Ireland,
it's spelt with an "e"
but in Scotland
it's real "Whisky."

So if you see Whisky
and it has an "e,"
only take it,
if you get it for free!

For the name is not the same
and it never will be,
a dram is only a real dram
from a bottle of "Scotch Whisky."

"A pub with entertainment," said Nick, hoisting his glass in a toast to her and downing a swig.

"That's Stanley Bruce, the Bard of Banff. Google him. His poem has earned me a lot of tips."

"I'll bet. What's your name?"

"Karen," she replied.

"I'm Nick," the corporal said, flashing his regimental badge.

"You can drink on duty?"

"Actually, I'm on my days off. But since I'm the only cop who can ski Boomer's Run, the local Horsemen called me in to assess the murder scene. Currently, though, I'm off duty."

"Poor Boomer. An ugly way to go. I guess he messed with someone else's chick one too many times."

"In here?"

Karen nodded. "This was his watering hole."

"Any chicks in particular?"

"That table would be a good place to start."

Turning from the bar, Nick followed her nod toward three striking women—a blonde, a redhead, and a knockout with raven hair—shedding their coats for what he suspected was an après-ski manhunt for Olympic champions. The Gilded Man was filling up with satisfied skiers and boarders from around the world, all of them lured here to test the waters before going for the gold in February. As North America's blue-ribbon resort, Whistler had always been the haunt of beautiful yuppies. But now the whiff of real money—*endorsement* money—had gold diggers like these three polishing their velvet claws. If they could hook a future owner of the podium, these foxes would be able to enjoy the money-is-everything lifestyle that spills from the bed of all platinum jocks.

Have you ever noticed how many multimillionaire sportsmen have Barbie dolls clinging to them?

Nick had.

As a cop from the wrong side of the tracks, the corporal felt inadequate in a gene pool like this. Somewhere, he had read about a speed-dating study that stripped away what people like to think they're looking for—a like-minded soul mate—and exposed the brutal reality that men are attracted to beauty and women to wealth. Women trade their attractiveness for higher-quality men, leveraging their looks for security, fitness, and commitment. A man wants the most attractive woman who'll accept him, so he can mate with good genes. Feminine beauty plus masculine money equals love, because evolution drives us to create more successful offspring. Not a pretty picture, but it had the ring of truth. And that's why Nick knew these three babes were out of his league.

"Karen!" one of the honey traps beckoned, lifting three manicured fingers above her expensive coif. "Guinness is good for you."

Accepting the advertising slogan as an order, the bartender popped the tops off three cans of beer, partially filled glasses with the dark, foamy brew, and arranged them on a small round tray for delivery to the table.

"I guess I should talk to them, eh?" said Nick.

"I thought you were off duty."

"Conscientious cops are *never* off duty, Karen."

"Not if the duty looks like that," said the barkeep, rolling her eyes. She passed Nick the drinks. "Here. Go introduce yourself. But return the tip to me."

SNOW BUNNIES

The music in the Gilded Man—strictly retro R&B—was played softly enough that drinkers didn't have to bellow to flirt, but loudly enough that they were induced to get it on. Nick weaved the tray through clusters of chatter to strains of "Money Honey" by the Drifters. A clumsy waiter, he served the sexy trio without spilling too much, then pulled back one of the vacant chairs at their table and sat down.

The blonde tossed him a "get lost" glare.

The redhead dismissed him with a cold pout.

The raven-haired goddess used mental telepathy to tell him to buzz off.

In reply, Nick flashed them all his bison-head badge.

"Boomer," he said.

When it came to cinematic thrillers, nothing irked Nick more than a director with a fetish for one color of hair. He'd sit there eating his popcorn, trying to figure out whodunit, and all the actresses in the movie would be blondes. In a long shot, the suspects were interchangeable. There should be a rule that femmes fatales must be color-coded so armchair detectives—and real detectives, in Nick's case—can keep them straight. The women at this table—the Blonde, the Redhead, and the Raven—were how it should be.

"What happened to your hand?" asked the Blonde. Mandy was her name, and she wore a scoop-necked sweater. Obviously, she hadn't come in from the slopes. She made Nick think of Lana Turner.

"A bad guy hacked it off," said Nick.

"Why?"

"He was evil."

"How strong is the *new* hand?" asked the Redhead. Her name was Jessica, and she wore a fuzzy green sweater. She reminded Nick of Rita Hayworth.

Picking up Jessica's empty can of Guinness, the cop crushed it down to scrap metal.

"Wow!" said the Blonde. "When you cop a feel, I bet a girl *knows* she's been felt up."

The buxom trio tittered.

"What's your strangest case?" asked the Raven. Corrina by name, she reminded Nick of Jane Russell. The Raven wore a clinging creamy sweater that hung to her thighs, with a black belt, black ski tights, and black riding boots. When she sipped her Guinness, a foamy mustache lined her Cupid's bow lip. Out flicked her tongue to lick it away like a kitten laps up milk.

If Nick had to choose …

(In your dreams, dude.)

… he'd take all three.

"You forgot your whisky without an 'e,'" Karen said behind him, and as she bent over his shoulder to set the drink down on the table, her chest brushed against him. Nick had always been a sucker for Hollywood's golden era. How had Bob Hope once introduced his radio guest? "Ladies and gentlemen, welcome the two and only Jane Russell?"

Karen went back to the bar.

"Boomer," Nick said. "I'm led to believe you ladies knew him in the biblical sense?"

"Everyone knew Boomer," replied Mandy the Blonde.

"He was key to the party circuit," Jessica the Redhead added. "Get on his list and you were in."

"Were you all on Boomer's list?"

"Of course," said Corrina the Raven. "The Olympics will be a blast."

"How did you get on his list?"

"It's Whistler," said Jessica the Redhead. "Everything has a price. You pay to play."

"Pay what?"

"Boomer's entry fee."

"Which was?"

"Entry."

The vixens laughed.

The answer reminded Nick of a quip someone once made about Ray Charles. To be a Raelette—one of his background singers—the joke went, you had to let Ray.

"I'm sure you all have boyfriends?"

"Had," corrected Corrina. "We're currently unattached and moving up in the world."

"Or *were*," groused Mandy, "until Boomer got himself topped."

"I'll need your ex-boyfriends' names."

One by one, the social climbers provided Nick with the names and addresses of the lovers they'd ground underfoot on the steps to their own Olympic podium. Each one had a motive for lopping off Boomer's head.

Ah yes, Whistler!

Gold, sex, and honey drippers.

"So what was your strangest case?" asked Corrina.

"Do you believe in ghosts?"

"No."

"Neither did I, until I went to Ireland for an extradition case. On a dark and stormy night, I ran out of gas on a countryside road. So there I was, walking along in the pitch black, the rain so hard I could barely see five feet in front of me, when suddenly this car crept up behind me and stopped. Relieved, I jumped in the passenger's door—but there was no one behind the steering wheel and the engine wasn't on.

"The AA Guide had told me this district was known for its ghosts, one of whom was called the Phantom Highwayman. I couldn't believe it when the car began to move! All of a sudden, as it rolled toward a curve, a ghostly hand came in through the window, yanked the wheel, and saved me from crashing! I was so spooked that I dove out of the car while it was still moving and ran on ahead until I spied lights beckoning from a roadside pub. It was called the Phantom Highwayman.

"As you can imagine, I dashed in, ordered a whiskey, and drank it in one gulp."

Raising his glass to the Blonde, the Redhead, and the Raven, Nick snapped the malt down his gullet. Wincing, he wiped his mouth with the back of his real hand.

"The locals were nodding their heads," he continued, "as I told my ghost story, and that's when two more soaked travelers burst in from the deluge.

"'Look, Paddy,' one said, pointing his finger at me. 'It's the fucking idiot who jumped in while we were pushing our car!'"

The snow bunnies groaned.

"You're a barrel of laughs," said Mandy.

"If you ladies want to pay the entry fee," said Nick, "I'll put you on *my* party list."

———•◆•———

Two hours later, Nick wandered out of the Gilded Man into the dazzle of Christmas lights sparkling throughout Whistler Village. He reached for his gloves to protect his hands and found a keycard to a room in the El Dorado Resort stuffed in the open end of one.

The keycard bore a Post-it Note.

Nick sucked in a deep breath to help focus his eyes through a fuzz of intoxication.

"Ten o'clock tonight," he read. "Be discreet."

TSANTSA

The head that emerged from the spaghetti pot had shrunk to half its size. The skin was as white as paper and smelled like cooked flesh. To the headhunter's fingers, Boomer felt rubbery.

"Behold the head of a poacher," the killer said to himself, holding up the trophy like French revolutionaries had with aristocrats topped by the guillotine.

Now to make it a *tsantsa*. A shrunken head.

He carried Boomer's flaccid face to the sauna off the rear bathroom. When he pulled open the wooden door, the blast of heat was as dry as a desert wind. The skin had shrunk, but Boomer's mane had not, so the killer hung the trophy by its hair from a ceiling hook and left it to dehydrate in the warmth.

"Enjoy the spa," he said.

Returning to the kitchen, the man selected round stones of various diameters from a metal box, then arranged them around a burner on the stove. Next, he partially filled a frying pan with sand meant to grit icy sidewalks and provide traction for snowbound cars. Molding a *tsantsa* from flayed flesh required the skill of a chef.

Poof! Poof!

Igniting both burners, the cook left the stones and the sand to heat.

By the time he'd retrieved the head from the sauna, the skin was dry enough—still pliable, but not squishy. He set it down on the kitchen table, flanking it with several tools instead of the usual knife, fork, and spoon. Then he lit a candle for macabre atmosphere.

Flick.

Out went the kitchen lights. As darkness closed in around him, he was back in the Amazon.

He fantasized he was Jivaro.

As a boy, he'd been led on a spirit quest by his headhunting father. The rainy season was at its height, and the jungle was steaming. Fog rolled in as they approached the waterfall, and mist choked the undergrowth the way the vines and tendrils did the branches overhead. Required to fast, he could drink only tobacco juice. When they reached the tumbling river, his father fed him nightshade to help him hallucinate and acquire his *arutam.*

Back and forth they paced, the boy's mind swimming in delirium until he saw a huge disembodied head. Running as hard as he could with his arm outstretched, he touched the vision sought by his spirit quest. As it exploded into a fireball, it filled him with an overwhelming desire to kill.

Suddenly, he was a man.

From that point forward, he would hunt heads.

"The power you feel," his father explained, "is the spirit of a *wakani,* an ancestor. *Arutam* will protect you from injury, disease, and most attacks. If you're killed by an enemy, your protective spirit will avenge your death, hunting down your killer and destroying him.

"Blood revenge," stressed his father.

"If you kill an enemy who has *arutam*, his protective spirit will come after you. To paralyze that vengeful ghost, you must trap it inside a *tsantsa*. If you do that, you will thwart his blood revenge and add the power of his *arutam* to your own. Turn enough heads into *tsantsas* and you will be *kakaram*, a powerful one. A warrior invincible to attacks by anything."

So here he sat, with gloom encircling him, shrinking Boomer's head down to the size of a fist. With a knife, he scraped the inside of the half-dried skin clean of tissue. He pulled the upper lashes down to shut the gaping eyeholes, then stitched the lids tight with black cord to blind any vengeful spirit. After skewering two-inch splinters through the lips, he lashed them together like sails cinched to deck cleats. The nose and ear holes were plugged with cotton. Finally, he sewed together the slit up the back of the head. Boomer now looked like an empty rubber glove.

"Gotcha!" the killer said to the spirit trapped inside. "You won't get out."

Donning an oven mitt to insulate his hand, he carried the trophy to the stove and used a pair of tongs to drop the largest stone from the burner into the gruesome pouch. The stench of barbecued flesh wafted to his nostrils. To guard the skin from scorching, he rolled the stone around like a gambler tumbling dice in a box. Minutes later, he gripped the head by its hair with his bare hand and dumped the cooling stone into the mitt's palm.

As each subsequent stone decreased in size, so too did Boomer's face. Eventually, even pebbles were too big for the task, so the killer stuffed the head with sand from the pan hissing on the stove. The hot grit filled crevices in the ears and nose the stones couldn't reach. Every four minutes the killer replaced the sand, and as the trophy shrunk to the size of an orange, he molded the features of Boomer's boneless face to maintain his likeness.

"Almost done," he said. "Is that a tight fit? You'll never escape to haunt me, so get used to it. Vengeance will not be yours. I own you body *and* soul."

Removing the splinters, he dried the lips with the press of a heated knife, then stitched them with a black thong that he could ornament with beads and fray into tassels. The only feature that hadn't shrunk was the hair, so it now seemed three times as long as it was when Boomer lost his head.

"Aren't you hirsute?" said the killer.

Normally, a Jivaro would rub powdered charcoal into the skin to blacken it and encase the spirit in darkness. But that would undermine what the headhunter had planned, so instead he reached for the glittering gilt of El Dorado …

A noise foreign to the jungle interrupted him. It was the sound of a door opening into his psychosis.

Poof!

The psycho morphed back to the here and now.

"I wish I had a hotrod," the killer said, "so I could hang you from the rearview mirror."

He set the shrunken head down on the oilcloth, then blew out the candle. Pushing away from the table, he opened the door into the living room of the chalet. As he stepped into the glare, he saw himself reflected in the full-length mirror.

His ugliness made him wince.

Not long ago, he'd been a strikingly handsome man. But then he'd tried to outwit the Mounted Police with radical plastic surgery, and the doctor had botched the job.

Now look at him!

The face he saw in the mirror rivaled that of the shrunken head in the kitchen.

"How'd it go?" he asked the woman shucking off her coat.

"I've hooked a Mountie," she said.

"Which one?"

"Nick Craven."

The headhunter grinned. Any Mountie would have fitted his plan, but Craven was a bonus.

"When do you reel him in?"

"Ten o'clock tonight."

"Good. Come here," he said, "and I'll show you what you'll use to kill him."

PITCHER PLANT

"Scarlett" had been her stage name for as long as she could remember. It came from her mother's obsession with the movie *Gone with the Wind*. "Fiddle-dee-dee!" her mom would say as she dressed her daughter up as a Southern belle for child beauty pageants. And whenever they lost to some "little tramp," her snarl of rejection was always the same: "Tomorrow is another fuckin' day!"

Even then, the girl was aware of her sexual hold over men. She'd seen the ogling eyes of those who attended the various pageants, had noticed how they fidgeted when she performed the vamp routine her mother had taught her.

"Let's play motorboat."

Her stepfather's name was Hake, but her mom called him Rhett. He was a cokehead who constantly hatched lowlife scams to make a buck, though he succeeded only once. Motorboat was the game they always played before Scarlett went to bed. With one hand, Hake would grab her around the side of her chest, below the armpit; his other hand would slip down to fasten onto her thigh. Like a weightlifter doing curls, he'd raise her horizontally in front of his face, nuzzling his mouth into the gap where the top and bottom of her pajamas met. *"Bbbbrrr."* His lips would vibrate against her naked tummy, mimicking the sound a boat motor makes, while his little finger tickled her crotch.

Fittingly, her mom had died *on* Scarlett O'Hara. Having taken the train to L.A., she located Vivien Leigh's star on Hollywood Boulevard—near Elvis's—then pulled a pistol from her purse, yelled "I don't give a damn, either!" and blew out her brains.

It made the papers.

After that, Hake assumed control of Scarlett's career. Internet porn was his obsession, and he finally made his bundle off "Scarlett, the Southern Belle." But the hardcore stuff also landed him a stretch in jail.

Left to fend for herself, Scarlett earned a tawdry living by role-playing in men's sexual fantasies. Modeling, peep shows, stripping, hooking—she had done it all. Finally, she took a job as a chorus girl in Vegas.

That's where she was when Hake got out of jail: kicking her legs in the air so men could eye her crotch. You've come a long way, baby, since those kiddie pageants.

Fiddle-dee-dee.

It wasn't far enough.

Hake had tracked her down and waylaid her outside the stage door on a sweltering Friday night.

"Yo, Scarlett. Miss playing motorboat?"

"Hake?" she gasped.

Oh, how she loathed his voice.

He stepped out of the shadows, rumpled, stubbly, and drunk.

"Daddy's home. And you owe me."

"For what?"

"Flaunting your naughty wares on the Internet cost me pussy for too many years."

"You ruined me, Hake."

"Tough luck, kid. From now on, Scarlett works for *me*. Damn if your T&A won't make ol' Hake a bundle."

"No way!"

"Want me to slash your face?" He waggled a barber's razor in the light from the stage door. "Let's go to my place so I can *see* what you got."

He had a room in a flophouse motel on the outskirts of town. Neon lights and walls so thin you could hear the tricks turn next door. A bed was banging the studs.

"Quite a rack you've got, kid. Yer all grow'd up. Are those titties real or fake? Give Hake a peek."

Without a word, she unbuttoned her top and stripped it off. Hands reaching behind her, she unclasped her bra. Hake was drooling when she shimmied out of the cups.

"Let's play motorboat," she said.

"*Bbbbrrr*," he replied.

Knees half-bent, Hake nuzzled his face into her cleavage, pressing his prickly mouth against her breastbone and shaking his head from side to side while his lips vibrated.

Motorboat.

The tit man's version.

Any smart Vegas showgirl carries a weapon for her own protection, and Scarlett was no exception. Sliding the ice pick, which was masked as a nail file, from the waistband at the small of her back, she aimed the tip at the nape of Hake's neck and plunged the steel into his brain as hard as she could.

Her breasts muffled his squeal.

Bang, bang went the bed next door as Hake dropped dead.

The next day, the Vegas cops hauled her in for questioning. "Ice Pick Killer Strikes!" screamed the newspapers.

Her relationship with Hake trapped her in suspicion like a spider's web. But stabbing him had felt so good that Scarlett yearned to stick another pig. If she got free, she knew she could become another Aileeń Wuornos—"Ice Pick Killer Strikes Again!" read the headline in her mind. Since the cops didn't have the weapon and their case was circumstantial, her lawyer advised her to say nothing. So she kept her mouth shut.

"You're free to go," a cop said a short time later. "Lucky for you, your alibi checked out."

What alibi?

A mystery man fell into step beside her outside the station. "I'm the guy who sprung you," he said. "May I buy you a coffee? You owe me nothing, but I do have a proposition."

"My life is one big proposition."

"Money, not sex," he replied. "I need someone with your looks. And your ... *cool*."

She laughed. "Save your breath. I won't confess."

"I don't expect you to. You obviously didn't speak to the police. That's why the alibi worked."

"What alibi?"

"Don't you remember? I hired you to strip for a private poker party. When I arrived to pick you up at the stage door after your show, a man was bugging you. He ran off when I approached. Turns out he was a child abuser who got iced while you were stripping for us."

"Says who?"

"All four players at the party."

"Why?"

"Let's just say I have the means. The cops had zilch on you except your past ties to a child pornographer. I came forward because of what I read in the paper, and you were cleared."

"So what's your proposition?"

"I'm offering you a fortune for about a week's work."

"Doing what?"

"Nothing you haven't done before."

———— • • ————

So here she was a few months later, in Whistler, British Columbia, shedding her overcoat and following the man who'd given the Ice Pick Killer an alibi across to the plants lining the sill of the window overlooking the El Dorado Resort.

"This colorful beauty," the man said, "is *Sarracenia purpurea*, the purple pitcher plant. An insectivorous meat-eater, it's the floral emblem of Newfoundland."

He picked up a jar squirming with bugs, opened the lid, and extracted a beetle with tongs. The pitcher plant was a squat tube with a frilled, sloping hood bristling with stiff hairs. Gingerly, the botanist released the bug on the crest of the garish trap.

"Watch," he said.

The hood was patterned with red veins baited with nectar. Slowly, the beetle followed the veins down the purple spout to the gaping mouth. The downward-pointing hairs kept it from climbing back up. At the rim of the pitcher, in which water had collected, the foothold changed to wax. The bug slipped and fell into the deadly pool.

Scarlett peered in and watched it thrash around.

"Cool," she said. "Will it drown?"

"Yes, then enzymes in the water will digest the beetle. That's how the plant feeds."

"I'll bet the bug is male."

"Why?"

"In my experience, men are more likely to succumb to the pitfall of a deep, wet cavity."

The headshrinker grinned maliciously.

"Well put," he said. "When you meet Craven tonight at ten, I want him killed with this."

He picked up a jewelry box from the sill next to the pitcher plant.

"For you," he said.

Lifting the lid, Scarlett peeked inside. Her eyes widened as she began to understand.

"*Wicked!*" she exclaimed.

WAIF

"Dad!"

Searching the hordes of people streaming in from the customs hall at the Sea Island airport, Chief Superintendent Robert DeClercq looked right past the waving teen who'd mistaken him for her father.

"Don't you recognize me?"

"Katt?" he said.

The young woman held up her passport. "According to this, that's me."

But the stylish girl leaning over the barrier to bestow a welcome hug looked nothing like the wild child in the passport mug shot. Kissing him on both cheeks as they do in Paris, she more closely resembled a Sorbonne student summoned home for Christmas break.

"Who says you can't turn a sow's ear into a silk purse?" DeClercq kidded.

"Oink!" replied Katt.

How does any cop come back from the death of his only child, especially when that child was killed as vengeance against *him*? Decades ago, kidnappers had shot DeClercq's wife and abducted little Jane, snapping the girl's neck before the Mountie could hunt them down. Guilt had squeezed him in its stranglehold for years, and eventually the stress of the Headhunter Case had crushed his will to carry on. Every man has a breaking point, and that psycho had found DeClercq's. The moment of reckoning flared in his mind like a camera's flashbulb.

Avacomovitch was moving.

Charging across the living room toward the greenhouse door, the Russian tucked his head tight to his body and pushed off hard from one foot. At six-foot-four and 285 pounds, he smashed the wood like a human battering ram. With a crack of protest, the door split in two. In a shower of splinters, the hinges gave and the lock tore free. Potted plants tumbled from shelves and dirt filled the air as Avacomovitch somersaulted across the floor and crashed a foot through the glass.

"Don't do it, Robert!"

With the muzzle touching his palate, DeClercq cocked the hammer and bit down on the steel ...

"You got him!"

His finger closed on the trigger to end it all ...

"A flying patrol brought him down!"

There was a frozen eternity while the Mountie sat at his desk with the gun in his mouth, staring down at the man sprawled on the floor tiles. Slowly, he withdrew the barrel and set the weapon down.

That was a narrow escape, and a lucky one, for as fate would have it, DeClercq found redemption in the aftermath of the carnage on Deadman's Island.

Another flashbulb lit up his memory.

"Someone's in the maze," Craven yelled over the din, indicating the tangled garden near the clifftop house. Snow

billowed up as the helicopter entered ground effect. The pilot jockeyed levers to set them down. While the whup-whup-whup *of the airfoils died to a whistle, DeClercq threw open the passenger's door and jumped onto the island.*

Trees flanked the entrance to the labyrinth. Wrapped in a rug, her eyes wild with fear, a girl of about fourteen stumbled toward him. The Mountie found himself reliving a dream that had tormented him for years. "Daddy!" Janie cries, running toward him with outstretched arms. He waits, and waits, and waits, but she draws no closer.

Then, suddenly, the shivering girl was in his arms, seeking warmth to ward off hypothermia. Only when DeClercq wrapped his coat around her did Katt's teeth stop chattering.

"Where's your mother?"

"Dead."

She glanced at the house of horrors.

"And your father?"

"Don't have one," Katt replied. "Now I don't have anyone left in the world."

How strange, the twists of life.

In the beginning, it was an act of charity. DeClercq had a houseful of empty rooms haunted by ghosts. Katt was a waif with nowhere to go. To give her shelter under his roof seemed the right thing to do—at least until a more permanent solution could be found.

But he must have had rocks in his head to take on a challenge like her, the spawn of a New Age poet and practicing pagan witch. He remembered one Christmas, when Katt suggested baking gingerbread men. "I've never had any," she protested, "my mom being a pagan and all." So they'd gone shopping for ingredients and a set of cookie cutters in the usual shapes. Having whipped up a batch of dough, they punched out identical men.

"How boring," Katt pronounced, and she began to reshape the lower leg of one man into a peg, adding the dough she'd removed to a lump on his shoulder.

"Who's that?" DeClercq asked while she squeezed icing from the tip of a pastry bag.

"Long John Silver. See the parrot?"

Next, she used a rolling pin to flatten the legs of another gingerbread man into a skirt, then she cut off his head and tucked it into the crook of one arm.

"Marie Antoinette," she explained, icing the gown with ruffles fit for a queen.

Not to be outdone, DeClercq trimmed dough from the sides of one gingerbread man and added it to the torso of another.

"Jack Sprat and his wife?" guessed Katt.

"No. Elvis in the early years and final Vegas days."

Slathering a gingerbread man from head to foot with icing, Katt used the knife tip to groove bandage lines. "The Mummy," she declared.

"I'll see your mummy and raise you this." DeClercq kneaded the leftover dough into a ball, then flattened it into a big circle with the rolling pin. Raisins were gobbled-up victims peering out of the brown ooze. "The Blob," he announced.

In the end, Katt had fostered *his* redemption. It used to be that he gazed into the bathroom mirror and watched a ravaged man emerge from the shaving cream. Life with Katt, however, rejuvenated him, and soon the face DeClercq saw each morning seemed to shed years, as if he were actually turning back the hands of time.

Then he learned that Katt's mom wasn't actually her mom. In fact, Luna Darke had kidnapped her as a baby, and the teen's birth mother was very much alive. DeClercq had uncovered the secret and could have kept it to himself, but having endured the loss of Jane, he knew he couldn't foist that torment on another human being. So he had let her go, and Katt was now living in England, where her mother, a Bostonian, had found work.

"How's your mom?" the Mountie asked, wheeling her suitcase through the airport from the arrivals hall to the exit for the parking lot.

"She met a man. I think she's in love! That's why I called you. My Christmas gift to her is *no me.*"

"Lucky me. And what's with calling me Dad? Didn't it used to be Bob?"

"'When I was a child, I spake as a child, I understood as a child,'" the teenager quoted. "'But when I became a woman, I put away childish things.'"

"A little education is a dangerous thing." DeClercq rolled his eyes. "What does that mean?"

"Absence makes the heart grow fonder. I now realize that you're a better father than any bio-dad could be."

"How much do you want?"

"Millions," Katt said, laughing.

They crossed the road between the terminal and the parking lot. Katt was on the lookout for his Benz—the car she had dubbed the "old-fogey-mobile"—so her eyebrows rose when they approached a brand-new, metallic red 350Z.

"Uh-oh! Midlife crisis?" she asked.

"It's a birthday present from Gill."

"The shame of it," Katt moaned, burying her face in the crook of her arm. "Dad's a kept man."

"I prefer to view it as Dad's got a rich girlfriend."

"Can I drive?"

"Well ..."

"Driving on the left has *vastly* improved my skill."

Sighing, he tossed her the key.

It was an hour-long trip from the airport—on an island in the mouth of the Fraser River—through the high-rise canyons of the downtown core to DeClercq's waterfront home on Burrard Inlet. Katt *was* a better driver—or so he thought, until she slammed on the brakes so hard that dear old Dad would have smashed through the windshield if not for his seatbelt.

Screeeech!

Standing bewildered in the headlight beams on the road in front of the car was a small, scruffy white cat. Katt gave it a short honk, but the animal didn't move. She gave it a flick of the high beams, but the feline didn't blink. Finally, she put the car in neutral, yanked on the handbrake, activated the hazard lights, and left it blocking traffic.

From the passenger's seat, DeClercq watched Katt crouch down in the glare and talk to the cat. When waving her hands before its eyes elicited no response, she bundled the feline up in her arms and carried it back to the car.

"I think it's blind," she said on climbing in.

DeClercq knew this was one of those "a man's gotta do what a man's gotta do" moments. He found himself eyeing his reflection in the glass: a middle-aged cop with dark, wavy hair silvering at the temples and eyes jaded from having seen too much death and cruelty on the job. The face in the windshield was watching to see how he would react.

"Poor little waif," said Katt.

Any ordinary cat a moral man could just shoo off the road. "Shoo, shoo, kitty. Go fend for yourself." But a *blind* cat, that was a test of ethics. If he abandoned the waif by the side of the road, it would most likely be crushed by the next car along. If he took it to the SPCA, kitty would probably get the needle. Either course of action would haunt him later.

No, fate had placed this cat in front of *his* car, and the best dad in the world had only one choice.

The same choice he'd made with another waif.

"Okay, we'll take it home—"

"Hooray!" said Katt.

"—for now," he added quickly. "Tomorrow, we'll board it at the vet's, and we won't make a final decision until we get back. Agreed?"

"Get back from where?" the teenager asked, combing the cat with her fingers.

Why do I get the feeling my household just grew by one? wondered the Mountie, gazing at the vacant eyes as the cat began to purr.

"Whistler," he said. "Come morning, I'm taking you with me on a working holiday. While I review security measures for the Olympics with Zinc and Nick, you can ski the slopes with Gill." He looked over at Katt and her new charge. "I'm thinking of popping the question."

"A rich stepmom! I won the lottery. How much will I inherit?"

WINTER HEAT

The Blonde? The Redhead? Or the Raven?

In the end, curiosity got the better of him. He had to know *which* snow bunny had slipped him that key while he was drinking in the Gilded Man.

Nick's relationships with women were a shambles. His love affair with Gill Macbeth had not survived after he'd caused the shipwreck that had made her miscarry. Gill had moved on to a future with Nick's boss, Robert DeClercq, while Nick had lost a hand and an ear to a megalomaniac. That torture had brought him romance with Jenna Bond, a sheriff's deputy in Washington State. But now that romance was foundering on the reef of irreconcilable differences. Jenna planned to run for sheriff south of the border, to fill the boots of her father, a legendary lawman of the San Juan Islands. Nick's family history was in the Mounted Police, and his disability had forced him to fight hard to keep his job. With a stretch of ocean between them and the ferry times a logistical nightmare, their ardor had chilled.

It was bad enough that long-distance love had claimed two more casualties, but Jenna's six-year-old daughter was caught in the middle. Becky had embraced Nick as a surrogate for the dead father she had never known. Nick feared it would tear the child apart to have him abandon her, too.

What a vise!

The stress had the corporal yearning for some form of escape—a night of respite from *all* commitment that would hold his guilt at bay. That's why Nick found himself riding this elevator up to the eighth floor.

Cherchez la femme, old boy.

If not for the booze, he might have sniffed the danger. After all, it was a femme fatale who had caused his mutilations, by luring him into a trap for Mephisto and cutting him apart to force the cops of Special X to find the Silver Skull, a relic rumored to reveal the secret behind Stonehenge.

But this was Whistler, the mecca of casual sex, where high-rolling jetsetters from around the shrinking globe gathered to get royally fucked.

So why not Nick?

A roll in the hay would do him a world of good in his depressed frame of mind. But would the farmer's daughter turn out to be the Blonde, the Redhead, or the Raven?

Hey, this was Whistler!

Maybe he was destined for a three-on-one.

Just kidding.

What decent guy would desire that?

Whistling, Nick used the electronic key to pop the door. Reaching into the dark, he flicked on the lights. The room could have been any one of a million in North America, with its queen-size bed, two night tables, armchair, writing desk, TV stand, and luggage rack. All that indicated this was a ski resort was the wooden door leading to a sauna off the bathroom.

Nick glanced around.

There seemed to be no one home.

The cell in his pocket buzzed.

"Craven," he answered.

"Hi. It's Jenna. Is now convenient to talk?"

"Sure."

"Are we still on for tomorrow?"

"You bet. I promised Becky I'd teach her how to ski."

"Do you know what you're going to say to her about our breakup? She'll take it hard."

"I'll tell her the truth, as gently as I can. And if it's okay with you, I'll add that she can always call on me as her friend. This is about me and you, not me and her. Neither of us can abandon our life and be who we want to be. But that doesn't mean I won't love *her* from now on."

"Expect tears."

"I will." Nick had a lump in his throat.

"We'll catch the early ferry and get there about noon. Where should we meet?"

"Have Becky bring her skates. Alpha Lake is frozen over. You'll see it on the road in to Whistler. I'll find you there and take you to the cabin."

"See you then," Jenna said, ringing off.

Suddenly, Nick was aware of how hot it was. His forehead beaded with sweat, and his clothes were plastered to his body. The blast from the sauna felt as searing as the heat from Death Valley. He turned to see a naked woman standing in the door frame, her skin trickling perspiration.

Well, well, he thought.

"Girlfriend troubles?" she asked.

"Nothing I can't handle."

"I don't doubt that."

"You look hot."

"I am."

"You dropped your room key in the bar. I thought I should bring it up."

"Close the drapes, lock the doors, strip off your clothes, and come on in," she said, crooking her finger at Nick. "I'll teach you the meaning of *winter heat*."

VENUS FLYTRAP

It was a sultry night in Laurel Canyon. The actress Grace Kelly stood in her bedroom with the lights on. The curtains were open, the blinds were up. As if she had just returned from a night on the town, she removed her hat and slipped off her gloves. Slowly, she slid the straps of her evening gown from her shoulders, then let the clingy crepe de Chine drop and pool around her high heels. A flick of her fingers unsnapped her bra, and she stepped out of her lace panties and—pausing to turn the tables on the master of suspense—snuffed the lights.

Across Laurel Canyon, a mile away, Alfred Hitchcock sat with his eye glued to a powerful telescope and watched the star whose Hollywood career he'd made strip for him. The scene was straight out of *Rear Window*, their second film together, in which James Stewart, immobilized by a leg cast, spies on his neighbors to keep from getting bored. Scopophilia, sexual gratification through gazing, was one of Hitchcock's many kinks, and Kelly's striptease was intended solely for him.

The man who had told Mephisto that story was the plastic surgeon who'd botched the work on his face, turning him from a notably handsome man into a deformed freak. The doctor had paid for his bungling with an operation of his own. By the time Mephisto was finished with his scalpel, the rejuvenator of aging Hollywood stars was unrecognizable as a human being.

That, however, was nothing but foreplay compared to the vengeance Mephisto would wreak on Special X. He'd planned out every moment of the revenge he intended to exact on those who had foiled him in the past.

First up was Craven.

Beheading Boomer was a calculated gamble. Craven had returned to Special X for the Olympics. Because he was recognized as the best skier among Whistler's Mounties, the odds were good he'd be called to the murder scene. Boomer's link to the Gilded Man would lead the corporal to Scarlett. And Scarlett would finish what Mephisto had started by taking Craven's hand and ear.

Now, the gamble was about to pay off.

No need for plan B.

This megalomaniac left little to chance.

So here he sat, like Hitchcock had across Laurel Canyon, with his eye to a telescope, spying at the darkened window of room 807 in the El Dorado Resort. Suddenly, the black square lit up, and there was Nick Craven framed by the open door, his hand on the light switch. Mephisto watched his prey answer a cellphone and carry on a conversation while the door swung shut. No sooner did the cop ring off than he turned his head and spoke to someone hidden from sight. Then he walked to the window and drew the drapes.

No matter.

Mephisto wasn't James Stewart.

There was no need for him to wonder what was afoot.

He *knew* what was going on behind those blinds.

Mephisto strode to his terrarium of Venus flytraps. Each one was a starburst of heart-shaped leaves tipped with yawning jaws. They were like human hands, the open palms and curving fingers poised to clap. Each red palm oozed a line of sweet nectar droplets along the base of the fingers. At the moment, a beetle had crawled up one leaf and was feasting on the honey.

Brush ...

The bug's leg tripped a trigger hair inside the trap.

Touch it again, Mephisto thought.

Brush ...

That did it!

The trap snapped shut, the fingers locking like crossed swords to clamp the beetle in both palms. A leg stuck out, flailing to free itself. But the Venus flytrap squeezed tighter, and there was no escape.

The bug was Nick.

And soon he would be clamped in a similar trap behind the closed drapes.

Along the wall were several bear traps, one with open jaws. In outline, the large steel frames resembled the flytraps on the windowsill. Mephisto enjoyed imagining the damage the bear traps would do. Reaching for a broom handle leaning against the wall, he rammed it down on the trigger mechanism that sprang the leg-hold jaws.

Snap ...

Crack ...

Splinter ...

Slivers burst out in all directions as the metal teeth clanged together, smashing the wooden pole like they would human bones.

Mephisto could hear the screams.

And see the pain twisting the features of his prey into masks of agony.

Yes, he thought. These will do.

He walked into the kitchen to fetch the cans of spray paint he had used to finish off the shrunken head. Then, after bundling up against the cold and hiding his disfigured face, he left the chalet to trudge down to the El Dorado Resort.

The madman had another trap to set.

FROM RUSSIA, WITH HATE

It wasn't hard to spot him.

Gill Macbeth stood behind the waist-high barrier outside the arrivals hall at the Sea Island airport—no more than a couple of feet from where DeClercq had waited earlier that day—and scanned the passengers exiting the customs area. The moment she spied a giant in a Russian fur hat with the earflaps tied at the crown, she knew this was her man. Gill tailed him along the barrier until it ended.

"Dr. Avacomovitch, I presume?"

"Dr. Macbeth?" he replied, taking the hand Gill offered for a gentlemanly kiss.

"My, my. You must teach Robert that."

"Would you prefer my bear hug?" the Russian asked.

The pathologist took in his girth—as massive as an old-fashioned, wood-staved beer barrel—and smiled. "I'd like to keep my skeleton intact."

Even with his hat doffed, Avacomovitch towered over Gill, and his slicked-back white pompadour added inches to his height. Luckily, he tended to stoop, which helped shrink him down to the size of most people, but even so he barely fitted into Macbeth's car.

"How kind of you to greet me."

"Robert sends his regrets. His daughter, Katt, arrived on a flight from London earlier today. They have a lot of catching up to do, and she hasn't seen her dog and cat for a long time. He thought it unfair to make her spend hours waiting at the airport."

"I could have taken a taxi, Dr. Macbeth."

"Call me Gill."

"I'm Joseph. Joe."

"It's the least I can do. If not for you, Robert says he would have blown his brains out."

The forensic scientist shook his head. "Those were ugly times. You had to have seen Robert with Jane to truly understand. How he loved that baby girl!"

Both were silent as Gill eased her car out of the parking garage and began to follow the same route to the North Shore that Robert and Katt had taken earlier in the day.

"When I defected to the West from the Soviet Union," Joe said, breaking the silence, "I knew no one here. I chose to resettle in Canada because it reminded me of home. The Mounties offered me a job because of my forensic work in Russia."

"I hear you're the best."

"I'm fortunate some governments think so," he said, shrugging his shoulders. "When the Mounties employed me, the first friend I made was Robert. Many a night, back when he was zooming up the ranks as a homicide detective, he and his wife entertained me in Montreal. We'd talk for hours, sipping cognac in front of the fire, with Jane asleep in his lap."

Macbeth was attractive—handsome, not pretty—with auburn hair and emerald eyes. She was independently wealthy, having inherited several Caribbean hotels, but she'd still chosen to follow the feminist trail her mother had blazed as a forensic pathologist. Gill sensed the Russian appraising her, and hoped she would compare favorably to Robert's dead wife.

"Robert blamed himself, of course, for what happened to Jane, and when the Headhunter Case came along, it brewed up a perfect storm," said Joe. "The killer was hacking the heads off women and sending Robert photos of them mounted on poles to taunt him. Eventually, panic fueled a riot in the streets, and there were calls for *Robert's* head. When he couldn't stop the killings, his remorse got mixed up with unresolved guilt about Jane. Those demons, combined with too much booze and Benzedrine, pushed him to the brink, and he ended up sticking his revolver in his mouth."

"Thank God you're so big," said Gill.

"It was just a greenhouse door."

"Joke all you want, but Robert wouldn't be alive today if not for you."

Joe shrugged again, embarrassed by her words. "Anyway," he said, changing the subject, "I was lured back to Russia after the fall of the Soviet Union."

"By what?"

"An offer I couldn't refuse. The end of Communism exposed a plague of serial psychos. Chikatilo—the Rostov Ripper. Ryakhovsky—the Hippopotamus. Onoprienko—the Terminator. Pichushkin—the Chessboard Killer."

"Was that the guy trying to kill one person for each square on a chessboard?" asked Gill.

"Yes," Joe replied. "The *new* Kremlin asked me back to head up a state-of-the-art lab. It was an opportunity to rub Communist noses in my Western success, and to go home a hero. Revenge and ego satisfaction make a potent cocktail."

"So what brings you back here?"

"The Winter Olympics in 2014 will be in Sochi, Russia. Terrorism is now a global business, so we're sharing information we've gathered with Special X. We help them now, and later they'll help us. With the added perks that I get to ski Whistler and see Robert again."

The BMW drove through the forest of Stanley Park, almost an island of evergreens caught in the throat of the harbor. Recently, the city had suffered a freak windstorm that had leveled trees faster than loggers with chainsaws. It would take generations for the park to recover. Ahead, the necklace of lights outlining Lions Gate Bridge was marred by dozens of burnt-out bulbs. At least those would get replaced for all the wallets coming to town.

"How's Robert now?"

"All patched up," said Gill. "He has Katt, and me, to fill the void."

"And no Headhunter."

"Actually, it's worse. Now he's hunting a monster who threatens to be his nemesis."

"Mephisto."

"You know about him?"

"From what Robert says in his emails, they've battled twice. First, when Mephisto kidnapped a member of Special X—"

"Corporal Nick Craven," Gill offered.

"—and began cutting him to pieces. From what I recall, he refused to stop until Robert found some sort of Scottish artifact. Was it something linked to Stonehenge?"

She nodded. "The Silver Skull."

"Why did Mephisto want that?"

"Only *he* knows for sure. But from what Special X was able to put together, Robert concluded that he was interested in the zodiac inscription on the skull, said to be the secret of the stones. It most likely has something to do with human sacrifice. Stonehenge has a Slaughter Stone outside the main circle, and the idea of sacrificing virgins to the summer solstice would be right up Mephisto's alley."

"Mephisto sounds like a *nasty* piece of work."

"According to the psych profile Special X worked up on him, he has a narcissistic personality disorder with psychopathic features, paranoid traits, ego-syntonic aggression, and a complete lack of conscience. It's a mouthful, but it basically means he's a megalomaniac of Olympic proportions. His obsessive-compulsive need for power manifests itself in delusions of greatness. All through Nick Craven's captivity, Mephisto wore the tartan of a Scottish laird. He's a borderline psychotic, and he relishes cruelty. Like Brady with Hindley and Bernardo with Homolka, he lured a woman named Donella into his fantasy. She played the role of his Celtic highland queen and mutilated Nick on his command."

"How did he get so warped?"

"We don't know," said Gill. "Malignant narcissists usually harbor a massive inferiority complex from some childhood trauma. He may have been rejected, abandoned, teased, bullied, or sexually abused. Whatever it was, it must have been severe for him to overcompensate in such a vicious way. Mephisto isn't the stereotypical asylum Napoleon, with one hand stuck in his shirt. He *kills* for his delusions of greatness."

"What happened to Craven?" asked Joe.

"He was saved by Robert and an American sheriff's deputy named Jenna Bond."

"So Craven can ID Mephisto?"

"Yes."

"And so can you, I believe?"

Gill nodded. "And so can Jenna's daughter, Becky Bond. Mephisto grabbed Becky for a series of bizarre experiments, and he lured me to his clinic on Ebbtide Island. The *same* island he had used for his first psychotic scheme."

"To thumb his nose at Robert, I assume?"

"Precisely. What a megalomaniac craves is a worthy challenger to defeat. A Moriarty needs his Holmes. A Mephisto needs his DeClercq."

"What sort of clinic was it?"

"I had a nip and a tuck. The clinic was supposed to be a recovery spa, but that was just the front. Behind the façade was a sick laboratory for human experimentation, just as his own slick façade hides as cold-blooded a reptile as a man can be."

"A chameleon?"

"Who changes his skin with each psychotic scheme. For the Silver Skull, he wrapped himself in the tartan of a Scottish clan. For the clinic, it was Egyptology and a plot that was somehow tied to a *reverse* Fountain of Youth."

"What is he? A mad Indiana Jones?"

"You don't take the name of the devil unless devilry is what you're plotting. Role-playing is how a malignant narcissist conquers his mental demons. Mephisto creates a *subjective* image of himself and inhabits it so completely that those around him are tricked into responding to his delusion *objectively*."

"The ultimate self-absorption. So where is Mephisto now?"

"Who knows? He escaped again." Gill turned the BMW off Marine Drive and followed a road down through the dark trees to a house fronting the ocean. "The only thing we do know is that one day, Mephisto will return for revenge."

"With another grandiose plot?"

"And a new delusion."

"It could be worse," said Joe.

"How?"

The Russian tapped the briefcase at his feet.

"He could be armed with this."

BIOHAZARD

Beyond the glass of DeClercq's seaside home, silver moonlight sparkled on the ripples of Burrard Inlet. Topping a knoll on the beach was a driftwood chair and an antique sundial. Each sweep of the beacon from nearby Lighthouse Park caught the words etched around the metal face: "The Time Is Later Than You Think."

Though it was cold and stark out there, inside the blazing fireplace cast warmth and cheer. The hearth was flanked by two overstuffed chairs, the Holmes and the Watson. The Katt of old had always claimed the Holmes chair—"I'm more flamboyant"—thereby relegating the chief superintendent— "You're staid and dependable"—to the role of sidekick. Tonight, however, the teenager was curled up in the doctor's seat, having said to DeClercq, "You're the great detective. How arrogant I was to usurp your sleuthful throne."

Would wonders never cease?

After cleaning up, grooming, and tending to Waif, they'd spent the night making pizza and gingerbread men. Now they sat in the armchairs by the fire, watching a *Monty Python* skit on TV and killing themselves with laughter. So there'd be no jealousy, Katt had Catnip, the resident cat, snuggled in her lap and Napoleon, the German shepherd, at her feet. DeClercq cradled the blind stray in the crook of his arm.

There was a knock at the door.

"I'll get it," he said.

On the threshold stood Joseph Avacomovitch. He was about to embrace the Mountie in the bear hug that Gill had turned down when he saw the scruffy cat. Instead of crushing it, the long-parted friends opted to shake hands. With a flick of his eyes, Joe glanced over Robert's shoulder at the greenhouse door through which he had crashed all those years ago.

"Long time, no see," the cop said.

"Too long," said the Russian.

Closing the door on winter, Joe and Gill hung up their coats and trailed the Mountie along the hall to the living room that overlooked the ocean.

Just half an hour later, Katt went to bed. She had sleep to catch up on before the morning's early start. They'd stop by the vet's to board both cats, then follow the Sea to Sky Highway up Howe Sound to Squamish and into the mountains to Whistler. The drive would normally take an hour and a half, but snow was in the forecast.

A heavy snowfall.

With whiteout conditions.

The kind of weather known to cut Whistler off from the rest of the world.

"So," said Robert, "let's see the DVD."

Joseph opened his briefcase and fished out the disk. As Robert fed it into the player, the forensic scientist cautioned, "A stiff drink will help us watch it."

"Name your poison."

"Vodka."

"Gill?"

"Are you having one?"

"Sure."

"Then make it three."

The Mountie went to the fridge for a chilled bottle and poured three shots.

"*Za vashe zdorov'ye!*" said Joe, raising his glass.

"To your health!" echoed Robert.

"Cheers!" said Gill.

As they watched, a black man with ruby red eyes shambled, shambled, lurched, and shambled toward the camera. Blood trickled from his eyes, ears, nose, and mouth, and bubbled through his pores from hemorrhages under his skin. Dissolving flesh hung from his bones, while his sagging face detached from his skull.

It could have been a schlocky Hollywood zombie movie.

But it wasn't.

"September 1976," said Joe. "The first recorded outbreak of Ebola Zaire, along the Congo River in the rainforest of central Africa."

The oozing man shuffled up an aisle squeezed by hospital beds filled with thrashing wretches in the grip of seizures. Gore pooled underneath them and inched across the floor. The lurching zombie slopped through the slime and stalked the camera out the door.

The living dead terrorized the street beyond, crawling among the corpses and clutching at those not yet infected. Women wailed in anguish and yanked out their hair. Babies cried for mothers who lay dying in the blood-soaked dirt. If they ever offered an Oscar for hell on earth, this place would win it hands down.

"Ebola Zaire is a perfect parasite," said Joe. "It assaults every part of the body, except skeletal muscle and bone. The virus lives to replicate itself, and it turns each victim into a seething bio-bomb. Spread around the globe, it would kill off 90 percent of the world's population in six weeks."

All of a sudden, the horror movie morphed into a science fiction film. Astronauts in biohazard suits, their heads sheathed in breathing equipment, filled the screen. They roamed the village collecting samples from the dead while their flesh liquefied into red gumbo.

A tiny Soviet emblem adorned each man's shoulder.

"The Vektor compound in Siberia," said Joe as the DVD switched scenes again, this time to a labyrinth of tunnels sealed by airlocks. "In the 1980s, forty thousand scientists worked for Biopreparat, the Soviet Union's biological weaponry agency. They had access to ten thousand viruses, including 140 strains of smallpox and three kinds of Ebola. The Ebola Zaire strain came from the village we just saw."

"Black biology," commented Gill.

The Russian nodded.

"Ebola's weakness is twofold. First, it kills too quickly, eating up bodies from brain to skin before victims can infect enough new hosts to sustain an epidemic. Second, like the AIDS virus, it spreads solely by direct contact with infected body fluids. To address this, the virologist you see here— Vladimir Grof—created an *airborne* strain."

"How?" asked Gill, about to drain her glass.

"He began by thinking about the worst scourge in history: smallpox. That disease has a longer incubation period and a much lower kill rate than Ebola, but it spreads more easily. Grof realized that if he could combine the virulence of Ebola with the infectiousness of smallpox, he would have a supervirus without compare. He found a way to insert Ebola genes into a smallpox shell to create a hybrid that could be spread by air."

"Phew!" said Gill. "What happened to Grof?"

The previous scenes had shown him going about his work in a secret lab at the Vektor compound, weaponizing viral agents for the Soviet military. In the scenes they were watching now, he'd become a living skeleton, his Slavic face merely angles of skin and skull.

"A Vektor virus wormed into his heart," said Joe. "This footage was taken shortly before he died. During the Soviet era, Grof had had it all. A dacha on the Black Sea and a hunting lodge in the Urals. But with the fall of Communism, he lost everything. Suddenly, he was working in a crumbling lab and went months without getting paid. He blamed American capitalists for his decline. For revenge, he sold his supervirus—in the form of three aerosol bombs—to a bioterrorist."

"Who?" asked the Mountie.

"We don't know."

"Where?"

"Seattle," answered Joe.

"How did he smuggle it in?"

"By diplomatic pouch. You see, the fall of the Soviet Union had created a new threat from broke, disgruntled Biopreparat scientists looking to sell their toxic wares to hostile states. To stop that, Washington funded several make-work projects through Russia's Academy of Sciences. Ironically, Grof was sent to America as an example of the program's success. He used the opportunity to transact his revenge."

"So you know what he sold and where he sold it, but not who the buyer was. How did you find out as much as you did?" asked Robert.

"He boasted about it before he died. We know the transaction took place, but we don't know why the bombs were never used."

Joe paused to let Gill and Robert take in all he'd just told them.

"Now here's the nightmare scenario," he continued. "Nowhere on earth is more than twenty-some hours away by plane. Nothing gathers an international crowd like the Olympics. If a bioterrorist were to release Grof's supervirus at Whistler in February—or at Sochi in 2014—he'd essentially create thousands of human time bombs, people carrying a potential airborne pandemic to all four corners of the globe."

Nightmare indeed, thought Robert.

He made a mental note to discuss Grof's Frankenvirus with Zinc and Nick at the next day's security powwow.

In a post-9/11 world, Robert knew, it was madness to hold the Winter Olympics at a site where the venues stretched over a hundred miles. It was going to cost a fortune in taxpayer money to police the games, what with skating down near the American border, curling and hockey in Vancouver, snowboarding up on the North Shore mountains, and the alpine events off hell and gone along one of the world's most precarious roads. To make the games palatable to the Canadian public, security had originally been budgeted at a laughable $175 million. But those costs had soon skyrocketed to around a billion dollars. And then the bottom had crumbled away from the national treasury, which left taxpayers barely able to afford to protect the *actual* games. There was simply no money in the kitty for *preliminary* tryouts like those being held at Whistler over the next few days.

As fate would have it, this was also the week that VISU, the RCMP-led Vancouver 2010 Integrated Security Unit, was fine-tuning its multi-threat detection system in downtown Vancouver. Called Safesite, this system boasts an array of sensors that can monitor entire city blocks and sniff out forty chemical, biological, radiological, and nuclear (CBRN) threats. If a terrorist organization like al-Qaeda wanted to attack the Olympics with sarin, mustard gas, anthrax, or ricin, or with a "dirty bomb" of radioactive waste, the target would be Vancouver, not Whistler. That's why all but a few of the Olympic defenders were now on a test run in Lotusland.

In tough economic times, hard choices had to be made. Until security ramped up for the *actual* games, still two months away, Whistler had let down its guard.

HELL DORADO

Mephisto's inspiration had come from *Dactylella*, a carnivorous fungus. The fungus looped its many threads into nooses. If a roundworm stuck its head into one of the holes, the ring tightened, strangling it like a hangman's rope. Then a penetration tube emerged from the thread to pierce the body of the worm and suck out nutriments. Sated, the fungus released its prey.

Good idea, Mephisto had thought.

And *voilà*.

The metal strangling device he'd created resembled a dog collar attached to a four-foot chain ending with a hook. The inside of the collar was ringed with a circular razor blade.

"How does it work?" Scarlett asked.

They had just returned to the mountainside chalet overlooking the El Dorado Resort, where they'd baited the trap designed to hook DeClercq.

The psycho demonstrated. The loop constricted when he yanked the leash.

"Wicked!" she replied.

"And *this*," her boss added, "I created for you. I got the idea from Jivaro headhunters." Mephisto handed her the weapon.

The Ice Pick Killer's eyes widened with admiration as she grasped how it worked.

"Wicked!" she repeated.

Her new favorite word, it seemed.

The most diabolic weapon, however, had come not from his brain but from Vladimir Grof. The two had linked up on the Internet, that godsend of sexual perverts and worldwide terrorists. What began with a discussion of biological plagues—with the Russian in Siberia and Mephisto in the United States—had eventually culminated in a face-to-face meeting. That meeting took place in a Seattle hotel room, on a sunny autumn morning when Scotch mist swirled over streets bustling with weekenders going about their chores.

"Bring out your dead," Mephisto had said then, gazing down at them as the bitter, dying virologist puffed on a Lucky Strike and blew out smoke rings.

"Bring out your dead!" The cry had echoed through the burghs of fourteenth-century Europe as street carts gathered up the twenty-five million victims of the Black Death.

Mephisto envisioned streets of panic.

Streets red with blood.

"What you have here," Grof said, tapping the box on the table, "is a plague of biblical proportions. The 1918 flu wiped out one percent of the human population. This will annihilate *ninety* times that, or nine of every ten people."

Mephisto did the math.

It took a million years to populate the earth with a billion people:

1 billion around 1800;
2 billion around 1930;

3 billion around 1960;
4 billion around 1975;
5 billion around 1987;
6 billion around 1999.

Seven billion were projected for 2011, the year following the Whistler Olympics.

A 90 percent cull rate would cut that to seven hundred million, or a global population about double that of the United States. Instead of a planet in peril from melting polar ice caps, receding glaciers, rising sea levels, freak weather patterns, vanishing species, food shortages, and mobs of climate refugees, we'd be left with the fallout of a biological killer unlike anything the world had ever seen, a weapon conceived to eliminate urban populations but save infrastructures. Gone would be the overwhelming pressures on the environment, energy sources, natural resources, food, water, and housing. Every survivor would have his choice of home from those already built, meaning slums could be demolished to recover green space. The last time the earth had had a population of seven hundred million was 1700.

Wouldn't that be El Dorado?

The elusive City of Gold.

Especially for the Gilded Man, who was immune to this plague, and thereby free to speculate for his self-interest.

Me, thought Mephisto.

The savior of humankind.

The only man with the balls to do what had to be done, while lesser men talked and talked at useless gabfests that accomplished nothing, staging silly Earth Hours and self-aggrandizing rock concerts, obviously afraid to deal with the real threat: too many people pumping too many people out of their loins.

"Bring out your dead!"

"Pandora's box," said Grof, caressing the lid of the oblong case in front of him. "The hard work is done. All you do now is release the monster in here—" he raised the lid to expose three cans of freeze-dried horror and a vaccination kit—"at a meeting of people about to fan out around the globe, and they will carry the incubating plague home with them. Six to seven days later, the world will be bleeding, and the blood won't clot. By day nine, most of the population will be dead. Fate will determine who lives and dies."

Grof tapped the vials and syringes.

"The Ebola genes are *inside* the smallpox shell, so all you need to protect yourself are smallpox antibodies. Smallpox vaccinations stopped in 1971, and the world was declared smallpox free in 1979. Because a smallpox vaccination lasts for ten years, no one alive today—with the exception of those who inoculate themselves with what is in this kit—is immune to this virus."

Mephisto's original plan had called for the simultaneous release of the supervirus in New York, Miami, and Los Angeles. Had DeClercq not found his hideout on Ebbtide Island and cleaved the boat on which he tried to flee, sinking Pandora's box to the bottom of the strait, he'd have succeeded. It had taken precious years for Mephisto's secret salvage operation to recover the box. And in those years, the U.S. military had launched a smallpox vaccination campaign among its forces, so the world was not quite as unprepared as it had once been. Still, the supervirus would wipe out most of the human population, in a world ill equipped for the double whammy of the smallpox-Ebola time bomb.

"Time for bed," Mephisto said. "A big day tomorrow."

"When do I get to see what's in the box?" asked Scarlett.

"Curiosity killed the cat."

"Meow," she purred.

"I guess it won't hurt to give you a peek, since you'll be the one to let loose the monster."

With Scarlett watching, Mephisto eased Pandora's box out of its watertight case.

Pausing for suspense, he raised the lid.

"Do you grasp the irony?"

"No," she replied.

"What's the second most recognizable logo in the world?"

"McDonald's Golden Arches?"

He shook his head. "The scarlet uniform of the RCMP. Canada's the only country with a cop as its national symbol. The image is trademarked."

"So?"

"What's the *most* recognizable logo in the world?"

Scarlett clapped her hands.

"Wicked!" she said.

Mephisto smirked.

"Wicked indeed," he concurred.

BLUE MURDER

The next day

Whistler awoke to a sky full of snow and the need to rethink plans. Only diehard skiers and boarders would spend the day on the slopes. Olympic hopefuls would give it a try—after all, that's why they were here—but if the forecast delivered, most would forsake the whiteout for indoors. And the El Dorado Resort would mine even more gold than expected. Eureka!

"Good morning," Jenny answered the phone in her perkiest voice. "Hospitality."

"Give me the manager."

"I'm sorry. Mr. Hawksworth is currently engaged."

"Interrupt him," snapped the female caller.

"Perhaps I can be of assistance," Jenny countered, deflecting rudeness with patience, as she'd been taught.

"There's a *dead* man in your hotel. Do I get to speak to your boss now? Or would you rather I grab his attention by screaming blue murder in the lobby?"

"One moment, please," Jenny said, just as lively as before. Then she got up from her desk, knocked on Hawksworth's door, and barged in to alert the hospitality czar.

"Impeccable" was the best word to describe Niles Hawksworth. He was a spiffy-looking gent in an elegant Armani suit, whose clean-shaven scalp emphasized his handsome face, as if hair was a distraction used to hide flaws. No detail was too small for the hawk-like eyes, and no function too big for the military tactician in his soul. In short, Hawksworth was a consummate hotelier.

"Not now, Jenny. I'm *not* to be disturbed. Didn't I make that clear to you?"

"Yes, Mr. Hawksworth, but—"

"No *buts* about it. The Olympics are a once-in-a-lifetime opportunity for any hotel. If 'Going for the Gold' is a success tonight, the El Dorado will be *the* place to be come February. A reputation like that will draw the elite for decades."

"But, Mr. Hawksworth, there's a *dead* man in the resort!"

The hospitality manager blinked.

"Who says?" he asked.

"The pushy woman on line one. She insists on speaking with you."

"A dead man! Good Lord. We can't have Olympians spreading *that* news at 'Going for the Gold.'"

Handing Jenny pen and pad to record what was said, he punched on the speakerphone.

"Niles Hawksworth, hospitality manager."

"There's a dead cop in room 807," mumbled the caller. "Have Special X figure it out."

———•◦•———

Scarlett slammed down the receiver and smiled to herself. With a gloved finger, she emptied her mouth of the gauze pads she'd used to muffle her voice.

Let the games begin, she thought as she opened the door to the confining phone booth.

———•+•———

Meanwhile, the clock ticked on …

About seventy miles south, in the heart of Vancouver, the Omega Countdown Clock ticked off the seconds remaining until the Winter Games began, on February 12. Back when that towering piece of wood, metal, glass, and Swiss electronics had its official kickoff, protesters had stormed the podium to shout what sounded like "4Q—2010!" into the microphone. Scruffy-looking people wearing bandanas booed, jeered, and waved placards stating "Stop the Clock!" "Bread, Not Circuses!" and "Smash the Wrecking Balls of Gentrification!" The officers sent to suppress that mini-riot were pelted with balloons filled with paint and papier-mâché balls stuffed with rocks. To thwart vandals from wrecking the clock, security cameras watched it night and day over the next three years. Because the cops in the Special X office in Whistler Village faced the same deadline, a digital image of the Countdown Clock was beamed via satellite to a screen mounted on the wall above Sergeant Dane Winter's head.

"It's freaking me out," said Corporal Jackie Hett.

"What is?" Dane asked, glancing up from his half of their partners' desk.

"The Countdown Clock. I chose the wrong side of the desk. Every time I look up, I see seconds slipping away. And the shrinking numbers remind me of the odds against."

"Against what?"

"Doomsday," she said frankly. "I can't shake the feeling that something wicked this way comes."

"By the pricking of my thumbs," Dane said, crossing himself. "I'm partnered with a *witch*."

Actually, Dane was the envy of every male cop in Special X. Who wouldn't want to be teamed with this Amazon? With her flaming red hair, hypnotic green eyes, and statuesque figure, Jackie was a fantasy female right out of Greek myth. Like the legendary warriors, she was also armed to the teeth. A blue Kevlar vest protected her chest, and the belt buckled around her waist held an armory: a nine-mill on one hip, a Taser on the other, and the whole thing backed up by pepper spray, extra magazines, a portable radio, an extendable baton, and a set of handcuffs. Unlike the Amazons, she hadn't cut off her right breast so she could shoot a bow more freely. But that was okay with the men of Special X.

Ooh-la-la.

As far as Dane was concerned, Jackie could slap her cuffs on him any day of the week.

All of which stayed unexpressed, since he was her boss.

But dreams are free.

———•—•———

Jackie Hett had a crush on her boss. As likely as not, when she glanced up from her work, it wasn't to look at the Countdown Clock but to feast her eyes on Dane.

But for the chevron on his shoulder—three stripes, plus crown, not her two—they were dressed like twins. Sandy-haired and cobalt-eyed, he stood just over six feet. Beneath the blue vest and long-sleeved gray shirt with blue tie, Dane was athletically slim. Basketball or soccer—not hockey or football—would be his game. The sexual balance at Whistler tilted Jackie's way. At 53.6 percent male, the town was the most testosterone-charged in B.C. Boy toys came up for a few years to ski and have fun, making it a woman's hunting ground. So why was Jackie attracted to the one guy she couldn't bag?

No sex, please, we're Mounties.

She was one Mountie who *wouldn't* get her man.

Sex with your boss was a snake, not a ladder.

"It's like playing with alphabet soup," Jackie complained.

"What is?" asked Dane.

"The number of acronyms in VISU," she said, waving the security report in her hand. "We've got CSIS and CSOR and JTF-2, and Christ knows how many more. Acronyms within acronyms fill every document. When I'm commissioner, we'll go back to labels with meaning. Scotland Yard, flying patrol— that sort of thing. When I was a girl, at least I could rearrange letters to spell *words*."

"In your alphabet soup?"

"Yeah. Didn't you?"

"Spoon around for letters to make words?"

"Uh-huh."

"Who didn't?"

"So what's the answer?"

"To what?"

"The obvious question."

Dane shrugged. "Obviously, the obvious question isn't so obvious to me."

"A, B, C, D," Jackie said. "That's a clue."

"It is?"

"E, F, G, H. That's another."

"Beats me."

"Tsk-tsk," Jackie clucked. "And you call yourself a detective? The obvious question for any kid is, Does *every* can of alphabet soup contain all twenty-six letters?"

"Does it?"

"Now that would be cheating. You know it's a sin to blab the end of a mystery."

The phone on Dane's half of the desk rang.

"Sergeant Winter," he answered while jotting "Buy alphabet soup" on his notepad.

"Niles Hawksworth, hospitality manager at the El Dorado Resort. It may be a hoax, but we just received a call to say there's a dead officer in room 807."

————

VISU had the staggering task of building an impenetrable shield against terrorist attacks during the Olympics. From its operations base in the old Motorola building, a huge office complex near the Fraser River, the unit was gearing up to protect more than one hundred venues. Its territory spread from the airport near the U.S. border to the mountain slopes, and included countless smuggling coves on the world's most indented coastline.

No event presents a better target for terrorists and political zealots than the Olympics. The massacre of eleven Israeli competitors by Palestinian gunmen at the 1972 Munich games had proved that. The threat was palpably real—the rise in militant extremism, the wars in Iraq and Afghanistan, bombs going off in London, Madrid, and elsewhere—and there were gaps in the shield. Security, by its nature, is never 100 percent foolproof. You can secure an Olympic village or an isolated venue, but you can't secure an entire city and a hundred-mile swath around it, unless you turn the area into a police state.

A Stalag behind barbed wire.

And even a stronghold can be breached.

VISU was assigned to protect 5,000 athletes and officials, 10,000 media, 25,000 volunteers, and 250,000 visitors from hazards ranging from fire to a hail of manmade junk plunging from outer space. The nightmare scenario was a dirty bomb, a radiation device offloaded from a ship at sea and smuggled ashore by a motorboat putting in to one of the coves.

Come February, air force fighters would patrol restricted skies, and navy destroyers would guard the waterfront. CSOR—the Canadian Special Operations Regiment—would defend against biological, chemical, and nuclear weapons. JTF-2 commandos, the 350 best counter-terrorists, would act as snipers and bodyguards.

Regular policing would fall to an army of cops with bomb-sniffing dogs, as well as to hostage negotiators and riot squads. There would be miles of fencing delineating safe zones with limited access points. Everything would be watched by surveillance cameras, and biometric software would identify known terrorists by measuring their facial features and analyzing their walks.

Special X was but a cog in that giant machine.

The Special External Section of the Royal Canadian Mounted Police predated the world's current obsession with acronyms. If not, it would now be known as SES or—with a little fudging of the abbreviation—SEX. Imagine the jokes that would spawn!

Tied to Interpol—the International Criminal Police Organization—Special X investigated crimes committed in Canada but with links outside the borders. It kept tabs on violent troublemakers and would hunt down any killer if a murder took place at the Olympics. With the countdown on and time running out, the last thing the officers stationed at Whistler needed was the death of one of their own.

Though it was a short trudge from the Special X detachment to the El Dorado Resort, Dane and Jackie were white with snow by the time they pushed through the revolving door. Bundled up in fur hats with earflaps, storm parkas, scarves, mitts, and boots, they brushed themselves off. Their plumes of breath evaporated as they entered the hotel, but their cheeks stayed flushed from the chill outside.

A fretting Niles Hawksworth met them in the lobby.

"This is *most* inconvenient," fumed the manager. "No doubt it's a hoax perpetrated by one of our competitors to undermine tonight's event. It's a cutthroat business, trying to go for the gold."

"You've touched nothing?" Dane asked.

"Of course not," Hawksworth replied, offended that anyone would think he didn't do things just so.

The three rode an elevator to the eighth floor and angled along a hallway wide enough to allow drunks to wobble shouldered skis. Even so, the wallpaper had scars. The door to room 807 was blocked by a security guard with a pair of bolt cutters.

The sergeant rapped on the wood.

"Police," Dane announced.

Three times he knocked, and three times got no reply.

"Who rents the room?"

"A company called Ecuador Exploration," Hawksworth stated. "They're new to us."

"How does the door work?"

"Three locks. Combination keycard and deadbolt, and a swing-bar door guard. I have a master key to override the first two. Ken here has bolt cutters for the bar."

"Allow me," Dane said, holding out his hand. "Fingerprints," he added.

Hawksworth passed him the master key, and the Mountie stuck it in the slot. That popped the electronic lock and automatically twisted the deadbolt. Cautiously, Dane used his gloved hand to depress the handle, careful not to smudge any prints. The door swung open about an inch before the knob caught in the swing bar.

"There," he said, indicating where the guard should cut.

Ken eased the bolt cutters through the gap between the door and its frame to snip the metal.

Crunch!

The knob fell to the floor and the door swung wide.

"Jesus Christ!" Jackie gasped, staring at the bed.

Dane stood stunned.

"There'll be hell to pay for this," he swore to himself.

It wasn't blue murder.

It was gold.

SHRUNKEN HEAD

Snow was falling in fat white flakes as the potential podium topper stood in line for the chairlift. Too bad the weather wasn't conducive to a little spying. With all the competitors here to test the terrain before the real thing, he'd hoped to be able to eyeball their performance-enhancement teams and compare them to his own.

Whiteout, however, meant a blind eye.

"Look upon the Olympics as going to war," Will's coach had said. "Strategy counts. So does spying."

As in war, it was all about national pride. As host of the world's top winter sports event, Canada had shoveled over $100 million into its Own the Podium program, designed to identify top athletes and whip them into shape. Will had been fussed over by a gaggle of physiotherapists, biomechanists, sports psychologists, and conditioning gurus. They'd put reflective stickers on his knee and ankle joints and then videotaped him jumping for a computer to detect any "muscle activation abnormality." Wind-tunnel testing had helped him shave seconds off the clock.

"We have a super skier," stated their report.

Meanwhile, 150 researchers at dozens of Canadian universities were at work on Top Secret, a high-tech program developed to give golden boys like Will the tenth- or hundredth-of-a-second edge required to nab a gold medal. Top Secret alchemists reduced friction on suits and helmets, matched ski waxes to weather conditions, and timed the release of their best innovations so it would be too late for foreign spies to copy them.

For Will, however, the ski was on the other foot. Wars, he knew, are won by spying on the competition, and today would have been the ideal opportunity to check out his rivals for clues to what was hidden up their sleeves.

If not for this veil of snow.

Sport could be *so* unfair.

But all that vanished from his mind as Will clomped onto the spot where the chairlift would sweep him away. A curvy creature filling out a red ski suit slid into place beside him. A pulled-down toque, a pulled-up turtleneck, and yellow goggles masked her face. But if her looks complemented the hourglass below, Will felt he just might salvage the day. The benefit of having a physique like his was having a physique like his. He had the stamina to rock the sexual fantasies of any snow bunny he considered worth his down time.

Show yourself, lady.

The chairlift scooped them off the ground and carried them up into the blinding snowfall. The only sound was the bending and flexing of the cable as it circled the bullwheel and slipped over the support towers. The mountain air smelled crystalline and misted from their lungs. Reaching up behind their heads, Will grasped the restraining bar and pulled it down so they could support their skis on the footrest.

"You're Will Finch!" the woman said, pushing the goggles up on her brow.

Her features *did* complement her figure.

"What's your name?"

"Scarlett."

"In from where?"

"Vegas."

"Sin City."

"So they say."

"What do you do?"

"Showgirl."

"I should have guessed." He looked her up and down. "Too bad I missed the show."

"You can still catch it."

"How?"

"By a command performance."

"You move fast."

The femme fatale pouted. "I've only got this ride."

"Is the show worth it?"

"You decide. I once worked as a stripper."

Like fish in a barrel, thought Will.

Flakes tumbled around them like dandruff off the scalp of God. They seemed to be the only skiers in this frozen Garden of Eden, and Will had no doubt they'd soon be as naked as Adam and Eve. The snake was stirring.

The sudden yelp of pain from Scarlett took him by surprise. One of her legs jerked like a frog hit by electric current in a school biology lab.

"Charley horse!" she gasped through gritted teeth.

"Stretch it out," said Will.

"I can't! The footrest's in the way."

Here was an opportunity for Will to play Galahad. The surest cure for a muscle cramp was to extend the leg, pushing down with the heel and pointing the toes toward the face. Slipping a hand under her thigh to lift the troublesome limb, Will grabbed the restraining bar and released it.

Bending forward, he reached down to massage her calf, and that's when Scarlett looped the metal dog collar about his neck. Hooking one end of the leash around the chairlift frame, the Ice Pick Killer pushed him as hard as she could. Will was propelled from the seat high above the slope and dropped like a prisoner through the trapdoor of a gallows.

Zzhhhh …

His weight cinched the noose tight, while the razor blade inside the collar sliced into his flesh and didn't stop constricting until it had sundered one vertebra from another.

Scarlett gripped Will's head by the hair as his decapitated body plunged in a geyser of blood that reddened the snow.

The siren swapped the head for the trophy she carried in her backpack and tied it to the chairlift frame. Just short of the bullwheel at the top of the run, she skied off on her escape route.

A voice from the chair behind was in hysterics.

———————

At the foot of the chairlift, an Austrian couple sidestepped onto the marks to wait for the next carrier. The seat spun around the bullwheel and scooped the lovebirds up. As the newlyweds leaned together to snuggle for the ride, they found themselves confronting a grisly chaperone.

A shrunken human head hung from the chairlift frame.

GILDED MAN

Robert's first thought on seeing the body was that he was back in Egypt. When the archeologist Howard Carter unearthed the tomb of King Tutankhamen in 1922, he found the boy pharaoh's mummy encased in three coffins, one within another in the oblong sarcophagus. Each coffin was molded in the king's image. The innermost was made of solid gold.

The view from the door of room 807 transported the Mountie back to the Cairo museum he and Katt had visited a few years earlier. Gilded gold from head to foot, the body on the bed reminded Robert of the innermost coffin, except that the image was a likeness of Nick Craven, not King Tut. Naked, Nick lay face up on a black satin sheet, his wrists crossed over his heart. One arm ended with a stump where his prosthetic hand had been. The hand was on the bedside table, alongside Nick's prosthetic ear.

I get it, Robert thought, clenching his fists to quell his roiling anger.

Dane Winter had called his cellphone as he, Katt, and Napoleon, their German shepherd, neared the outskirts of Whistler on the Sea to Sky Highway. Despite their early start, they had slowed to a crawl as the weather deteriorated. Behind them in her car, Gill and Joe had faded, then vanished in a scrim of blurry snow.

"DeClercq," he'd answered.

"Chief, it's Dane Winter. Brace yourself ..."

The link between Nick's gilding and the scene of the crime struck the psycho hunter as he drove past the Gilded Man pub in the El Dorado Resort. As a lifelong historian with several books in print, he was well read in the literature of the Holy Grail, Atlantis, Shangri-La, King Solomon's Mines, and El Dorado. The banner flapping above the hotel's entrance confirmed the link: "Meet Olympic Hopefuls at 'Going for the Gold.'"

"Why are we stopping here instead of driving to the cabin?" Katt had asked. She knew Nick well, so Robert had yet to tell her.

"Something I must check."

"Was it bad news?" Katt pressed. "You've been spacey since you took that call."

"Time will tell. I need half an hour. Park the car and take the dog for a walk."

Napoleon barked his agreement.

"Goody," Katt said with exaggerated glee, rubbing her palms together. "It's joyride time!"

Moments after Robert's car disappeared, Gill's materialized ghostlike from the snow, and the Mountie's cell hummed again.

"DeClercq," he responded.

"It's Corporal Hett, Chief. Looks like we've found the head from yesterday's snowboarder. It's shrunken and painted gold, and what's more, we have *another* beheading."

The digital image that zoomed to his phone from Jackie's showed a miniature human head dangling from a chairlift frame. Nick's gilded body linked him to the golden severed head, which in turn reminded the chief of the Headhunter Case. Was someone trying to jab his memory?

Who would do that? he wondered.

And *love* doing it?

Now, they stood at the threshold to room 807—the psycho hunter, the pathologist, and the forensic scientist—while Dane indicated the path he'd taken to the bed to check Nick's vital signs. He had hugged the walls in the hopes that would keep him from trampling on vital clues.

The four pulled on latex gloves and plastic booties, then approached the body. Gazing down at the man he had saved twice from disaster—when Nick had stood trial for the death of his mother, and when Mephisto had cut him apart piece by piece—Robert struggled to view the crime scene objectively. The tradition was etched in stone: kill a Mountie and you take on the entire force. And history had shown that in those instances, they *did* always get their man.

But the chief didn't want emotion blinding his logic. He knew the run-of-the-mill serial killer was a slave to fantasy. Acting out that fantasy created a normally subconscious "signature" that could be profiled by crime scene analysts. In this case, the signature was not subconscious but displayed on the bedside table for the chief and all the world to see.

The gilded man had been stripped of his prosthetic hand and ear. By returning Nick to his handless, earless self, this killer had left his signature in the overblown, gilt-edged scrawl of a malignant narcissist.

Goldfinger!

The first connection cracked through Gill's mind like a bolt of lightning. In Ian Fleming's book, the megalomaniac with an obsession for everything gold could attain sexual climax only by romping with gilded women.

Megalomaniac …

That was the second connection.

Mephisto, she thought.

Strange, how at times like this, you remember only the good parts. Looking back, their love affair had been doomed from the start. Gill and Nick had come from different places and were going different places. She was classical music, while he was rock 'n' roll. Gill was born into money, raised in the sun of Barbados, and blessed with a mother who set an example as a leading pathologist. Nick was born prematurely on a bathroom floor during a blustery winter storm in Medicine Hat, Alberta. Later that night, his dad shot himself. His mom toiled in the laundry of a mental hospital to keep the roof over their heads and food on the table. Having raised hell as a teenager, Nick became a cop to atone for the disappointment he'd caused her.

What Gill and Nick had in common was what they did in bed. She was a champagne partner for him, and he was a hot young stud for her. That she was turning forty was a factor in the equation. But when the ghosts of his past came haunting, that wasn't enough to see them through the turmoil.

Now, scowling down at Nick's gilded body, Gill was sickened by the stench of lacquer. So thick was the coat of paint that she couldn't even see the tattoo on his upper arm: an hourglass running out of sand, with the words "Here Comes" above and "the Night" below. But worst of all were his eyes. The killer had left them open, gazing vacantly at the ceiling, then had sprayed the eyeballs with glittery gold.

Gill couldn't help it.

Tears rolled down her cheeks.

————•—•——

Having never met Nick, Joseph Avacomovitch was all business.

"I don't see a wound on the body, do you? He looks serene, as if he's simply fallen asleep."

"Poison?" Dane suggested. "Spiked with a syringe? Maybe there's a puncture wound beneath the gunk."

The Russian turned to Gill as she wiped away her tears. "It seems to me that Nick was painted postmortem, yet there's not a trace of gold on the black satin. That indicates the killer changed the linen so he or she could display the corpse for maximum shock value. May I turn him over to look for a wound?"

Gill glanced at Robert for approval.

The chief nodded.

The paint was sticky to the touch as Dane and Joseph gripped Nick at the shoulder and hip and eased him onto his side. The sheet adhering to his back was peeled away. There wasn't a patch on the underside that wasn't gold, and a careful examination revealed no signs of trauma.

"Poisoning by mouth?" Dane suggested.

"Likely," Joe replied.

"Where can I do a postmortem?" asked Gill.

The question drew Robert's focus to her. The image of Gill dissecting her former lover furrowed a deep crease into his brow.

"He's gone," she said, aware of what Robert was thinking. "All that's left are Nick's remains. The answer to *who* killed him lies in the cause of death. Your pool of suspects will scatter before his body even reaches Vancouver. I'm the pathologist *here*. I owe it to Nick to help catch his killer."

"I'll assist," Joe offered, sealing the deal.

"Instead of the medical center," Robert suggested, "use the trauma room that's been created for officers hurt while securing the Olympics. It's nearby and private."

"Hopefully, when we wipe the gilt off Nick, we'll see how he died," said Gill.

"There's another puzzle," Dane interjected. "The room was locked from *inside*. So how did the killer escape?"

An aisle led from the door of room 807 to the far window. The bed flanked the left-hand wall. Above it hung a framed painting of Whistler and Blackcomb mountains, the rising sun adorning their ski runs in gold. Between the bed and the window, on the side where Joe and Dane stood, there was a door giving access to the adjoining suite.

"The only way in or out," said Dane, "is through one of these two doors. The window doesn't open, and there's no egress whatsoever in the right-hand side."

He gestured from the window to the writing desk, TV stand, luggage rack, bathroom, and wardrobe.

"The deadbolt on the connecting door was engaged when we broke in through the main one."

"As it is now?" confirmed Joe.

"Yes," agreed the sergeant. Turning to the lock, Dane gripped the thumb-turn by its narrow ends, not its flat sides, to avoid smudging any prints, and gave it a quarter twist to vertical. The connecting door opened to reveal no keyhole on the outer side. The wood was intact, as was the wood of the door securing the adjoining suite.

"See the problem?" asked Dane. "Each deadbolt securing each door has an *exit-only* function. The rod will retract only if someone rotates the cylinder by twisting the knob on the *inside* of his door. A deadbolt can't be jimmied with a card or a tool, and because there isn't a keyhole, it can't be picked with a bump key. To lock this door, you need someone alive on this side, and Nick was obviously dead when the killer escaped."

"Puzzling," Joseph mused, examining the oiled lock.

"To join the rooms, each occupant unlocks his deadbolt from *inside* his suite. If the killer fled through this door to the next room, how did he lock it behind him?"

"It would appear," the Russian replied, "that he escaped by way of the entrance door."

"I don't see how," said Dane. "That puzzle is even tougher. There were three barriers preventing us from breaking in: an electronic lock, a deadbolt, and a swing bar. Setting the deadbolt and swing bar again requires someone alive inside the room. To break in, we needed the hotel's master key and a pair of bolt cutters to sever the knob in the swing bar."

"So," said Joseph, "who set the three locks?"

"A woman," Dane replied.

"Why do you say that?" asked the chief.

"In searching his clothes, I discovered this in Nick's pocket." The sergeant held up a magnetic keycard in an evidence pouch. "It springs the lock on the entrance door. The door keeps a log of the times the card is used. This card was used at ten last night, and the door wasn't opened again until we broke in this morning."

"So why a woman?" asked Gill.

Dane produced a second evidence pouch containing a yellow Post-it Note.

"This was stuck to the key."

The note read: "Ten o'clock tonight. Be discreet."

Gill's glare darkened. "It looks to me like Nick got picked up in a bar."

SLIT

The Sea to Sky Highway had almost cost Whistler the Olympics.

During the last ice age, the Pacific coast sagged under an immense weight. Creeping glaciers gouged cliffs and valleys into the bedrock. Once the ice retreated, the land rose up and the sea surged in, forming fiords such as Howe Sound. It took dynamite blasts to cut through the granite so train tracks and a cramped road could snake along the shore. Nature constantly threatened to block the only route to Whistler under crushing landslides.

"What's that, Mom?"

"What's what, Becky?" Jenna Bond was afraid to take her eyes off the icy, winding road. Along the so-called Killer Highway, deaths were common.

"Those windows up the mountain."

Chancing a glance, Jenna squinted through the veil. A sob of wind from the sea buffeted their car, almost pushing it onto the shoulder of the slippery road. Beyond the window, Jenna could just make out a staircase-shaped structure climbing the mountainside.

"That's a concentrator, Becky," Jenna explained, passing on something Nick had told her during a romantic ski weekend. "It's a gravity mill for a copper mine. The story is that a long time ago, a doctor shot a deer on this mountain. The thrashing legs of the dying buck exposed some copper ore. That's how Britannia Beach became a huge copper mine."

"Poor deer," mourned the girl.

A train chugged past them on the twisting ribbon of track. Becky shoved a CD into the player and started singing along with "Jingle Bells." As she warbled, she rolled down the passenger's window, filling the car with blizzard.

"Becky!"

"Mom, we need an open sleigh."

At spots, the road hugged nearly vertical slopes. The frozen Shannon Falls plunged as hundreds of yards of ice.

"Know how the falls were formed, Becs?"

"Uh-uh," said the girl.

"A two-headed sea serpent named Say-noth-ka used that spillway to slither up the mountain."

"Cool," said Becky, cupping her hands around her eyes to take in the falls.

On the outskirts of Squamish, a lumber town that had buzzed with life until the pulp mill closed, there was a massive granite face almost two thousand feet high. Known as the Stawamus Chief, it was a climber's dream in summer, but today it was shrouded in white.

"Does that look like an Indian's head to you?"

"Yes," said Becky.

The imagination of youth, Jenna thought. All she saw was a hump of snowy rock.

At Squamish, the road cut away from the sea and followed the Cheakamus River into the Coast Mountains. Back in the Cariboo Gold Rush of the 1860s, fortune-seekers had trudged into this harsh wilderness to reach the Lillooet Shortcut, an ancient Native trail through the mountains.

"Did you know that old-time miners once used camels to pack their supplies up this valley, Becs? The camels refused to behave, though, so they were released to fend for themselves in the bush."

"Are they still there?"

"I doubt it. That was a long, long time ago."

"Poor camels," said Becky.

Luckily, a snowplow had preceded them inland, so the highway here was in better shape than the stretch along Howe Sound.

"Mom?"

"Yes?"

"Are you going to marry Nick?"

Oh no, Jenna thought, her hands tightening on the wheel. "Why do you ask?"

"'Cause I think he'd be the best dad I could ever have. Why don't I see him more often?"

"He's a busy Mountie."

"Can't we move up here?"

"It's not that easy. We're Americans. Nick's a Canadian. A border separates us. And anyway, your granddad was the sheriff of San Juan County."

"He died with his boots on," the girl said, repeating the legend she had so often heard.

"Yes, he did. Serving the islands. Don't you want me to be sheriff, too?"

"I want a dad more."

Hearing Becky talk like that broke Jenna's heart. San Juan County elected its sheriff every four years. Jenna's father, Hank Bond, had been returned to office twelve times before he was cut down by a stroke at his desk. Tough as nails on the outside but loving within, he was the best dad a tomboy could desire. For as long as she could remember, Jenna had wanted to follow in his footsteps. Lured from Orcas Island to Seattle's FBI office, she had married an agent with the Drug Enforcement Administration. But instead of the happily-ever-after she'd always dreamed of, their marital bliss had morphed into a horrifying nightmare.

"Something's up, Jen," Don had said over the phone one night. "Got a meet tonight. May be a lead on the cartel."

"But it's your birthday!"

"I won't be late."

"I'll wait up."

"Lots to celebrate if this works out."

That was the last time they'd talked. Don's body was never found—all that was left was his voice on a tape sent to the DEA. They wouldn't let Jenna hear it. Hours of Don being tortured by the cartel, every last minute recorded in an attempt to get the law to back off.

A week later, Jenna learned she was pregnant.

Every time she looked at Becky, she saw Don. They were as alike as she and Hank. Same fox-like face, slender chin, unruly russet hair, mischievous grin. Same hunting for an opening to crack a joke. Because she'd grown up in the protective shadow cast by Hank, Jenna knew how much the girl yearned for the love of a father.

And Jenna still had the dream …

Don's screams echo up and down this hall of a hundred identical doors as Jenna searches frantically for her abducted husband. Time is everything. Don can take no more. He begs the Colombians to finish him off. "Oh, Jesus! Please, not another piece!" A hundred doors! Where is he? Tears salt her lips. Each door sticks as she tries to push it open. Damn island weather—too much moisture, wood expanding so every door always sticks. "Oh, Jesus! Not that! Leave me a man!"

Jenna reaches out to shove open door 13, but it opens a crack by itself, and the DEA agent who will later refuse to let her hear the tape of the torture session peers out at her. "Don't worry, Jenna. It's all under control. I'll make sure the Geneva Conventions get followed in here. They won't disturb your daughter with the way Don looks. He'll be long gone before she's born."

"Oh, Jesus!" Don gibbers. "Don't cut off my—"

"Mom?"

Jenna turns sharply.

Oh, God. No!

Becky stands behind her in the hall.

"What are you doing here?"

"I can't sleep."

"Jesus!" Don beseeches. "Don't let her see me!"

"Back to bed, honey."

"I had a bad dream."

"Go back to bed, back to sleep, and it'll be gone by morning."

"Mom ...

"Mom ..."

"Mom?"

Jerking out of her reverie, Jenna returned her attention to the treacherous highway.

"What, Becs?"

"Are we there yet?"

"Almost."

"Where's Nick gonna meet us?"

"Alpha Lake. A-L-P-H-A. Watch for the sign."

Function Junction—an industrial park with a recycling facility—marked the beginning of Whistler Valley. The map on her lap told Jenna that the mountains owned the right flank of the road. She could sense them, rather than see them. Along the left side of the road ran a string of lakes: Alpha, Nita, and Alta. The railway clung to their far shores. Like the mountains, the lakes were lost to sight.

"Turn, Mom! Turn! It's Alpha Lake!"

Blind faith guided Jenna through the maze of streets to the parking lot. No sooner had the car stopped than Becky jumped out and trudged to the basketball court. The hoop was hung with icicles, the wire mesh full of snow. Left to lug her daughter's skates, the equipment manager caught up with the girl just as a well-aimed snowball snapped the last icicle off the ring.

"What an arm!"

Becky grinned and was off again.

A footbridge arced over a small creek to a windbreak of white-barked birches. White, white, white, wherever the eye focused. A white pagoda and swing set in the play area. White willows and picnic tables beside the lake, which itself was frozen white and blanketed with snow. Jenna felt caught in the snow globe at the start of *Citizen Kane*.

Rosebud, she thought.

"Hurry up, Mom! Bring my skates!"

Becky was kneeling on a bench, rocking with excitement. The girl rubbernecked, trying to spy Nick. The wind was picking up, and random gusts tore sightlines through the snow. Now you see them, now you don't. A skater with a shovel cleared the ice. A showoff with his face masked by a balaclava spun and jumped like an Olympian. Kids supported by both parents wobbled around for their first skate.

Down on one knee like Prince Charming fitting Cinderella with a glass slipper, Jenna laced Becky into her skates. The bench was so close to the lake that ice froze her kneecap numb.

"Stay on the shoveled path," cautioned Jenna. "No thin ice."

"Watch for Nick."

"I will."

"Marry him, Mom. *Please!*"

Jenna's sigh was stolen by the gusts. Off went Becky to circle the rink. She was like Halley's Comet, slipping off on a far-flung orbit that would eventually return her to Mother Earth.

Rosebud, Jenna thought. Innocence lost. That word of regret in the dying gasp of Charles Foster Kane. Her daughter had lost her father to Colombian thugs. God knows what psychological damage was done while she was kept caged by Mephisto. In Nick, she'd found a surrogate father who helped heal those wounds. But he couldn't abandon the job that made *him* feel whole again, and that left Jenna with a major impediment to *her* ambition.

Guilt made her shudder.

What would Hank think, she wondered, if he knew she was willing to put aside Becky's happiness to fill his boots as sheriff of San Juan County?

I can't do that, she thought.

So, sitting on the bench at the edge of the ice, Jenna rummaged in her pocket for her cell. As she scrolled through the menu for Nick's name, she took her eyes off the ice. From out of the snowfall came the man in the balaclava, winding up for his Olympic stunts. He bent his torso forward and extended one leg straight behind him, forming his body into the shape of a T.

"Look out!" someone shouted.

Jenna glanced up.

Exposing her throat.

Within striking distance of the bench, the skater whirled on his supporting leg to execute a camel spin. His razor-sharp blade spun 360 degrees, slashing across Jenna's neck and slitting her throat to the bone.

MURDER BAG

Joseph Avacomovitch never attended a murder scene without his Murder Bag. He even traveled with it.

Television these days was wall-to-wall forensics. Quirky but lovable CSI nerds were the new detectives, working in state-of-the-art labs and solving murders through magic. A machine jiggles test tubes or whirls them around, then miraculously tells a computer the results. On scene, a tech opens a stainless steel case packed with glowing wands that catch stains the human eye can't see. A squeeze of fluid from an eyedropper and the cell door clangs shut.

All of which dates back to a handful of guts.

The Crumbles Case.

The patron saint of CSIs—for those who know their history— is Sir Bernard Spilsbury. The British pathologist shot to fame through his work in the Crippen Case, the Brides in the Bath Murders, the Brighton Trunk Murders, the Blazing Car Murder, and other forensics puzzles of the early 1900s.

In 1924, Spilsbury traveled to a rented bungalow on a barren strip of the Sussex shore known as the Crumbles to help Scotland Yard piece together a dismembered woman. Patrick Mahon had butchered his lover, Emily Kaye, to keep her pregnancy from ruining his life. A trail of blood ran from the sitting room, where Mahon had struck Kaye with an ax, across a hall and through a bedroom to the scullery. There, using a knife and a saw, he'd cut his mistress apart for disposal.

Blood and body grease were splattered everywhere. Boiled human flesh slimed a saucepan and a tub. Kaye's heart and other internal organs were stuffed in a biscuit tin. A trunk bearing her initials contained rotting body parts. Over a thousand charred bone fragments littered the fireplace.

When Spilsbury entered the bungalow, he was shocked to see a detective chief inspector using his bare hands to scoop up mounds of putrid flesh and dump it into buckets.

"Are there no rubber gloves?" he asked.

The Yard man gave him a puzzled look. "I never wear gloves. No one I know has worn gloves in the seventeen years of the Murder Squad. This is how we do it."

The smell was so foul that Spilsbury set up a table outside. There, with hundreds of locals gawking over the fence, he reconstructed Kaye's body like a jigsaw puzzle. Pieced together, it was found to be missing its head, uterus, and right leg.

Mahon confessed to having thrown portions of the corpse from the train on a trip to London. He said he burned the head in the fireplace during a thunderstorm. The heat had caused Kaye's eyes to pop open just as a clap of thunder shook the room. Shocked, Mahon fled from the house. Later, he smashed the skull to bits with a poker.

To test that tale, Spilsbury burned a sheep's head at the bungalow. He thereby established that fire did make a skull brittle enough to reduce it to splinters.

Mahon was hanged that fall.

Since 1842, when Scotland Yard established its detective branch, homicide investigators had been collecting evidence with their bare fingers and wrapping it in paper or envelopes for safekeeping. Spilsbury suggested introducing a Murder Bag, a standard kit to be carried by any detective responding to a homicide. The bag contained rubber gloves; brushes to dust for fingerprints; a ruler to measure distance; a compass to establish direction; a magnet, tweezers, and other means to lift clues; swabs, bags, and containers to store evidence; and although it wasn't on Spilsbury's official list of contents, a bottle of whisky to fortify detectives at the grisliest of crimes.

Although Joe had traded the whisky for vodka, the Murder Bag he fetched from Gill's car was in all other ways based on Spilsbury's original design. That's because he believed in the principle of Occam's razor: "All other things being equal, the simplest solution is the best." Or, put another way, when you hear hoof beats, think horses, not zebras.

Keep it simple, stupid.

With that in mind, the Russian bypassed the entrance door to room 807. It had three locks, one of which was electronic, making it much more complicated than the connecting door. That infringed Occam's razor.

Skirting the end of the bed to reach the other door, Joe set down his Murder Bag and knelt on the floor in front of the deadbolt. As he opened the bag, Dane joined him, squatting down on his heels to see what was up.

"Find something?" asked the sergeant.

"Not yet, but I have a theory."

"Give me a clue?"

"What's the first step a salvage yard takes when it receives a load of scrap metals?"

Dane had been to junkyards. "Ferrous and nonferrous. Divide iron and steel from other metals."

"What's the first thing we learn about iron in school?"

"It's magnetic."

"Why?"

"As I recall, it's something about electrons lining up."

Joe nodded. "Every electron, by its nature, is a tiny magnet. For a metal to be magnetic, it must have electron spin. Normally, the countless electrons in a metal are oriented in random directions. A metal is ferromagnetic—like iron and steel—if its electrons line up when drawn by a magnet. A metal is diamagnetic—like copper and zinc—if its electrons don't line up. You'll note that the thumb-turn on this door is copper."

"So it's not magnetic?"

"Supposedly," said Joe, fetching a handheld electromagnet from his Murder Bag.

Dane watched the Russian apply the prongs to the outside face of the door, so they lined up with the arms of the thumb-turn on the other side. Flicking a switch electrified the tool. A quarter-turn of Joe's wrist turned the knob of the deadbolt as well. The rod emerged from the lock in the edge of the door.

"So it isn't copper?" said Dane.

"Let's see." With a screwdriver, the scientist removed the screw in the center of the thumb-turn. Holding the knob in his fingers, he showed the Mountie the edge that usually faced the wood. "What color is that to you?"

"Gold," said Dane.

"The same color as Nick's skin."

With the blade of a knife, Joe scraped off the layer of paint to reveal two iron plugs set into the outer tips of the thumb-turn.

"I'll be damned. How'd you twig to that?"

"The lock on the entrance door is released by the keycard's *magnetic* strip. That got me thinking of magnets. And I noticed that this lock had been oiled when we examined it earlier. I put one and one together." He shrugged.

Joe tried the electromagnet on the locked door to the other suite, to no avail.

"What if the killer had access to *both* rooms?" he suggested. "The door of the next room was left unlocked while she— I assume it's a she—waited in here for Nick to arrive. After using the key, he triple-locked the entrance door for privacy, then fell prey to the trap. Maybe an accomplice lurked next door?"

"That's probable," said Dane. "Can you imagine one person lifting Nick's body?"

"Unlock the thumb-turn on this door and step into the next room. Turn and close this door, and lock it from the outside with the magnet. Then close the other door and turn its dead-bolt from inside the next room. Would that not present us with the puzzle we face—and allow escape from the adjoining suite?"

"Tricky," said Dane.

Just then, a far-off explosion boomed loudly enough to rattle the snow-flaked window.

"What was *that*?" asked Joe.

THIN ICE

Winter was Inspector Zinc Chandler's favorite season.

Most adults, the Mountie knew, loathed the winter months. To them, exile to Siberia would be no worse than suffering through a deep freeze on the Prairies. How many folks died from heart attacks while shoveling snow? How many homeless men and women froze to death? How many drivers trapped in snowbound cars asphyxiated while running the engine for heat? Did you hear about the guy who crawled out of his trapped vehicle and made it to a phone booth? While he was talking to his wife, telling her not to worry, a snowplow passed in the whiteout and buried him alive.

Ah yes, winter in the Great White North!

Zinc, however, still saw winter through the eyes of a bundled-up schoolboy. Two pairs of socks in thermal boots, two pairs of mitts tethered by a string around his neck, long johns beneath a flannel shirt and jeans inside a snowsuit. His mom would throw open the door of the farmhouse in Rosetown, Saskatchewan, and let in a blast as cold as Jack Frost's breath. No sooner would Zinc step outside than he'd have to pee.

Brrrrr …

People who weren't from Saskatchewan didn't *know* snow. Spraying the yard produced a personal skating rink. Freezing a snowdrift made a slide. Burrowing under the surface created a maze of tunnels and caves. Zinc could glide on the frozen sloughs or play hockey on the road. Lash the toboggan behind a horse and off he'd go. Drifts became forts for snowball fights. Easter egg dye gave him snow churches with stained-glass windows. On flat days bled of color, snow would fall, and Zinc, facing skyward, would capture flakes on his tongue. Once, he'd stuck his tongue to a piece of cold metal, learning a lesson to last a lifetime.

Ouch!

When he came in from the blizzard, he'd be struck by a wave of heat. Standing by the wood-burning stove in a cocoon of warmth, Zinc would peer out at the white world, stark and eerie, through an overlay of reflected Christmas lights. The next morning, he'd draw faces in the rime on the pane.

Winter ...

Now that boy was a man on the cusp of forty. Transplanted to the gray blahs of Lotusland, where the rain, rain, rain replaced the requisite white, Zinc was forced into the mountains to enjoy his favorite season. Luckily, this year the Olympics had moved him up to Whistler, so the back of his Range Rover was stocked with all his winter gear: downhill and cross-country skis, snowboard, toboggan, and skates. That afternoon, he was slated to meet with Robert DeClercq, which had severely limited his options for outdoor exercise. That's why he was seated on an icy bench beside frozen Alpha Lake, lacing up his blades, when the Latvian Iceman slit Jenna's throat.

———•-•—

A spurt of blood arced across the falling snow, its warmth melting the flakes into drops of red rain. The skater completed his slashing spin with a reverse check that left him facing the carnage. His toe pick gouged a crimson hole in the ice.

"Mommy!"

The shriek of raw horror raised the hackles on Zinc's neck. Out of the snowfall emerged a girl on wobbly skates, obviously circling the rink for Mom's praise. Eyes wide and mouth agape, the child was transfixed by the spewing blood. Her howl of anguish shattered the brittle air.

Ka-boom!

———•·•———

The explosion was loud enough to reverberate off the heights of Whistler Valley, setting off avalanches that could be heard but not seen. The Latvian Iceman nodded, for that meant the other Icemen had launched their assaults, too.

Once professional soldiers trained in the tactics of winter warfare, the Icemen had been hand-picked for this work, the money from which would provide each killer with a platinum retirement plan. Their history went back to 1242 and the legendary Battle of the Ice, when Roman Catholic Teutonic Knights advanced against Russian pagans. During the battle, fought on frozen Lake Peipus, the pagan cavalry forced the knights onto thin ice, which gave way under the weight of their heavy armor, causing many to drown. From that point forward, the armies of northern Europe developed their winter warfare tactics, culminating in the greatest battle in the history of the world: the 1942 Battle of Stalingrad.

Winter warfare was defined as armed conflict in exceptionally cold weather and snowy, icy terrain. Survival depended on sub-zero equipment: warm clothing and footwear, nutritious food, white camouflage, tents and thermal sleeping bags, heaters and adequate fuel. Winter warriors learned that snow holes made good shelter, and that frostbite and hypothermia were constant enemies. For ambushes and attacks, ski-equipped troops could rival the speed of and distance covered by light cavalry.

Also, the Latvian could figure skate.

That's why he was assigned to kill Jenna and Becky Bond.

Frozen with shock, the child stood on the ice in front of the bench, watching as two women tried frantically to stanch the spurts of arterial blood. Others in the park were also rushing to help, so the Iceman decided to put some distance between himself and the do-gooders, in case they mobbed him while he was busy killing the girl.

Pushing off with one blade, the Latvian stormed toward Becky, wrapping an arm around her waist and scooping her off the ice. Captor and captive shot into the blizzard, heading for the middle of the lake. If not for the child's colorful clothes, they'd have vanished completely, for the Iceman wore the white camouflage of a winter warrior.

Snow, snow, fast-falling snow …

Hurled in all directions by the erratic wind …

Here, thought the killer, skidding to a halt.

Yanking the toque from her head, he dropped the girl on her back on the cold crust of the lake. The blade of one skate pinned Becky's hair to the snow-covered ice. The other—blood-splattered from what it had done to her mother—stood poised above the girl's throat like the blade of a guillotine.

———————

What's the roughest sport? British rugby? American football? Canadian hockey?

At six-foot-two, with 195 pounds of brawn, Zinc Chandler was built to throw the bodychecks of the bullish northern game. Though he lacked the fancy footwork of the masked blade runner, the Prairie boy knew how to power a puck across the ice and shoulder his bulk to take out anyone blocking his path.

Whack!

The guillotine was coming down when Zinc's bodycheck cracked the killer's ribs and launched him off the ice. The Latvian went spinning in an incomplete Axel jump. Figure skaters, however, learn the tricks of quick recovery, and the Iceman landed on both skates and kept going, intent on escape. Zinc was hot on his heels, fumbling to draw his Smith & Wesson through too many layers of clothes.

The Iceman was better prepared.

Zinc burst out of snow-blindness into a wormhole tunnel cleared by the wind. The Latvian was skating backwards, and the muzzle of his Beretta took aim at the pursuer's heart.

Bang!

The bullet should have ripped through Zinc's chest. But instead, the Iceman was airborne again. The bang was not a gunshot but the sound of the mercenary hitting the edge of a summer swimming platform—hidden by the snowfall—and flipping into a reverse somersault.

Bam!

That was a real shot, but it went wild.

The platform had marked the end of solid ice. The crust at the heart of the lake wasn't thick enough for human weight, and the Latvian's hard landing cracked it into a spider's web. When that gave, in he plunged.

Zinc finally cleared his gun of its confining outerwear as he shaved the rink of ice to halt his forward motion. Still moving, he tucked his ankles up and hit the platform on his knees, skidding across to the far edge, just shy of taking an ice bath, too.

Gun in hand, the Iceman surfaced directly in front of Zinc. But before the swimmer could shoot, the inspector fired from his hip. The Latvian's head snapped back as a red hole appeared in the white balaclava. The frigid water turned crimson as the bloody mask sank.

Ka-boom ...

Boom ...

Boom ...

More explosions made avalanches tumble down the peaks. But these were to the north.

Boom!

STOPWATCH

Buddy Hopkins was singing along with T. Rex when the vee-bid blew sky-high. "Vee-bid" stood for VBIED, and that stood for "vehicle-borne improvised explosive device," which was just a fancy way of saying "truck bomb." Unknown to Buddy, the device was affixed to the cargo tank behind his cab. It wasn't a particularly powerful explosive—but then it didn't need to be when his vehicle was a tanker full of gasoline.

Convinced that he was the only North American able to appreciate Marc Bolan's voice, Buddy was warbling along with "Raw Ramp," the music blaring at ear-bleed volume, when the remote trigger tripped. Buddy's wasn't the only vehicle wired to explode. It was simply the first to reach the bridges.

The attack on the three bridges was a work of saboteur's art. This was the weakest point on the Sea to Sky Highway. Here, the railway and the highway came together to cross a creek. The creek bed was a manmade concrete V, hardened so the banks wouldn't erode. One bridge accommodated trains. The other bridges, to and from, were for the steadily increasing Whistler traffic.

As the self-appointed world's authority on boogie music, Buddy had stuffed his iPod with tunes like John Lee Hooker's "Boogie Chillen," Canned Heat's "Going Up the Country," and

ZZ Top's "Tube Snake Boogie." It was hard to play air guitar with his hands on the wheel of the rig, so Buddy was bobbing his head to Marc's sexy ode when the remote triggers tripped. The bomb on his truck and the mines on the bridges were electronically set to blow when he reached a certain point in the road.

Ka-boom!

The tanker truck exploded into a roiling fireball, hurling chunks of shrapnel hundreds of feet in the air. Waves of fire belched up and down the highway, frying other motorists to crisps as black as charcoal. The thunderous roar blew the sky clear of snow and filled it with an oily smoke so dark that night swallowed day. The mines under the bridges added to the havoc, buckling steel beams, melting bolts and rivets, and turning concrete to rubble. With the three spans destroyed, the creek bed became a castle moat cutting Whistler off from everything to the south.

The electric warrior who had mined the bridges was miles away to the north. A Germanic mercenary, he went by the codename Stopwatch.

Stopwatch came from a long line of Doppelsöldners, or "double mercenaries"—soldiers of fortune who were paid extra for battling on the frontlines. His ancestors had been Landsknechts, foot soldiers famous for using long pikes to dismount charging knights in a crunch of armor. After 1500, Maximilian I, the Holy Roman Emperor, decreed that the Landsknechts could hire themselves out for pay, and they were soon the most feared troops in Europe, fighting in every major campaign for centuries.

Of his ancestors, folks had often said, "They are as good as the gold you pay them, and last about as long as the beer."

But Stopwatch had had no interest in the life of a modern mercenary. The world's hellholes—jungles where the insects eat you alive, and deserts where the broiling sun bakes your brains—were not for him. He preferred the concrete jungle, where his skills as a military marauder earned him more than his ancestors could ever have dreamed of.

Stopwatch began at the top.

The family villa in Salzburg had a war room where toy soldiers fought famous battles. His father had taught him how to recreate those turning points of history, the moments when victory was snatched from the jaws of defeat.

Armchair maneuvers.

As a man, Stopwatch had put that guidance to lucrative use. He got a thrill from pulling off the perfect heist. Like a climber scaling Mount Everest just because it's there, Stopwatch was a soldier of fortune who stole fortunes just to prove he could.

Mephisto had linked up with Stopwatch through the Internet. For their first collaboration, he'd wired him money through several shady Asian banks, and in return the soldier of fortune had stolen a priceless Rembrandt. The painting was now in the secret collection of a Russian tycoon, who planned to have it buried with him when he died.

Who says you can't take it with you?

Not Stopwatch.

He thrived on the law of demand and supply.

His most recent mission for Mephisto had been the theft of an Egyptian mummy. In that operation, timed to the minute by a stopwatch he wore around his neck, he'd extracted the mummy from an armored car by blasting through it with a thermal lance. His mercenaries had diverted the vehicle to a red light, where it stopped over flat metal doors that opened to the cellar of a British pub. Wearing a fireproof Nomex suit, Stopwatch opened the doors and applied an acetylene torch to the undercarriage. Then, using the lance—which was similar to a Second World War flamethrower—he shot raw oxygen down a magnesium tube and ignited the hot spot beneath the driver's seat.

Foom!

At 8,000 degrees Fahrenheit, a thermal lance will slice through a foot of steel in seconds. The driver exploded in a sizzle of steam, and Stopwatch removed the mummy like a doctor performing a Caesarean birth. That night, the loot was flown to Mephisto.

"We need to meet," said the email that had set up this subsequent mission. That broke the rules. Anonymity was the blind protecting both men.

"Why?" wrote Stopwatch.

"The planning required is too intricate. We need to discuss tactics face to face."

"What job is that big?"

"The Olympics."

Stopwatch couldn't resist the challenge, and he agreed to meet Mephisto in Venice. The mercenary came in conventional disguise. The psycho came wrapped in bandages that made him look like the Invisible Man.

"That's extreme," said Stopwatch.

"The bandages are real."

"What happened?"

"I was thwarted by a Mountie named DeClercq. He ruined my plans for the mummy you provided and forced me to flee before I could eliminate those who'd seen my face. So I had to change it, resulting in *this*! The plastic surgeon botched the reconstruction." Mephisto seethed with anger. "Mark my words: DeClercq will rue the day he was born. No one thwarts me. *No one!*"

Stopwatch respected the settling of scores. "Is this about revenge?" he asked.

"Yes. For geopolitical reasons I'm sure you can imagine but I'm sworn not to reveal, various European and Middle Eastern interests place a lot of value on sabotaging these Winter Olympics. It's the price Canada pays for being in Afghanistan. And since DeClercq has such a pivotal role to play in providing Olympic security, ruining the games will also ruin him. He'll piece together the clues and know it's me, and this will be checkmate."

"A win-win situation."

Mephisto smirked. "All on my side."

"Security doesn't come tighter than the Olympics," said Stopwatch.

"That's why we'll strike *before* the shield is in place. To sell an Olympic bid to a frugal public, the organizers low-balled the cost of security. You couldn't protect an outhouse with what they budgeted. After Vancouver won the games and couldn't back out, the actual cost was revealed. The price tag was so exorbitant that there was nothing left to protect any qualifying competitions. The only money available is being spent on the *actual* Olympics in February 2010."

"So when do we strike?"

"In December."

"We'll need a team of winter warriors," Stopwatch said.

"Is that a problem?"

The Austrian shook his head. "There's not much call for soldiers of fortune with winter skills. I'll find killers hungry for cash. I'll call them Icemen."

———·•·———

"The skater," Mephisto had said the night before. "I need his expertise. Scarlett overheard Nick Craven talking on his phone just before she snuffed him. He was making plans to meet Jenna Bond and her daughter, Becky, at Alpha Lake at noon. I want them both killed. My face may be different, but my body and my voice are the same. I can't chance being recognized."

So Stopwatch now had three missions in play. The blast that echoed up the valley from the south meant that the route linking Whistler to Vancouver was blocked. The time told him that the Latvian Iceman was taking care of Bond and her kid. And meanwhile, Stopwatch himself was blocking the route linking Whistler to the north.

———·•·———

Who the hell would build a log cabin today?

Sure, Whistler was developing at the speed of light, with some celebrity chalets selling in the multimillion-dollar range. But December was the month to hibernate, not build. So why was this contractor offering a bonus to have these logs delivered now?

Some people!

Treetop—"T.T." to his logging camp buddies—had been a high rigger before his accident. No fir had been too tall for him to scale until a chainsaw bucked and chewed into his leg. After that, he had switched to hauling loads, which didn't earn danger pay but did put grub on the table.

Today, T.T. was dressed like the quintessential Canuck: red-checked flannel shirt and blue jeans over steel-toed boots, stubbled chin beneath a peaked Molson beer cap, and a quilted, sleeveless green jacket zipped up his chest.

"Timber!"

The Cowboy Junkies were on the radio, singing their cover version of Lou Reed's "Sweet Jane," as the rig trundled down the slope, approaching Whistler from the north. Because this stretch of highway ran from the ski resort to the sticks, instead of down to Vancouver, there'd been no reason to widen it for the games. Just two lanes zigzagged above the junction where the road, the railway, and the electrical towers powering Whistler met.

Through the foggy windows of the cab, T.T. could barely make out the passing Slow signs. The trees alongside the highway were like skeletons scratching bony fingers at the somber, smothering sky. As T.T. cleared the windshield with his hand, the railway bridge crossing the road ahead suddenly materialized.

Could there be a worse road in the world for truckers?

"No," T.T. answered himself.

It was bad enough that snowstorms like this could close it down, and that Mother Nature could sever the route at will with avalanches and erosion. What was worse—at least to T.T.'s mind—was the snooty Olympics. For the duration of the games, the road would be closed to all but "permitted vehicles," which didn't include his. Two weeks! Do you think those Olympians gave a rat's ass about a hard-working trucker just trying to—

What happened next wasn't amorphous, hazy, or cold. Since light travels faster than sound, T.T. was first blinded by the dual explosions around the supports for the rail bridge. Perhaps he heard the booms, but if so, it was only for the split second before the shards of metal crashed like spears through the windshield. The span above the road smashed down like a portcullis sealing a gate. The rig, with its driver spiked to his seat, caromed into the bridge and flipped on its side, spilling the timber onto the highway like a giant playing pick-up sticks.

———•◆•———

The problem with public officials is that most don't have criminal minds. That's why the powers-that-be had assumed there was a backup system in case of a power failure.

Stopwatch knew better.

The dams that power British Columbia were in the north. Electricity was transmitted to the Lower Mainland by the shortest possible route, so both the primary and the backup feeds hummed down this valley side by side. To plunge Whistler into darkness, all Stopwatch had to do was cut *all* the power lines.

Boom! Boom! Boom!

From his ambush platform along the valley, the mercenary punched the button to blow the charges the Icemen had packed around the base of each hydro tower. One by one, they toppled in an explosion of sparks. Stopwatch averted his eyes as live wires snapped and lashed about like sizzling bullwhips. Those that landed across the highway formed another barrier.

Ozone fouled the air, stinking of weak chlorine.

Satisfied that he had earned the cash in his Swiss bank account, the soldier of fortune pointed his snowmobile toward Whistler, heading for the black hole spawned by the blackout.

BURNING BRIDGES

Chief Superintendent DeClercq was questioning Niles Hawksworth, grand poobah of the El Dorado Resort, when all hell broke loose. The hotelier sat frowning behind his compulsively organized desk. Try though he might, he could express no real sorrow for the three murder victims. It was obvious that his only concern was his threatened business.

"Two skiers killed on the slopes," he said, "is outrageous enough. But a policeman murdered in *this hotel* just hours before 'Going for the Gold'? It's obscene." As he spoke, he rolled an egg-shaped worry stone back and forth in his palm.

"It's more than that," said DeClercq, his voice as dry as autumn leaves.

The hotelier agreed. "The Olympic Games will put Whistler—and the El Dorado—on the map for decades to come. Bodies on the slopes hurt everyone. But a murder in *this hotel*! Jesus Christ!"

"I'm sorry for your loss," the cop said sarcastically.

"Thank you," said the oblivious hospitality manager. "And thank you as well for removing the body by the service elevator and taking it out the back door. Imagine it going through the lobby!" Hawksworth shuddered at the thought. "Now, how soon can we reopen the eighth floor? Every room is booked tonight because of 'Going for the Gold.'"

"The show must go on, Mr. Hawksworth?"

With his power suit, his manicured hands, and his scalp shaved to corporate perfection, Niles Hawksworth embodied everything DeClercq disliked about the Olympic Games. If the games were really about sport and the human spirit, wouldn't it make sense to stage them in the same place every four years, stripped of all the commercial nonsense that bleeds them of meaning? Greece could be the home of the Summer Olympics and Chamonix–Mont Blanc the Winter Games. The cash saved could be spent on humanitarian causes, and security could be state of the art.

That made sense to Robert, but not to the world's businessmen.

Men like Hawksworth saw the Olympics as a giant money-making opportunity. They gambled with the public purse, squandering millions on a bidding process that only one country could win. A fortune more was spent on massive sports facilities needed for only a brief moment in time. Corporate shills milked the carnival for every dollar they could. Meanwhile, cops like Robert were expected to provide impregnable security at rock-bottom rates.

"Combing a murder scene takes as long as it takes," said the chief. "So if you want 'Going for the Gold' to proceed, you're going to have to give me all the help I need."

The hotelier clenched his worry stone. "You'd shut us down?" he said.

"I will if I think the El Dorado remains a hunting ground."

Suddenly, Hawksworth was all business. "How can I help?" he asked.

"This woman who called to report the murder—did you recognize her voice?"

"No, I think she'd disguised it."

"What did she say?"

"I can tell you precisely. I put her on speakerphone so my assistant could write down her exact words." Hawksworth consulted a series of squiggles on a shorthand pad. "'There's a dead cop in room 807,'" he read aloud. "'Have Special X figure it out.'"

"So you called us?"

"Yes."

"I want those notes."

Hawksworth passed him the pad.

"Your assistant is?"

"Jenny."

"I want to question her."

"She's with the chef, discussing the menu for tonight, but she should be back soon. I know she didn't recognize the caller's voice either. Do you think that woman is the killer?"

The Mountie showed Hawksworth the Post-it Note in the evidence pouch. "Does this handwriting look familiar?"

The hospitality manager shook his head. "'Ten o'clock tonight. Be discreet,'" he read. "That sounds like a pickup in a bar."

"Is the Gilded Man the only bar in the El Dorado?"

"You don't think …" Hawksworth's earlier frown was nothing compared to the glower he took on now.

"Who worked the bar yesterday?"

"Jenny will know."

"Are the same people working today?"

"The entire staff's doing 'Going for the Gold.'"

"This company that booked room 807, how do I—"

Ka-boom!

That's when the first explosion roared in from the south, rattling the windows of the hospitality office and the murder room on the eighth floor, where Joe had just solved the puzzle of the deadbolt.

"What was that?" asked Hawksworth.

———•·•———

It wasn't long before the chief's cellphone went mad. Calls were coming in like waves washing a beach. The first to reach Robert was Jackie Hett, who had just returned to the Special X detachment after responding to the decapitation of the skier on the chairlift.

"Chief, a tanker truck explosion has blocked both the road and the rail links to Vancouver. It took out three bridges and caused a major pileup. I called the local clinic. Doctors are responding, but all available medical help is urgently needed at the scene."

"I'll see what I can do. Keep me informed."

"Roger," said Jackie.

By the time the Mountie finished his call, the manager's assistant, Jenny, had returned from consulting with the chef. Like her boss, she hadn't recognized the voice of the woman reporting the murder. Nor could she identify the handwriting on the Post-it Note.

"Who tended the bar yesterday?" asked the chief.

"Karen and Stew in the afternoon," said Jenny. "Marco and Trixie took over at night."

"Are Karen and Stew here now?"

"No, but they will be soon. Everyone's working the 'Going for the Gold' event."

The Mountie turned to Hawksworth. "Do you have medical staff on call?"

"Why?" the hotelier asked suspiciously.

Ignoring him, Robert phoned Gill Macbeth on his cell. The pathologist had accompanied Nick Craven's corpse from the room on the eighth floor to the nearby trauma facility. She was to be joined there by the Russian forensic scientist as soon as he had finished examining the crime scene.

"What's going on?" she answered. "That's more than thunder."

"A tanker truck explosion has caused a lot of injuries. We need every doctor on scene."

"But what about the postmortem?"

"Joe can start without you, searching Nick's body for wounds and stripping off the paint. When you're finished at the accident scene, you can conduct a full autopsy." Robert looked back at Hawksworth. "Hold on, Gill. You may have passengers." He covered the phone. "Well?" he asked. "I need medical personnel."

"We use doctors from the nearby clinic. If they've already been called out, I can only suggest trying one of our guests," said Hawksworth.

"Who would that be?"

The hospitality manager turned to his assistant. "Jenny, what's the name of the Finn who's trying to land a sports medicine job at the Olympics?"

"I can't pronounce it, but he's in room 312."

"Call him down," the Mountie said, returning to his cell. "Gill, it looks like I'll have someone to ride shotgun at your—"

That's when a succession of explosions rumbled in from the north, shaking the town of Whistler like an earthquake. Suddenly, all the lights in the El Dorado went out, plunging Hawksworth's office into dimness.

ICE PICK

With her skis and poles balanced on her shoulder and a backpack strapped to her spine, Scarlett could have been any one of a number of disappointed Olympians forsaking the mountains for the safety and comfort of the bars and restaurants of Whistler Village. What differentiated her from the rest of the pack was the concealed weapon she carried and the head of the skier she'd stored in a waterproof bag in her backpack.

With one mission complete, the Ice Pick Killer was now stalking Gill.

Architecturally, Whistler Village was a nest of snakes. There wasn't a straight street or walkway to be had in the hoity-toity community sandwiched between the highway and the mountains. Twisting and turning back on themselves, pedestrian rambles hid countless nooks and crannies. One of these was an oblong yard of virgin snow tucked away behind the RCMP's trauma center. Come the Olympics, heavily armed response teams would muster here. But this afternoon, only Scarlett waited.

She checked for a text message and found one glowing on her cell.

Kill time, she thought.

From the service bay at back of the El Dorado Resort, the Ice Pick Killer had followed the hotel's delivery van the short distance by road to the trauma center. Emerging from the van with a somber expression, Gill had wheeled the gurney carrying Nick's body in through the street door. Now she was locked inside the makeshift morgue.

Time you joined him on the slab, thought Scarlett.

Like the Olympics itself, Whistler was besieged by commercial hangers-on. If there was a buck to be made, Whistler was the place to make it. So in addition to skiing, you could dogsled, bungee jump, heli-ski, snowmobile, snowshoe, go tubing, or ride a sleigh drawn by giant Percheron horses. Or for a change of pace, you could "strengthen your core" in spas catering to your wellness needs with yoga, Pilates, facials, waxing, acupuncture, massages, aromatherapy, Vichy showers, and mud baths. Shucks, you could even get little yellow happy faces painted on your toes.

But then …

Boom! Boom! Boom!

… the juice stopped, and the fantasy faded.

One minute, Whistler had been a fantasyland of lights and sounds, with neon signs beckoning folks to come on in and spend, and rock 'n' roll cajoling drinkers to chugalug. Then, in the blink of an eye, the mirage was extinguished and the jukebox fell mute. This gaudy manifestation of the Winter Olympics had been transformed into a ghost town.

———————

"What are you making?" Scarlett had asked Mephisto days earlier in his mountainside chalet.

"Curare," he'd replied. "South American arrow poison."

"Where'd you learn that?"

"In Brazil. From my father. He was an archeologist. When I was a boy, he took me on an expedition to the Mato Grosso. He hoped to pick up the trail of Colonel Percy Fawcett."

"Who's he?"

"A British adventurer who vanished in 1925 while searching for El Dorado."

"Like Indiana Jones?"

"Only the *real* thing."

"Did you find him?"

"No, but I learned some useful skills. Like how to shrink a human head and how to make curare."

Scarlett watched Mephisto mix bark scrapings from the poisonous *Strychnos toxifera* and menisperm plants with venom harvested from the fangs of tropical snakes. The concoction was boiled in water for a couple of days, then strained and evaporated to extract a dark paste with a bitter taste.

"Watch," he said, lifting a frog from a jar.

Freed from captivity, the feisty amphibian hopped across the kitchen floor. Fetching it, Mephisto pricked it with a pin dipped in the paste. When he set it down so it could hop again, the frog collapsed after one leap.

"That's strong curare," he said with a satisfied smile.

"Who's it for?" asked Scarlett.

"You," Mephisto responded. "It's what you'll use to snuff a Mountie."

———•—•———

Now, as planned, the Mountie was dead from curare poisoning. His body, hiding the method, lay inside the trauma center. His killer stood in the shadows by a rear corner, where the outside walkway rounded the building from the front door to the backyard. Sheltered by the overhang of the roof, the walk bore only a smattering of snow. From there, Scarlett had a clear view of the untouched yard.

Abruptly, a square of light from the rear window fell across the snow. All Olympic venues and most hotels had backup power supplied by diesel generators or long-life batteries. So even in the midst of this debilitating blackout, some lights came on. Obviously, the trauma center was equipped for power cuts, and Gill had found the switch.

Scarlett watched a silhouette form on the square of white as Gill approached the window to draw the curtains shut. She wondered if the pathologist had figured out how the poisoning was done. Probably not. She hadn't been in there long enough before the lights went out.

Soon, as one of too few doctors on hand, she'd emerge to help the casualties from the explosions. The shortest route from the trauma center to her car in the El Dorado lot was across this yard of virgin snow, then out through the back gate. That's when Gill would die from an ice pick to her neck, making it obvious to DeClercq who had killed his lover.

Nick Craven was dead.

By now, an Iceman had killed Jenna and Becky Bond.

Gill was the only one left who could identify Mephisto. With her dead, it would be safe for him to come out of hiding.

Scarlett cocked an ear.

Was that a knock around front?

Her mind conjured up a knock-knock joke.

Knock, knock!

Who's there?

Police.

Police who?

Police let us in. It's cold out here!

The knock repeated.

Gill was at work in back.

Scarlett nodded.

Kill time, said the clock.

CURARE

Guided by his flashlight and a map sketched by Hawksworth's assistant, Jenny, Joseph Avacomovitch, with the Finnish sports medic in tow, followed the snowy sidewalk from the El Dorado to the trauma center's front door.

It took three knocks for Gill to answer.

"Dr. Gill Macbeth," Joe said by way of introduction, "meet Pekka Viljakainen."

"I won't shake your hand," Gill replied, holding up a gilt-smeared latex glove.

The Finn grinned. His eyes were masked by yellow goggles designed to enhance dull light, and his angular chin sported stubble worn for style. He was the athletic type, the sort of jet-set skier you meet in top-notch resorts.

"Pekka's not a doctor, but he excels at sports medicine," explained Joe. "He's offered to help."

"Good," said Gill, smiling back. "I'll get my coat. But first, you must excuse us for a moment. Joe and I need to talk."

They left the Finn on a chair by the front door and retreated along the hall to the makeshift morgue at the back. It opened on the left, halfway to the rear exit.

In every case, the corpse of a murder victim must be protected from contamination until the postmortem is done. Usually, it remains in place as crime scene investigators do an initial search.

Sealed in a body bag, it's then transported to the morgue by the body removal service, shadowed by a police car. There, it rests in a secure locker until the pathologist can perform an autopsy, at which time evidence samples are collected for forensic analysis.

Because Whistler was cut off from Vancouver, Gill had to improvise some. But the RCMP trauma center was a poor substitute for a hospital morgue. Nick's gold-painted body was stretched out on an examination table, nothing protecting it except the lock on the door. In a crisis, you make do with what you've got. And now Gill was about to hand over the search for Nick's cause of death to a forensics wizard from Moscow.

"My gut says Nick was poisoned with curare," she said. "There's no sign of overt trauma on his body. A needle prick would be covered by the lacquer."

"Why curare?" asked Joe.

"Because I know Mephisto, and that's how he operates. He's obsessive-compulsive. Pieces must fit together. This headhunter stuff is aimed at Robert, because that's what made him crack before. Mephisto is taunting him. Shrunken heads are the hallmark of the Jivaro, and they also used curare as arrow poison. So of all the poisons Mephisto could have chosen to dispatch Nick, that's the one that fits."

"What an ugly way to die."

Curare's an alkaloid that blocks impulses between our nerve axons and the contracting mechanism of skeletal muscles. It kills by asphyxia, by relaxing those muscles until they paralyze. The heart goes on beating even after breathing stops. The horror of curare poisoning is that victims remain aware of what's happening to them as paralysis progresses and they slowly suffocate.

In effect, Nick was buried alive in his own body.

"I'll find the wound. Trust me," said Joe.

"The wound will be in his back," said Gill.

"Why?" asked the Russian.

"Because Mephisto set a honey trap. Nick got picked up by some femme fatale in a bar, and his body was left naked on a bed. What better way for a killer to take a man by surprise than to jab him in the back during intercourse? He'd think it was her fingernails until it was too late. And she'd get the erotic thrill of feeling him expire in her clutches."

Joe blew out a long sigh, then removed his hat and overcoat, and got down to business. Opening his Murder Bag, he pulled out a magnifying glass worthy of Sherlock Holmes.

"I'll be going," said Gill. "Call me with what you find."

"Here," said Joe, passing her another map drawn by Jenny. "It's a shortcut through the backyard to the El Dorado lot."

"I know the route. Having a chalet at Whistler makes me a local."

Joe followed Gill into the hall, where she motioned Pekka toward her from his seat by the front door and donned her ski parka. Opening the rear door, she stepped out into the cold. The blizzard had faded enough to reveal the far gate. As Gill and the Finn began their trudge across the pristine yard, the deepening snow squeaked under their boots.

Joe shut the door and locked it.

From her hiding place in the shadows, Scarlett raised her ice pick for the kill.

EYEWITNESS

The myth of the Royal Canadian Mounted Police was inspired by cops who triumphed in winter weather. Sam Steele, the hard-assed lawman of the Klondike Gold Rush. The trackers who chased Albert Johnson, the Mad Trapper of Rat River, across 150 snowbound miles of the Northwest Territories in February 1932. The crew of the *St. Roch*, under Sergeant Henry Larsen, who cracked through the polar ice in 1942, becoming the first men since Roald Amundsen to conquer the Northwest Passage.

There were still rugged cops like that in the Mounted Police, and the chief had two under his command. But Sergeant Ed "Mad Dog" Rabidowski had almost been stabbed to death, and he was still on leave with his wife, Brit, recovering. Inspector Bob "Ghost Keeper" George was a full-blooded Plains Cree from Duck Lake, Saskatchewan, who was more comfortable in the woods than in the city. Unfortunately, Ghost Keeper was stuck in Vancouver, having been left in charge in the absence of both DeClercq and Chandler.

"Mephisto's playing us, G.K. Of that, I have no doubt," DeClercq said into his cellphone as he peered over the shoulders of Hawksworth and Jenny to see what they'd pulled up on-screen. He had commandeered the office of the El Dorado's hospitality manager, much to the annoyance of the hotelier, who was still whining about his "Going for the Gold" event. The man seemed unable to grasp that something more important than the Olympic Games was happening.

The chief wished he could slap him out of his economic hysteria.

"I don't know how he killed Nick—Gill's at work on that—but he lured him to a room booked by a company called Ecuador Exploration," Robert said into the phone. "The hotel has pulled up everything it has on the company, and I'm about to send it to you. I need whatever you can find on them ASAP."

The Mountie reached between Hawksworth and Jenny to hit the Send button.

"What in hell's going on up there?" Ghost Keeper asked. "Reports say the highways north and south—"

"Hold on," interrupted the chief. "Zinc's been out of contact, but my call display says that's him." Switching from one inspector to another, he barked, "Where are you?"

"I'm on my way from Alpha Lake to join you, Chief. A skater slit Jenna Bond's throat with his blade, then he grabbed Becky."

"Is Jenna dead?"

"Yes. But Becky's safe."

"And the killer?"

"He's dead. He fell through the ice as we shot it out. His body's still in the lake."

"Where's Becky now?"

"She's with me in my Rover. So is her mother's body. She won't let go of it."

"I'll meet you out front of the El Dorado Resort. If anyone tries to waylay you, shoot to kill."

Robert switched back to Ghost Keeper. "First Nick," he said, "and now Jenna Bond has been killed. Zinc foiled an attempt on the life of her daughter, but Mephisto is obviously out for revenge. He's the mind behind Ecuador Exploration. Hopefully, you can track that company's cyberspace dealings back to an address in Whistler. Meanwhile, I need a guard detail, armed to the teeth, to protect the girl against another attack. Get on the radio and round up a team. Have them out front of the El Dorado as soon as possible."

"Will do," confirmed the inspector.

Robert hung up and made for the door.

Behind him, Hawksworth asked, "Does that mean we can carry on with 'Going for the Gold'?"

Forget about a slap.

The Mountie yearned to punch him.

———•·•———

The El Dorado Resort was trying to have it both ways. The Beautiful People demanded all the amenities of a five-star hotel, from beauty salons offering the latest styles and tints to ski shops selling gear so expensive that no one would dare use it on the slopes. The decor, however, harked back to the rustic days when this was London Mountain, known locally as Whistler because of the shrill sound made by the western hoary marmots living among its rocks. A century ago, when Myrtle and Alex Philip opened a fishing camp called the Rainbow Lodge, it was a three-day journey—by steamer, horse, and foot—up from Vancouver. From the pioneer photographs hung on the walls to the totem carvings decorating the lobby, the El Dorado was an imitation of the real thing. But if friends at home wanted proof that you were hardy enough to survive in this wilderness, a shop off the lobby would sell you a genuine Bullwinkle moose wearing Mountie garb.

Superimposed on all this "authentic" Canadiana was the essence of the Olympic Games. Banners invited one and all to the "Going for the Gold" event, where any schlub could rub shoulders with the champions of tomorrow. The banners were festooned with logos lauding the official sponsors for the Winter Games, including Coca-Cola, Petro-Canada, Panasonic, McDonald's, 3M, and—rather tellingly—the Royal Canadian Mint and the B.C. Lottery Corporation.

Katt now knew every detail of the El Dorado's lobby. After Napoleon's walk, she'd waited just inside the entrance—ready to retreat if someone approached to complain about the dog—until Robert had returned with the gut-wrenching news that Nick was dead.

Ever since, she'd been crying quiet tears for the man who had seen her through Luna Darke's death. Although DeClercq had taken her in after the carnage on Deadman's Island, it was Nick who—having lost his own mom shortly afterwards—had truly understood her misery.

So now, while Robert was in the office of the hospitality manager, Katt mourned Nick as she and Napoleon paced the lobby, from the door to the Gilded Man pub to the Grand Ballroom at the far end. There, Katt could see a bartender constructing a pyramid out of what had to be hundreds of newly branded cans of Coke.

As an official sponsor of the Whistler games, Coca-Cola was also going for the gold.

Ka-ching!

When Robert emerged from Hawksworth's office with his cell to his ear, Katt and Napoleon were gazing into a huge glass case displaying the three Olympic mascots in their many commercial forms: stuffed toys, T-shirts, ball caps. Whatever would make a buck. There was Sumi, with what appeared to be a colander on his head, the wings of a thunderbird, and the legs of a bear. A sign said Sumi liked skiing and hot chocolate. There was Miga, a sea-going "spirit bear" with a dorsal fin as a cowlick. A sign said Miga liked snowboarding and eating salmon. And there was Quatchi, an ear-muffed, mukluk-sporting sasquatch with a goatee, an inukshuk tattoo, and Olympic rings on his chest. A sign said he liked playing hockey and dreamed of becoming a world-famous goalie.

Weren't they the cutest little profits you ever saw?

Katt frowned.

How spiritually depressing!

To think that what had once been a celebration of the prowess of amateur athletes had degenerated into a billion-dollar cash grab.

Get back to the basics and cut the crap, thought Katt.

She turned on hearing Robert's approaching voice. His brow was furrowed with concern, and the cell still hugged his ear.

"I can't reach Gill. That's not like her, Joe. How long ago did she leave the morgue?" The chief listened, then said, "I'll give her five more minutes."

"What's up?" Katt asked.

"Come with me." Robert led the teenager and the dog through the revolving door to the hotel's front entrance. The street was filled with frightened skiers straggling in from the avalanches, some so exhausted from their struggle down the mountain that they were using their equipment as crutches.

"Jenna has been murdered," Robert informed Katt. "Zinc saved Becky, but she's traumatized. He's on his way here with her now. A guard team will drive her to Gill's chalet for safekeeping. Until I know what's going on, I want Becky hidden away. Not in the middle of the crowd in Whistler Village."

A Range Rover came into view.

"Here's Zinc now."

Not long after, a four-wheel-drive bearing the insignia of the RCMP also pulled into the loop.

"The guard team," Robert said. Then he saw who it was and rolled his eyes.

"What's wrong?" Katt asked.

"Nothing," he lied.

The cop who climbed out of the driver's seat was Sergeant Rachel Kidd. The cop riding shotgun was Corporal Rick Scarlett.

As if that wasn't bad enough, the chief's entire plan was overheard. For one of the seemingly exhausted skiers, slumped nearby for a much-needed cigarette, was the mercenary who'd blown the bridges to cut Whistler off from outside help. His toque, caked white with snow, hid an earplug that picked up every word Robert said to Katt with a parabolic mike.

LOST CITY OF Z

So what became of Percy Harrison Fawcett, rumored to be the inspiration for Indiana Jones? Did he fall prey to wildlife in the steaming jungle of Brazil's Mato Grosso, that huge, swampy wilderness that holds secrets to this day? Was he murdered by headhunting cannibals in the unexplored area beyond Dead Horse Camp by the Upper Xingu, a tributary of the Amazon River? Or did he "go native" and leave his culture behind to populate the jungle with blue-eyed offspring?

Mephisto's father had told him Fawcett's tale as they huddled around the fire in their isolated bush camp, listening to the sounds of the Amazon night closing in. Fireflies streaked through the blackness, and nighthawks snapped at insects over the river. The shrieks of a jaguar's prey cut through the pulsing rhythm of croaking frogs. Blood-sucking vampire bats owned the night.

"Do you know anything about Bolivia?" Fawcett had been asked by the president of the Royal Geographical Society in 1906.

"Nothing," he'd replied.

"Look at this area," the president said, showing him a sketchy excuse for a map. "It's full of blank spaces because so little is known of it. The border between Bolivia and Brazil is poorly defined. That's raising tension and could lead to war. As a neutral third party, we've been asked to mount an expedition to mark the borders. It's a perilous task. The natives are known for their savagery, and could at any moment kill a surveyor and serve him up in one of their macabre feasts. The Royal Geographical Society wishes to know if you will take on the job."

"I'm your man," Fawcett replied, seizing on this ticket to adventure.

Before training as a surveyor, Fawcett had been an artillery officer in Ceylon and a spy in Morocco. Still, he was unprepared for what the New World jungle had in store. At night, poisonous spiders scuttled up his arm and across his throat. Though he slept under a mosquito net, it was poor protection against the fangs of the vampire bats, and he'd awake to find his hammock soaked with blood. Nature sought to kill him at every turn. Surging down rapids, Fawcett's raft shot over a waterfall, plunging him into the roaring depths. On the trek, bushmaster snakes and anacondas lurked around him. Fording rivers gave piranha fish the opportunity to strip him to the bone, and one of his companions lost two fingers washing his bloodstained hands in a stream.

Hostile natives were also a constant threat. Amazonians wanted revenge for years of enslavement by rubber traders who hacked ears, fingers, and hands off those who failed to deliver their quota. Once, while Fawcett and his group were canoeing down the wild Heath River, they rounded a bend and ran into Indians encamped on a sandbar. Dogs barked and women ran to gather up their children as men shot arrows and blew curare-poisoned darts at the explorers.

"Can you guess how they survived?" Mephisto's father had asked his son.

"With guns?" the boy replied.

The father shook his head. "Fawcett pulled his men back out of missile range, then had them sing 'Swanee River,' 'Onward, Christian Soldiers,' and 'A Bicycle Built for Two.' So perplexed were the natives that they stopped shooting, and Fawcett quickly approached with gifts."

"Good trick," said the boy.

Fawcett had an interest in the occult that went back to his years in Ceylon, where he'd stumbled on a large boulder inscribed with a strange script. When he learned that it was a form of writing that only a small group of Buddhist monks could understand, he became obsessed with the idea of lost civilizations hiding just beyond the fringe of explored territory.

"Fawcett befriended many famous occultists, including Arthur Conan Doyle and H. Rider Haggard," said Mephisto's father.

The boy's eyes shone. "The authors of Sherlock Holmes and *King Solomon's Mines*?"

"He told Conan Doyle about Brazil's tabletop mountains, which are completely cut off from the jungle below by vertical cliffs. Imagining the unique plants and animals that lived there, the writer penned *The Lost World*, populating a similar moun-taintop with dinosaurs."

The boy was thrilled. What a book that was!

"Fawcett endured the trenches of the First World War, win-ning a Distinguished Service Order and rising to the rank of colonel. By 1920, he was back in Brazil. In Rio de Janeiro, he discovered an eighteenth-century Portuguese document describing a lost city that natives said was populated by a tribe of red-haired, blue-eyed Indians. Fawcett dubbed the outpost the Lost City of Z and began raising money for an expedition.

"Funding came from a group of financiers called the Glove. With his son, Jack, and Jack's buddy, Raleigh Rimell, the colonel—then fifty-eight years of age—set out for this black hole in 1925. His plan was to travel to Dead Horse Camp, then head northeast to the Xingu River and on through the jungle to the Serra do Roncador, where the Lost City of Z was rumored to be hidden.

"Fawcett's final words to his wife, sent from Dead Horse Camp on May 29, were 'You need have no fear of failure.' Then—like the city he sought—he vanished from history."

Mephisto's father went on to explain that many expeditions had tried to pick up Fawcett's trail, and more than a hundred men had perished along the way. In 1928, the first search party found a metal plate from one of the colonel's trunks strung around the neck of a native chief's son. In 1932, Indians from another tribe said Fawcett had passed through, producing his compass as proof. In 1951, Kalapalos Indians confessed to clubbing the colonel to death, but the bones recovered from them weren't his.

The story the boy liked best, however, was this: "In 1932," Mephisto's father said, "a German stopped at an Indian village near the Xingu River. With persistent questioning, the village chief finally produced a small bag made from tree bark. Loosening the tie with his teeth, the headhunter withdrew a shriveled trophy. The features of the shrunken head, the German later swore, matched those of Colonel Fawcett exactly."

———·•·———

How lucky Mephisto was to have an adventuresome father, an archeologist obsessed with finding lost realms. His father had taught him many things, including how to make an Amazonian blowgun. "Split that palm stem with this." He handed the boy a knife. "Hollow out the pith and rub the bore until the tube is smooth and free of snags." He passed the boy a length of stripped liana vine, the kind of creeper Tarzan used to swing through the trees. "Bind the halves together with this, and you have a blowpipe."

Next, his father taught him how to make darts. "Cut the midrib of that palm leaf into two-inch lengths." The boy did so. "Now sharpen the points." He whittled the end of each missile. "Stick a wad of pith on the other end, so each dart fits snuggly into the blowpipe."

The boy made a slew of small arrows.

"Good," praised his father. "Now where's your poison?"

From his knapsack, the boy withdrew a glass jar full of the curare his father had made from ingredients purchased in a Mato Grosso village.

The archeologist ruffled his son's hair.

"Tomorrow, we go hunting."

Dawn brought another day of insufferable heat. Mist rose from the river as father and son slipped downstream in their dugout canoe. The languid air was thick with the smell of rotting vegetation. The lower branches of overhanging trees sank into the festering water. Caymans crawled through the underbrush and a boa constrictor stretched along a limb, waiting to drop on floaters-by.

Forsaking the river for the rainforest, they hid the canoe and crept toward an isolated hut on the edge of a glistening pool. Choked by vines as taut as garrotes, towering trunks reached for the burning sky. Up where howler monkeys screeched, the canopy was shot through with sunbeams. On the ground, as the hunters picked their way around backwater marshes, the citrine smell of ants swarming through hollow logs promised they'd be eaten alive if they stumbled against the bark.

"Stop," his father whispered.

The boy crouched beside his dad.

An Indian had just come out of his hut. Necklaces of jaguar teeth and boar tusks looped down his naked chest. Iguana skins ringed his wrists, and parrot feathers crowned his brow. His lips were dyed indigo, and a macaw feather pierced the septum of his nose. He was painted to look like the spirit people a shaman meets in visions, and it was clear the man was stoned on *yagé*.

The visionary vine.

The sounds of the jungle masked their approach. The Amazonian was lost in another reality. As the shaman saw serpents wrapped in fire and angry claws tearing at the sky, the boy unscrewed the lid on his jar of poison and dipped the tip of a dart. As the Amazonian sucked the breast of a jaguar woman, the boy carefully inserted the dart into his blowgun. As the visionary rode a viper to heaven, where he was introduced to the spirits of the dead, the boy aimed the blowpipe at his neck. Standing before a solitary tree, the shaman watched a door open into nothingness as the boy blew the dart from the blowgun.

Phhhh!

The poisoned missile hit the Amazonian's jugular vein, and the curare went to work. The shaman's legs buckled, and by the time the stalkers had reached their prey, he was gasping for breath.

"Here," said Mephisto's father, unsheathing a machete. "Hack off his head and we'll shrink it."

———•—•———

Now, decades later, Mephisto studied his butchered face in the bathroom mirror. The longer he eyed his features, the angrier he got. Not at the surgeon, who had already suffered for his crime, but at DeClercq for forcing him to erase his father's image. The face in the mirror no longer resembled the son of the fantasy father Mephisto's psychotic imagination spawned years ago. Erasing those features had sparked his severe case of body dysmorphic disorder. He was like an astronaut whose lifeline to the space station had snapped, leaving him drifting into nothingness.

His *actual* father wasn't a globetrotting archeologist, and he had never ventured into the Amazon with him.

He had repressed all memory of his early life and replaced it with a fantasy because of a long-ago atrocity committed in a hellish jungle on the far side of the world.

HEADHUNTERS

Inspector Zinc Chandler's steel-gray hair—the source of his name—had been that way since birth. His eyes were the same metallic hue, and so was the two-inch scar along his right jaw line. His sharp-angled features made for a ruggedly handsome face, and he moved with the fluid stealth of a panther. Savvy people sensed that Zinc should not be provoked, understanding instinctively that this man thought well under pressure and would be most dangerous with a knife at his throat.

Something about the inspector was sexually attractive to prowling women, so that made him the ideal bait for the femme fatale who had waylaid Nick Craven. DeClercq was certain she worked for Mephisto, and he knew that megalomaniac wouldn't be able to resist the temptation to squash the chief's second-in-command.

White knight to black king 4, thought the Mountie.

The chief circled around to the driver's door of the inspector's vehicle and pulled him aside to brief him on all that had happened while he was out of contact.

"Nick's dead too!" Zinc exclaimed.

"Yes, but we don't know how. The evidence suggests that he was picked up in a bar and was killed while engaged in sex in this hotel. So far, we've found no wounds on his body, so poison is likely."

"We're talking the bar in the El Dorado?"

"That would be my first guess. But the only solid lead we have is this Post-it Note found stuck to a room key in Nick's pocket."

The chief gave Zinc a Xerox of the note and showed him the original to compare.

"If Nick got picked up in the Gilded Man, it was probably yesterday afternoon. If we find the woman, she could lead us to Mephisto."

He passed Zinc Nick's driver's license to show to the bartenders, Karen and Stew.

"Smoke her out," he said.

"What about the girl?" The inspector glanced at the child curled up in a fetal ball in the Rover's backseat.

"I'll take care of her. Mephisto must be trying to eliminate survivors of his prior schemes. Nick, Becky, and Gill were the three people who could identify him. Nick's dead, and I'm off to look for Gill. To safeguard Becky, Rachel and Rick will hide her at Gill's chalet."

"Why not use our detachment in the village?"

"This crisis has too many strangers going in and coming out, and the staff's stretched too thin responding to all the emergency calls. Becky may not be safe enough at the detachment. It's a risk, but I doubt that Mephisto would suspect I'd hide Becky at Gill's chalet."

"Right. That doesn't seem likely."

"Can we use your Rover instead of the marked car?"

"Sure," said Zinc. Lowering his voice and arching an eyebrow, he asked, "Why Rachel and Rick?" Both had lost the chance to join Special X when they'd botched important cases.

"We're shorthanded." The chief shrugged. "I know it's not ideal, but I guess they were the best Ghost Keeper could get me under the circumstances. As soon as Dane and Jackie are free, I'll send them in as relief."

Zinc tossed him the keys.

Unnoticed by the Mounties, the weary skier who'd been regrouping with a cigarette across the road began to approach. Passing in front of Zinc's vehicle, he lost his footing and slipped off the curb, crashing to the ground in a clatter of equipment. Sheepishly, he struggled to his feet, then gathered up his skis and poles to shuffle his leaden legs into the hotel.

While on the ground, out of sight, Stopwatch had stuck a GPS tracker to the Rover.

DeClercq's beef with Corporal Rick Scarlett went back to the Headhunter Case.

Everything about Rick was wound too tight. Athletic and lean, he looked strained even when he was relaxed. Every strand of his short brown hair was slicked into line, and his mustache was clipped as neatly as Errol Flynn's. The swashbuckler in him, however, had little respect for rules, and his "ends justify the means" attitude had run him afoul of DeClercq on more than one occasion.

Rick was too free with his fists.

And that lost cases.

Sergeant Rachel Kidd had overreached as well. There was a time in the tenure of Mounties still on active duty when there were no women and no blacks in the ranks. As the first black female to make corporal, Rachel had been a PR man's dream.

Everyone knew her rocket was shooting up to inspector or beyond, and all she needed to reach the stars was a high-profile conviction. To that end, she had charged Nick Craven with the death of his mother, only to watch the case crumble when DeClercq proved his innocence.

The chief had not been impressed.

Rachel's rocket had sputtered and crashed, stalling her career at sergeant.

Now, the two minders leaned against the fender of the marked four-wheel drive, cooling their heels until DeClercq finished talking to Zinc. As he approached with their orders, the two pushed away from the vehicle and stood at loose attention.

"You know what's going on?" he asked.

"Mephisto," Rachel replied.

"Three eyewitnesses can ID him. One's dead. Gill's another. And the third is the girl you see in the backseat of the Rover. I want her taken to this address"—he passed Rachel a slip of paper—"and kept safe until I call."

"Yes, *sir*," Rick said, seeing his chance for redemption.

"You defend her with your lives. Understand?"

Both nodded.

"Do this properly, and I'll forget the past."

———✦———

Joseph called as they were walking to Zinc's vehicle. Robert stepped away from the bodyguards for privacy.

"Can you come to the morgue?" asked the Russian. "I think we've found the head from the body on the chairlift. Use the front door to preserve the crime scene."

"I'm off to look for Gill."

"No need. She's here," said Joe.

———•—•———

While Robert was on his cellphone, Katt peered into the side window of Zinc's vehicle. Inside, the terrified girl clung tenaciously to her mother's blanketed corpse, as if to hold her in this realm by refusing to release her to whatever might lie beyond. Dry sobs had replaced tears.

Gently opening the door, the teen crouched and leaned in.

"Hi. My name's Katt. You must be Becky. I know the hurt you're feeling. I lost my mom, too."

"She's *dead!*" the girl rasped, her face twisted from heartache.

"Let her go, Becky, and come to me. What you need now is your sister."

"I don't *have* a sister!" wailed the girl.

"Yes, you do. From now on, I'm your sister."

Katt held her arms open and waited patiently. Becky was afraid to let go, but she desperately craved comfort. She needed someone to make it all right.

Just then, a tear rolled down Katt's cheek, and that convinced the miserable girl. Loosening her grasp on the lifeless bundle, she crawled through the space between it and the front seat, burying her face in Katt's shoulder and enclosing arms.

Behind her, Zinc cracked the far door and retrieved Jenna's body. Rick helped him transfer the remains to the other vehicle.

Becky didn't look back.

Pocketing his cellphone, Robert rounded the Rover and poked his head in through the far door. "Becky, I want you to go with these two officers," he said. "They'll keep you safe."

"I'm going, too," Katt said. "Sisters stick together."

Whatever magic they'd used at that London "finishing school," Robert thought, had worked a charm.

My, how Katt had grown up.

———————

Stopwatch reported in to Mephisto.

"DeClercq just drove away in a marked car with the body of Jenna Bond."

"He's going to the morgue," said the psycho killer. "He's in for a shock."

"We've got a tracker on the unmarked car transporting the girl to Macbeth's chalet. Two cops, Becky Bond, DeClercq's daughter, Katt, and a dog. The Icemen are following. They'll strike at the supposed safe house."

"Katt, too!" Mephisto was thrilled. "That's a bonus. Bring me the heads of *both* girls."

PHANTOM FOOTPRINTS

Crouched on his haunches in the tumbling snowfall outside the rear door of the trauma center, Robert found himself face to face with horror. The head of the skier decapitated on the chairlift had been mounted atop a ski pole and stuck in a snowdrift on the inside edge of the yard. The tangled hair was matted with blood, and the eyes had rolled back in the skull so only slivers of pupil met the chief's gaze. Blood trickled from the nostrils down the yawning jaw. The tongue protruded from purple lips. The handle of the ski pole was rammed up the neck to the base of the brain.

The Russian had been waiting for the Mountie at the front door of the makeshift morgue and immediately ushered him down the hall to the rear exit. The moment they stepped out into the storm, the bodiless head was in their faces.

"After we spoke, I came out to look for Gill," said Joe. "That was waiting for me."

"So where is she? You said Gill was here."

Joe placed his hand on Robert's shoulder. "I couldn't tell you on the phone. Steel yourself, my friend. Gill and the sports medic are both dead."

DeClercq sucked in a gasp of air. Bile rising to his throat, it took all the self-control he could muster to keep from throwing up.

"Take me to her," he said.

"When I came out," the Russian explained, "the storm was lighter than this. I could see both bodies in the middle of the yard. The ground was undisturbed, except for these two sets of boot prints." He indicated tracks extending into the yard. "Had I not spotted the bodies, I would have followed the trail by stepping into the impressions. They had to lead to Gill."

Joe directed Robert to a third set of prints off to the left.

"Instead, I kept to one side to avoid ruining their tracks. My prints are a safe path to the bodies. I'll sweep the flashlight if you'll carry this." He passed the Mountie his Murder Bag.

Single file, they followed Joe's footprints into the whiteout. So thick was the snow that it had already erased the patterns made by the soles of his boots. With flakes flying at their faces, the two men used the flashlight beam to keep them on course to the victims.

The bodies lay side by side in the red snow, their boots facing the trauma center. Joe and Robert arced in from the left, the side on which the Finn was sprawled. Joe's footprints ended at his neck, where two long grooves indicated that the Russian had knelt beside the corpse.

"He died from a single stab wound through the neck," the scientist said. "The attack came from behind. The diameter of the hole suggests an ice pick."

The Mountie ignored the male victim. His eyes were locked on the snowy figure beyond.

"Gill was stabbed three times in the back," said Joe. "Once in the nape of the neck, like Pekka, and twice in the torso. One of those jabs spiked her spine. The other went through her heart, as you can see from the location of the ice pick still sunk in her back."

The Russian's footprints arced like a halo around both victims' heads, ending in two more grooves along Gill's right side. Robert trudged across and stood next to his murdered lover.

Gill's death put to rest any doubts he'd had that Mephisto was the mastermind behind this scheme. But if that madman thought he could crack the chief's psyche like the Headhunter had before, he was mistaken.

Robert was stronger, not weaker, at the broken places.

In the tropics, you learn firsthand the value of a hurricane room. On a vacation with Gill at one of her resorts, the chief had weathered a powerful storm in such a sanctuary—a strongly built cell designed to withstand the ravages of rampaging winds.

In the concrete jungle, you learn how a panic room, with its walls and doors of reinforced steel, can protect residents against robbery and rape.

The military equivalent is a redoubt, a fort within a fort for making your last stand.

That's what Robert was doing now: building his redoubt. Grieving would come later, when he had time. For now, he inured himself to the horror at his feet, then filled that vacuum with cold resolve to thwart this toxic monster.

"How do you see it?" the Russian asked, challenging the detective in his friend. "Walk me through the crime."

"The killer snuck up behind them as they trudged across the yard. First, the Finn was stabbed through the back of the neck. Then Gill was stabbed before she could turn. Three jabs in quick succession to the back of her neck and torso. The killer left the ice pick stuck in her heart and retreated to the trauma center."

"I agree that all the wounds were fatal," said Joseph. "So there was no fighting back. Both were paralyzed instantly by the stabs to their spines."

"I see the problem," the chief said. "There are only *two* sets of footprints in the snow."

The scientist nodded. "So how did the killer reach them?"

"In Western movies, the villain always erases his trail by dragging sagebrush behind his horse."

"Not here," said Joe. "Once the snow is compacted, you can't erase your trail. And if you try to fill your boot prints with snow, you'll leave other indentations behind. I scanned the area carefully when the snowfall was lighter. I'll swear that the yard was untouched except for the footprints you see."

"No marks from snowshoes or cross-country skis?"

Joe shook his head.

"Tarzan?" suggested the chief.

"The buildings aren't tall enough to allow someone to swing in on a vine. I can't see a tightrope either. And anyway, how would that work? The lack of disturbance around the bodies tells us that both were stabbed to death before they could react."

"Taken by complete surprise?"

"Yes. Stab, stab, stab, stab, and it was over," said Joe. "Gill didn't suffer."

"So what does that leave?"

"No," said the Russian, "I'm not the killer. I didn't sweep in from the side, pretending to bring them a message, and explain away my tracks by claiming I found the bodies."

"I never thought that, Joe."

"Well, all we have are footprints from the severed head to here."

"Maybe that's the answer," the chief replied. "The killer crept up behind them by stepping in the Finn's footprints. After both murders, he or she walked backwards in the same tracks."

"But *that's* the puzzle," said Joe. "The evidence is telling us we have an impossible crime." The scientist followed his own footsteps to Gill's feet. "Hand me my Murder Bag," he said to Robert, "and I'll show you what I mean."

Setting the forensics kit down in the snow, he withdrew several soft brushes. With the flashlight in one hand, he dusted fluffy flakes off the soles of Gill's boots.

No need to explain to Robert what he was doing. Footwear tracks are made up of both class and individual characteristics. The class characteristics, common to all boots of the same make, include size, style, and above all, tread design. The individual characteristics, which set each unique boot apart, include random defects, cuts, wear patterns, and stones wedged in the treads. Individual characteristics can identify a *particular* boot, to the exclusion of all other footwear.

Earlier, Joe had used his scarf to cover several of the footprints, protecting them from the falling snow. Removing it, he lightly brushed the surface of one print, exposing the tread pattern Gill's boot had left in the snow. Robert picked out both the class and the individual characteristics.

"My initial trudge from the morgue to the crime scene left sharp prints like these," said Joe. "I ruined them when I tried walking back in the same holes. The new patterns did not mesh exactly with the old."

"What about the Finn's tracks?"

"They're as crisp as these. There's no doubt in my mind that *all* the prints leading to Gill's feet were made by her, and *all* the prints leading to Pekka's feet were made by him. Not including the two of us, the *only* people who trudged to the center of this yard were the victims. Whoever stalked and stabbed them did it in a way that left no footprints."

"How?" asked Robert.

"I have no idea."

VAMPS

Before departing for the morgue, the chief had given Zinc Chandler Nick Craven's notebook to check for leads. In it, the corporal had jottings about Mandy the Blonde, Jessica the Redhead, Corrina the Raven, and their respective ex-boyfriends. His notes compared Mandy to Lana Turner, Jessica to Rita Hayworth, and Corrina to Jane Russell. Thanks to him, Zinc had nothing but sex on his mind as he weaved his way through a throng of paranoid barflies talking violence in a smattering of tongues.

He was hunting for a femme fatale.

"What'll it be?" the server asked when he finally bellied up to the bar.

"Are you Karen?"

"Is that not what's printed here?" The brunette tapped the name tag on her breast.

"I wasn't looking," Zinc replied, his focus on her eyes.

"You're *supposed* to look. It bumps up my tips."

The inspector dropped his gaze for a moment to her low-cut top. If she bent over the bar, he'd have a glimpse all the way down to her navel.

"Your tips don't need bumping up," he said, deadpan.

Karen laughed.

Zinc placed his regimental badge and Nick's driver's license down on the counter, side by side, and indicated the photo. "Did you serve this fellow yesterday?"

"He's the Mountie who was killed upstairs, right?"

Zinc nodded.

"Yeah, I served him. Scotch on the rocks," she said. "We kibitzed about whiskies, with and without the 'e.' He told me he was investigating the murder of the guy who got his head cut off on the slopes. Sorry—the *first* guy who got his head cut off on the slopes. This was Boomer's watering hole. I told Nick he must've moved in on the wrong chick."

"Like maybe Mandy, Jessica, or Corrina?" asked Zinc.

"Yeah," said Karen. "All three were here, sitting at the same table. Nick took their drinks over and sat down. He left his Scotch behind, though, so I followed."

"Did you overhear their conversation?"

"Just a snippet. Corrina was asking Nick about his strangest case. I knew they were playing with him."

"Why?"

"Because that's what those three do. Whistler attracts gold diggers by the hundreds. Rich guys plow the slopes, then hit the bars to get laid. Mandy, Jessica, and Corrina have the claws it takes."

"Think one of them picked off Nick?"

"Not to kill him. But I wouldn't be surprised if one was used as a lure. He told me he was mixing business and pleasure. Dabbling in the case because he could ski Boomer's Run. From the amount of time he spent with those three vamps, he seemed more interested in pleasure than business."

To the badge and license, Zinc added the Post-it Note.

"Recognize the writing?"

"No," said Karen. "Do you carry a gun?"

"What does that have to do with anything?"

"You look like you can take care of yourself in a fight. How'd you get the scar on your jaw?"

"In a fight."

"What happened to the other guy?"

"You don't want to know."

"Actually, I *do*."

"Let's just say it took more than stitches."

"Ever kill anyone?"

"Where's this going?" asked Zinc.

"Look, two skiers have lost their heads. A cop got killed in this very hotel. And now I'm hearing rumors that a woman's throat was cut at Alpha Lake." She shuddered. "Those vamps may want a man with money, but I want a man with a gun." She scribbled a note and passed it to Zinc. "Here's my cell number. Think it over."

Zinc Chandler had lost the love of his life to violence and was scarred both inside and out. Since then, he'd sought nothing from women—and had offered nothing in return—but brief physical flings. Emotional commitment was for other men. He was open to free spirits who played by their own rules.

"Mandy, Jessica, and Corrina. Where do I find them?"

"Looking for a better offer?"

"Unlike Nick, I am on the job. Business, not pleasure."

"Turn around and look for blonde, red, and black hair together," she said. "And if you change your mind about the other thing, I'll make it worth your while."

———

At first, Zinc hadn't spied them through the pack of beefcake besieging their table. Now, he tried to bypass a hulk reeking of rum to reach the Venusian trio.

"Back off, buddy," snarled Mars. "If you know what's good for you."

Zinc flashed his badge. "Talk to the hand, pal." He held the badge to his ear. "The hand says you should get lost. If you know what's good for you."

"That's what I've been trying to tell him," said Mandy. "Get lost."

"You heard the lady," Zinc said. "Don't play the fool. I'm looking for an aggressive drunk to yard in. Know someone who fits that bill?"

From how they quickly abandoned the table, Zinc figured these lunkheads weren't really planets. Theirs was more the elliptical orbit of a comet, zipping off into space to return in seventy-odd years.

"Okay if I join you?" he asked, grabbing a seat before there was any reply.

Corrina, the raven-haired beauty, sized him up, as if trying to decide whether he was worth her time. "How'd your hair go gray?" she finally asked. "You look too young for Viagra."

"I had an English granny. She used to read the Brothers Grimm to me. Cackling witches, grumbling trolls—she did all the voices. She scared me so silly I went completely gray."

"Pull the other one."

"It's true! Remember 'The Wolf and the Seven Young Kids'? In that tale, a mother goat warns her kids to be careful while she's out shopping. When she comes home, she finds her house torn apart and a wolf sleeping outside. He has something struggling in his stomach, so she cuts him open and out come her kids. After replacing them with stones, she sews the wolf shut again. He wakes up and goes to the well for a drink. When he stoops over, the stones drag him down and he drowns.

If you'd heard Granny acting out the screams of the kids being eaten alive and the howls of the wolf drowning in the well, your hair would be gray, too."

"Now tell *me* a story, Daddy," Mandy the Blonde implored, batting her baby blues like Little Bo Peep.

Was this what it was like to live in the Playboy Mansion? Probably.

"My favorite was the one about the chopped finger."

"What was that one called?" asked Mandy.

"'The Robber Bridegroom.'"

Zinc chose a mini pretzel stick from a bowl on the table and balanced it on his thumb like a coin about to be tossed.

"A miller betroths his daughter to a secret robber. To find out who she's marrying, the bride-to-be sneaks into his house and hides behind a barrel. The robber returns with his drunken gang, dragging a young girl with them. They force the captive to drink wine until her heart bursts. Then they tear off her garments, stretch her out on the table, chop her body into pieces, and sprinkle the morsels with salt. As they prepare to eat her—"

"This is a *children's* story?" the Redhead exclaimed.

"Sure. Look it up."

"Is your warped childhood the reason you became a cop?"

"It was either that or a horror writer," said Zinc.

"Finish the story," cooed Mandy.

"The bride trembles behind the barrel. She knows this is what will happen to her. One of the gang spots a gold ring on the girl's little finger. When it won't come off, he takes an ax and whacks it like a butcher." Zinc judo-chopped the table, causing the vamps to jump, and flicked the pretzel stick off his thumb … and right down Mandy's plunging neckline.

"Nice shot," the Redhead said, clapping her hands.

The Blonde leaned forward and tipped her head back like Marilyn Monroe would do. "Want to fish for it?" she asked.

Zinc was no fool. Cops had lost their careers over less. And anyway, it was time to get serious, now that he knew each woman's dominant hand.

"Actually, I'm tying up some loose ends on Boomer's death," he said. "A corporal talked to you yesterday afternoon." He set Nick Craven's driver's license down on the center of the table. "I'm sure you've heard that corporal is now dead. Just to be thorough, I must eliminate your ex-boyfriends. I'd like each of you to write down the name and address of your most recent beau, and tell me why you think he isn't—or *is*—a suspect in Boomer's death."

Zinc watched them scribble, two using the same hands with which they'd raised their drinks.

"You write and drink with opposite hands, Mandy."

"I'm ambidextrous."

"Show me," said the inspector.

The Blonde switched hands and finished scribbling.

"That must come in handy."

"Ask my ex-boyfriend," she said, winking.

Actually, Zinc had all he required, for he'd seen that the handwriting on one of the sheets matched that on the Post-it Note found in Nick's pocket. At the bar, Karen had inspired him to set a trap with her comment about wanting a man with a gun. Removing three business cards from his wallet, the inspector had jotted on the back of one: "Want a bodyguard to see you through the night? Room 412. After 5 p.m." He'd carried the cards to the table, where he distributed them now.

"If you remember anything, give me a call."

The vamp whose handwriting matched the Post-it Note got the card baiting the trap.

Two could play at that game.

———————

"Another fool's got the hook through his cheek," said Scarlett.

"Who?" asked Mephisto.

"Zinc Chandler."

"I want him, too. If it's safe."

"It can't hurt to feel him out. If he's looking to get fucked, he won't tell anyone. If it's a trap, I'll have an out. He'll be the wolf who set up the assignation, and I'll be the innocent lamb who fell for his charms."

"How will you kill him?"

"The same way I killed Nick Craven."

ICE AX

Rick Scarlett literally rode shotgun from the El Dorado Resort to Gill Macbeth's chalet. Gripped in his hands was a Remington shotgun loaded with four shells. Beside him, wedged against the door, was a Winchester bolt-action rifle with a four-cartridge clip. Both he and Rachel Kidd had nine-mills holstered on their hips.

"Near as I can tell, we're there," said Rick.

Rachel eased the Rover off the snowy road and let it claw them up Gill's drive. From the El Dorado, at the base of the mountains to the north, they'd snaked south through the blacked-out village and across the deserted highway to this upscale housing estate. The flat light of winter was fading fast as they slipped through a landscape that was assorted hues of blue.

"Park here," Rick said, jerking his thumb at a shoveled clearing that bulged off the driveway, downhill from the chalet.

Rachel pulled in.

Thick snowflakes tumbled through the somber gloom and mottled the Mounties' winter wear as they got out of the Rover. White speckled their muskrat hats, heavy storm coats, blue scarves, black gloves, and calf-high boots. Slinging the Winchester over his shoulder, Rick swept the shotgun down the drive.

"Climb out, kids," Rachel said, "and follow me." The dog tailed Katt and Becky.

They trudged up the hill through untouched drifts, their boots kicking up puffs of powder that whitened them from head to toe. The evergreens alongside the driveway resembled alpine huts, their sloping branches shucking snow before the weight could break them. Twilight cloaked the chalet with fear.

"I'm scared," said Becky, clutching Katt's hand.

"I'm not," the teenager responded. "Let's make snow angels." She fell back, arms spread, and fanned her limbs, prompting the younger girl to follow suit.

Gill's chalet was a sturdy log house, its upper story tented by a steep, dormered roof. A thaw between storms had lined the eaves with icicles. By now, the light was so dim that Rachel needed a flashlight to see where to insert the key.

Inside, the power failure had killed the lights and the electric heat. The beam of Rachel's torch swept the interior, picking out details: the stone hearth, a wood-burning stove, leather furniture surrounding a low coffee table. A staircase ascended to the bedrooms upstairs. Gill's chalet was bigger than most people's homes.

The first thing Rachel did was ignite a kerosene lamp. It burnished the woodwork with a bronze glow. Then she set about preparing a fire in the glass-windowed stove.

"Do you have any toys?" Katt asked Becky.

"A coloring book."

"Where?"

"In my backpack. With my skates."

Outside, Rick stood with his back to the chalet, sweeping the area one more time. The cold and the darkness, the darkness and the cold. Ice-crusted trees and snow were all he could see. Whistler seemed to slumber in the depths of hibernation.

Satisfied they were safe, he stepped inside, then closed and locked the door.

———•—•——

The mercenaries huddled in the white Pathfinder were camouflaged by white gloves, white pants, white boots, and white masks in the hoods of white parkas. Like ghosts in a ghost car, the five killers crept through this crystalline landscape, the headlights of their vehicle sparking off the whirling, swirling, twirling white flakes.

Now you see them, now you don't.

The Iceman in the passenger's seat held the receiver for the GPS tracker on the bumper of Zinc's Rover. Thanks to this technology, the soldiers of fortune had been able to shadow the Mounties and the girls from the El Dorado to the not-so-safe safe house without fear of being spotted. They were armed with Uzis, and each also packed a Glock pistol with a silencer.

Pfft. Pfft. You're dead.

No fuss, no muss.

"They've stopped moving," the Iceman said, pointing to the static blip on-screen.

In addition to the weapons they all carried, the Siberian had a mountain climber's ice ax in a shoulder holster. The ax was a double-headed tomahawk with one head like a chisel. Climbers used it to chop steps into hard snow. The other head was a sharp-pointed pick used to hammer a hold into ice, and the tip of the handle was spiked with a deadly ferrule.

Joseph Avacomovitch wasn't the only one steeped in Russian history. The Siberian knew that Leon Trotsky had been killed by an assassin armed with an ice ax on August 20, 1940.

Inspired by that, he'd made the mountain climber's tool his weapon of choice.

As long as he got the heads to torment DeClercq, Mephisto wasn't averse to a little skull cracking.

Ice Ax's mission was to kill the girls.

MY LAI

Decades ago, a frantic call had come in to 911.

"He's got a gun! He's gone berserk! He's going house to house to kill his neighbors! Oh God! Not *me*!" The sound of a door being kicked in was followed by gunshots and then silence.

The first cop on the scene was shot dead as he stepped out of his patrol car.

Bam! Bam! Bam!

The dead cop, shot in the head, was sprawled half in and half out of his cruiser. Discarded leaves stuck to the spreading pool of blood. The wail of a siren shattered the autumn afternoon as the backup police car screeched to a halt. Before those officers could swing open their doors, the madman sprayed them with machine-gun fire, blowing windshield shards at their startled faces.

In his mind, the gunman was back in Vietnam, caught in the chaos of Pinkville on March 16, 1968. Pinkville. The code-name for the hamlet of My Lai, where, according to military intelligence, the gooks were lurking in tunnels under the huts of their families. Charlie Company's mission was to search and destroy. "Go in there aggressively, engage the enemy, and wipe them out for good," they were told. Burn the houses, kill the livestock, destroy the food, and pollute the wells.

Fucking A!

These draftees had been dropped in 'Nam just three months earlier. Already, they'd lost five to mines and booby traps. Here was a chance to pay the Viet Cong back with higher body counts and kill ratios.

At shortly after eight in the morning, they'd stormed Pinkville with firearms, grenades, and bayonets, shooting, blasting, or spiking anything that moved. Quickly, the massacre had spiraled out of control. Smoke billowed from thatched homes the GIs set ablaze, turning the rice paddies into hell on earth. Women were gang-raped, and entire families were lined up in ditches and mowed down by furious gunfire. A praying old man was shot by a crying soldier. The slaughter heaped carnage five feet high.

"It's getting away!" a soldier yelled, pointing at a baby trying to crawl out of a ditch.

His buddy took a shot.

The shot missed.

Those watching laughed.

The GI moved closer and fired again.

The shot missed.

More laughs.

Finally, pissed off, the errant marksman strode over and plugged the baby at point-blank range, then tossed it back into the ditch.

Gooks that refused to come out of their huts were blown out with hand grenades. Body parts hung from the silkwood and papaya trees like Christmas ornaments. The sun cast macabre shadows on the dirt as trophy hunters roamed among the bodies, harvesting scalps, tongues, hands, or ears.

Whup, whup, whup …

A helicopter descended as the psychotic soldier watched a pair of GIs carve the words "C Company" into the chest of a mutilated Vietnamese. Even before he turned, he somehow knew it was *them*: the three traitors who'd landed their chopper at My Lai and threatened to shoot anyone who tried to stop them from saving the enemy.

"Turncoats," he cursed, about to open fire on the bleeding hearts.

That's when a sniper in the hovering police helicopter took a shot that hit the madman between the eyes, dropping him like a chestnut in the gutter of his terrified neighborhood.

The tale his neighbors later told homicide detectives was of a paranoid teenage draftee who'd come back from Vietnam to find himself a pariah to those on both sides of the political divide. Counterculture protesters had branded him a war criminal, while conservative patriots blamed those at My Lai for turning public opinion against the war.

In the end, the troubled vet had been unable to hold a job. He'd married his childhood sweetheart, and they'd had a son. But she'd eventually fled from his abusive drinking, and he'd turned into a nasty recluse hiding away in his dead mother's run-down house. With all that pressure seething inside, was it any wonder he'd snapped and wreaked vengeance on his neighbors?

The cops who later searched the madman's home found the pigsty they expected: piles of dirty dishes, cartons of crusty takeout food, and empty booze bottles. The door to the cellar was padlocked, so they used a crowbar to bust it open.

Christ, what a stench!

One corner of the basement had been converted into a "tiger cage" like those found on Con Son Island, off the coast of Vietnam. Built by French colonialists, the pens were later used by South Vietnamese torturers to break political prisoners. This cage was a concrete container, five feet wide, nine feet long, and six feet high. Steps led to a mesh catwalk that doubled as a roof. The stench—now recognizable as the smell of decaying human flesh—came from the cage.

The first cop down to the cellar followed his flashlight beam up the steps to the grate. Straddling the bars, he shone his torch into the dark, dirty, hot, humid pit—and illuminated the remains of a decomposing female on the floor. A matted tangle of hair adhered to her scalp, but the flesh of her face had been gnawed away. The ghastly skull, with its toothy grin, glared up at the cop. The rest of the corpse was a bloody mush of half-chewed organs and jutting bones, as if a scavenging jackal had been chased away from its meal.

Obviously, the madman's wife hadn't escaped from her husband's abuse after all.

The spooked cop jerked, rattling the grate, when something down there moved. His flashlight beam swarmed with flies as it slid along a chain bolted to the floor. At the end of the chain was a shackle clamped around the ankle of a naked, gore-smeared boy. The cowering child was curled up in a ball, his skin pocked with cigarette burns. To survive, he had been reduced to feasting off his mother.

The army dog tags around the boy's neck were strung with a dozen Vietnamese ears.

The child psychologists assessing the traumatized orphan were dismayed by how serene the boy became after he was released from the tiger cage. It was as if his every memory from before that moment had been erased. He was a walking example of tabula rasa: the theory that individuals are born with no built-in mental content, and that knowledge is built up gradually from life experiences. In the boy's case, however, the blank slate dated not from birth but from the day he was freed from the cage.

"Imagine a stage that hides a chamber of horrors," said one of the shrinks. "The boy has no recollection of what happened to him. He's like an actor who's forgotten what the stage hides, so he's fooling both himself and his audience."

To this day, Mephisto still lived on that stage.

And when he looked in the mirror, he had no memory of that tiger cage buried in a corner of his mind.

BLOWGUN

Standing in the snowdrifts outside the makeshift morgue, Joseph Avacomovitch was in his element. The forensic scientist had an impossible crime to challenge his brain, and solving it would help Robert DeClercq, the man who, more than anyone else, had helped Joe adapt after he defected.

"Gill and Pekka were the only ones who crossed this yard. No one stepped in their tracks or marked the snow in any way. Both victims were stabbed in the back while standing, then pitched forward, the way I found them. A single wound to the top of his spine either paralyzed the Finn or killed him instantly. Gill was stabbed three times in the back with the ice pick that's still in her heart. Do you agree that's what happened?"

"Yes," said Robert. "But it doesn't make sense."

"We're missing something."

"Uh-huh."

"So first things first," said Joe. "We know the killer brought three things with him—or her."

"Or they. There could be more than one."

"The ice pick," said the Russian, indicating the handle that jutted from Gill's back.

"The ski pole," added the Mountie, glancing in the direction of the morgue.

"And the severed head. Before we do anything else— including moving Gill and Pekka—let's examine the hardware the killer left behind for clues."

Gill's wound had frozen around the ice pick, so the investigators removed the spike from her heart with difficulty. Then they retraced their steps to the edge of the yard. There, Joe pulled the ski pole—with the head still mounted on top—from the ground. Having wrapped the head in a plastic bag, he trailed the chief through the rear entrance to the morgue. Pausing in the hall that linked the front and back doors, Joe held the pole like a spear, then gave the bagged head a twist to try separating it from the handle.

Shewww ...

A streak shot past Robert's ear and pierced the wall to his left in a spew of plaster. It took a moment for Joe to grasp that he had almost skewered his friend.

The chief glanced over his shoulder and asked, "Is this the missing piece?"

The ski pole was more like a headhunter's blowgun. Instead of blowing in one end to propel a dart, though, you activated a compressed-air mechanism hidden within the hollow metal shaft. Twisting the handle—as Joe had done—shot a projectile down the tube and out a hole at the tip. The spike jutting from the wall behind the chief had a taut nylon line leading back to the blowgun, like the tether on an underwater spear gun.

"Check it for blood," said the Russian.

The Mountie advanced to examine the projectile in the wall. The metal was streaked red. "Affirmative," said the chief.

"Let's see what happens in reverse," said Joe. "Better move along the hall in case there's any backlash."

Robert stepped toward the front door.

When Joe turned the head back to where it had been, the line whipped back into the shaft, yanking the ice pick with it. It reminded him of a tape measure retracting or a fly-fisherman backhanding a cast.

Now, except for the grisly trophy on the handle, the ski pole looked like any other on the slopes.

"You're right," said Joe as the chief closed the gap between them. "There were two killers: Pekka and the phantom. The phantom must have been lurking along the path that skirts the side of the trauma center."

Robert picked up the narrative, as was their style. The friends had worked as a team on numerous murder cases. "After moving into position near the back door, he or she aimed the blowgun at the Finn's spine."

Joe nodded.

"Meanwhile, as Gill and Pekka reached a point halfway across the yard, the Finn stabbed her three times in rapid succession. He left the ice pick stuck in her heart as Gill pitched forward into the snow."

Robert flinched but quickly recovered. To quell his emotions, he focused on the puzzle. "That's when the phantom took Pekka by surprise," he said. "Gill's killer didn't know that he was marked for death, too."

"The phantom fired the blowgun as Pekka stood over Gill's body." The Russian's eyes gleamed with the thrill of the chase. "The spike stabbed him at the base of his skull. I wouldn't be surprised to find it's poisoned with curare. As the pick got yanked back by its tether line, the Finn pitched forward beside Gill. The second killer left no footprints, and if blood was cast off as the spike recoiled, the snowfall soon covered it."

"Leaving the ski pole behind as a mount for the head is the sort of arrogant taunt Mephisto favors," said the chief. "He feeds off our stumbling over how smart he is."

"So where do we go from here?" asked Joe.

"The first thing we need to know is *how* Nick died. Zinc Chandler—my second-in-command—is hoping to flush out the woman who gave Nick the room key. I don't want him falling prey to the same outcome."

"Leave it to me," said Joe.

"I can't leave you here alone with who knows how many psychos on the loose."

"If I was a target, would they not have killed me by now?"

"I don't know, Joe. I really don't like the idea of leaving you without protection. But this manpower shortage has us in a bind. There's literally no one to spare."

"Robert, I appreciate your concern, but I'll be fine. Trust me."

"Okay. But I'll get you some help as soon as I can. And I don't want to leave Gill's and Pekka's bodies out there any longer than—"

The chief stopped talking.

"What's wrong?" asked the Russian.

"It's clear from how this scheme has unfolded so far that Mephisto's henchmen are armed with all kinds of high-tech gadgets." The chief was thinking aloud.

"And?" Joe pressed.

"Just before the girls left for the safe house, a skier fell down, out of sight, at the Rover's front bumper."

CROSSBOW

"Hi."

"It's your dad."

"I guessed that from the caller ID," said Katt, laughing.

"Are you settled in?"

"It's cold as hell in here. No, wait a sec. Make that cold as the last ice age."

"Build a fire in the wood-burning stove."

"That's what Rachel's doing."

"You'll soon warm up. That stove pumps out enough heat to thaw Gill's entire chalet."

"Wish we had electricity so I could crank on the sauna. I'm living in the stone age. All these kerosene lamps and flashlights will ruin my eyes."

"Is Becky near you?"

"Yes, we're coloring. Zinc stuck her skates in her backpack, so the book's a little wet. Luckily, it's colored pencils, not crayons."

"Tell her you're going to the bathroom. I'll wait till you've closed the door."

Katt's voice was muffled as she covered the phone. Then Robert heard her footsteps crossing the hardwood floor. He imagined her chasing her flashlight beam down the hall. Soon, she came back on.

"What's up?"

"There's no easy way to say this," Robert replied. "Gill's dead."

There was a stunned silence on the line. Then he heard a sharp intake of breath and a choked sob. "Oh no, Daddy!" Katt gasped. "It can't be!"

Not since the day he had lost Jane all those years ago had someone called him "Daddy." Suddenly, tears welled up in his eyes.

"Leave the bathroom and climb to the upper landing. You'll find the main bedroom at the head of the stairs. Listen closely as you go. Gill was killed by Mephisto. So were Nick and Jenna. I suspect he's trying to eliminate everyone who can identify him. I don't want to frighten you, but you need to know the danger. The only eyewitness left is Becky Bond. Backup is coming. Rachel and Rick will guard you until it arrives, but I want you—"

"Napoleon," Katt interjected. "I've got him."

"He'll protect you with his life. You *know* that. He saved me from death, remember? Police dogs don't come any better." He paused while Katt opened the door to the bedroom. "You said you wanted to be a Mountie, right? Well, here's your induction."

"I'm ready," said Katt.

"There's a secret panel beside the bed. See the knot in the wood to the left of the headboard? Push it."

——————

As soon as he hung up, the chief swapped his cellphone for his police radio. He broadcast a call for Dane, Jackie, Rachel, and Rick to switch to an alternative channel for a secure conversation.

All four Mounties wore belt radios with shoulder mikes, so they complied instantly.

"Dane, Jackie, where are you?"

"I'm at the three bridges, Chief. What a mess," replied Dane. "The carnage is horrific."

"Jackie?"

"Opposite end, Chief. The bloodshed's not as bad, but the toppled hydro towers are sparking like fireworks."

"Listen up. We have a crisis situation. I suspect Mephisto will go after Becky. Rachel and Rick, there may have been a GPS tracker under the bumper of the Rover. If so, Mephisto's henchmen know where you are. Dane and Jackie, do you know where Gill's chalet is?"

"Affirmative."

"Get over there as fast as you can. Rick?"

"Chief?"

"Check the Rover. But don't take any chances. We can't afford to lose you. If there's no tracker, this could be a false alarm. But if there is, destroy it before the goons close in."

"I'm on it."

"Be careful. These guys are pros."

Gill's bedroom was walled with wooden panels sectioned like chessboard squares. The paintings on the walls were reproductions of Emily Carr's evocative totem poles. Very West Coast.

Pressing the knot beside the headboard released a panel, swinging it open like a wall safe. Robert DeClercq was an expert bowman, and the woods out back of Gill's chalet were ideal for target practice. To hide his crossbow from those who might break in, the chief stored it behind the wall.

The device Katt had pulled from the recess was a shrunken bow across the snout of a rifle stock. The stirrup attached to the nose was for the bowman's foot when he cocked the weapon. There was a scope mounted above the trigger. Unfortunately, the nook hid nothing to fire. As an extra precaution, Robert had decided not to store the "arrows" there.

"It's William Tell," Rachel said as Katt came down the stairs carrying the crossbow.

A fire was crackling in the wood-burning stove. If not for the fact they were probably surrounded by several paid assassins, this would have been a rustic, cozy scene fit for a travel brochure.

"Cock this for me?" Katt asked Rick. She had nowhere near the strength to arm the weapon.

The corporal was gearing up to venture outside. He set down his shotgun and took the crossbow. Standing it up, he stuck the toe of his boot into the stirrup, then tugged the bowstring up to the trigger like a weightlifter curling a barbell.

Becky glanced up from her coloring book. "You need arrows," she said.

"You're holding one in your hand," replied Katt.

HONEY TRAP

They met outside the door to the Gilded Man. Mephisto passed Scarlett a wooden case designed for a fountain pen. Both wore gloves so as not to leave fingerprints.

"Careful," warned Mephisto. "It's loaded and ready to squirt. This dose of curare would kill Godzilla."

Scarlett opened the case to admire the syringe within. Nestled in a bed of satin, the spike was sheathed in a plastic cap and the plunger was primed to push.

"Good," she said. "I'll bait the honey trap."

"Stopwatch called. The other traps are set. It won't be long before we hear the crack of breaking bones."

"Music to my ears."

"You're my kind of gal."

———— • • ————

Up in room 412 of the El Dorado Resort, Zinc Chandler sat waiting for the witching hour. He'd repositioned an armchair so he could gaze out at the snow.

Snow, snow, fast-falling snow …

Snow on the rooftops …

Snow on the streets below …

He wondered if he'd ever find a woman to replace Alex Hunt. On stormy days like this, they used to settle in beside a roaring fire and watch a double bill of DVDs. Hitchcock films, for instance. Or back-to-back film noirs. Or *All the President's Men* and Linda Lovelace in *Deep Throat*. There was always a connection. His picks one week, hers the next. Before long, the connection was as tricky to guess as the ending of a locked-room mystery. *The Maltese Falcon* and *The Vikings*, in which Tony Curtis releases his pet falcon to tear out Kirk Douglas's eye.

"No fair," Zinc complained. "I thought it was a hawk."

"Bullshit," Alex said. "You were raised on a farm. No way do you confuse birds of prey."

Eventually, a game of hangman had cost him her love. Like DeClercq, Zinc had learned the hard way that some crazies couldn't resist taunting the Horsemen. One of those madmen had challenged him to a game of hangman, with Alex playing the condemned.

She died at the end of a rope.

A fitting term for the current state of Zinc's sex life was "uncomplicated." He and a woman he'd met during a case would set the date for their trysts a year in advance, linking up somewhere hot for even hotter sex. For three weeks, each would escape from the reality of a lifestyle to which the other would never adapt. They'd swim in a turquoise lagoon and snorkel around the reef, sun themselves on a golden beach devoid of other people, take a walk along the surf beneath a dome of stars, and then screw themselves silly until it was time to fall asleep.

It wasn't love.

But it was carefree, and sometimes that's enough.

As Zinc checked the time on his watch—it was five o'clock—a memory from their recent tryst on Aitutaki brought a smile to his face. They'd traveled from one island to another by single-engine plane. Including the pilot, there were six passengers aboard. Zinc's date was up front in the empty copilot's seat. Just after takeoff, as the plane was in a climb out over the Pacific, the hatch on one of the luggage compartments in the wings flipped open. The top suitcase popped, releasing its contents and plastering panties all over the cockpit windshield. Its airflow disturbed, the plane lurched sideways in a sharp dive.

"Hang on," yelled the pilot, trying to level the plane. He managed to pull them out of a crash just in time, then circled back to the airport from which they'd departed.

The passengers deplaned while the latch was fixed. Sitting on the grass, sipping fruit juice, Zinc sighed deeply and said, "It can't get worse than that."

"It could have been a lot worse," his date countered.

"How so?"

"The underwear could have been *mine*."

A diet of film noirs teaches you to beware of femmes fatales. The sobering lesson here was that Nick had let down his guard, and that had cost him his life. Hopefully, the honey trap Zinc had set with his business card in the Gilded Man would prove too alluring for Nick's killer to resist. The trick for Zinc was to make sure he didn't get himself killed in the act of trying to nab her. That would be a whole lot easier if he knew the *means* of Nick's death.

Operating on the theory that forewarned is forearmed, he fished in his pocket for the number Karen had passed him earlier in the bar and punched it into his cellphone.

"Hello?" the barkeep answered, pushing the receiver to her ear to overcome the background noise.

"It's Zinc Chandler."

"I knew you'd call, big tipper."

"I need a favor."

"So do I. Remember my offer?"

"Yes."

"What's the favor?"

"Are the vamps still at their table?"

"Uh-huh," she said, glancing over to Mandy, Jessica, and Corrina. "I just took them another round of drinks. Your ears must be burning."

"Why?"

"They were talking about you."

"Good things, I hope."

"Dirty girl stuff."

"I left one a note asking her to meet me at five."

"It's five now."

"If one of them gets up to leave, I'd appreciate a call."

"You'll get a call if I get a call. Do we have a deal?"

"You drive a hard bargain."

"You can drive the hard bargain, if you want."

Zinc smiled to himself. "Okay. If I can get free of work— that's a mighty big 'if'—you've got a deal. I'll be your bodyguard for the rest of the night."

"And you're in luck. One of them just stood up."

"What's she doing?"

"Grabbing her carryall off the back of her chair. Stupid girl. That's how your wallet gets pinched."

"Is she leaving?"

"Wait a sec. Yep, she's taking her coat."

WET JOB

Rick Scarlett stepped out of the two-story chalet and closed the door behind him. With icicles spiking down from the eaves and firelight turning the windows into glaring eyes, the house looked like an open-jawed Windigo monster. And the Mountie looked like its next meal.

Shotgun at the ready, Rick eyed the wooded white waste around him. He felt as if he were the only man alive on earth, the sole survivor of a new ice age. The land seemed to slumber under a blanket of snow. When the tree branches dumped their heavy burdens, it was as if hibernating winter was turning over in its sleep.

Rick listened intently but heard nothing.

Shotgun leveled before him, ready to blast if necessary, he descended the dark drive without the aid of light. If there was a sniper down there, a flashlight would make him an easy target.

The corporal's career had all but stalled since the Headhunter Case went foul. He'd shuffled around a slew of small detachments since then, moving laterally instead of up the totem pole. As he walked toward Zinc's Rover, now cocooned by snow, he almost wished the bad guys would come creeping along the road. Spotting them, he'd crouch in hiding until they approached the chalet, and as soon as he saw a weapon—this would be a righteous kill—the overlooked hero would scattershot those fuckers until they were mincemeat.

Inspector Rick Scarlett.

It had a nice ring to it.

Superintendent Rick Scarlett.

Even better.

Commissioner Rick Scarlett.

Why not go for the gold?

Top cop of the Royal Canadian Mounted Fucking Police.

Reaching the vehicle, Rick set the Remington down on the snowy hood. From his parka, he withdrew a small penlight. Then, stretching out along the front bumper, he shielded the beam as best he could and shone it up under the front of the Rover. At first, he saw nothing troubling. But when he scraped off the crud, there it was affixed to the undercarriage: a magnetic GPS tracker.

Tearing the device from its hold on the metal, the cop wiggled out from under the chassis. Rick was under no illusions about the peril. The bug in his hand meant that Mephisto knew where Becky was, and *that* meant that every second brought death closer to her.

The moment he saw the snow rise, Rick knew he'd made a foolish mistake. He should have set the shotgun beside him on the ground, not on the hood.

Ice Ax wore white so that when he lay flat in the snow, as he did near the Rover, his camouflage made him part of the landscape. Wet jobs were his specialty. Silent bloodlettings. He could lie still for hours without twitching, waiting for his prey to appear. He'd gone to ground within striking distance of the Rover because he wagered that if one of the Mounties ventured from the chalet, it would be to fetch something from the car or to drive it somewhere else.

And now his bet had paid off.

Having surveyed the wooded lot for signs of movement, Rick was convinced that the bad guys would ascend from the lower road, and that he'd have time to react if they came into view. There was just enough space to gaze down the drive between the Rover's undercarriage and the flat on which the car was parked. The mistake he'd made was in overlooking the heaps around the clearing, the piles of shoveled snow. Rick had an image of mercenaries as tough guys fighting it out in deserts or jungles. He didn't picture the killers being at home in the snow.

The shotgun was out of reach above his head.

His nine-mill was holstered under his parka.

A layer of clothing separated the corporal from his sidearm.

Scrambling to reach a weapon—*any* weapon—Rick launched a desperate bid to widen the gap as Ice Ax pressed his advantage. The mercenary sprang from the snow pile onto the driveway beside the Mountie. Hiking up his jacket as he struggled to gain his footing, the cop grasped the butt of his gun. Above him, the abominable snowman swung his weapon.

It seemed to Rick as if the oncoming collision between the ice ax and his skull was happening in slow motion. He could make out the curved T against the hoary trees. His hand found the shotgun as the pick began to plunge. Down it came as the Remington's barrel swiveled toward the breath billowing from the mercenary's mouth. Down it came as the nine-mill cleared the holster on his hip. In the blink of an eye, both firearms would be aimed at his attacker—

Crack!

The steel tip of the ice ax tore the fur of his cap, smashing through the crown of Rick's skull. The shotgun clattered to the hood and the pistol dropped from the corporal's hand as the pick sank deep into his gray matter.

The mercenary wrenched the weapon free as the cop crumpled to the ground. The squeak of steel on bone was accompanied by a gush of blood.

Next, the kids.

UMBRELLA ASSASSIN

As Joseph Avacomovitch methodically stripped Nick Craven's corpse of its layer of gold paint, he mulled over one of the most notorious of Cold War crimes: the umbrella assassination of Georgi Markov on September 7, 1978.

Markov was a Bulgarian novelist, playwright, and anti-Communist dissident. After his defection to London in 1969, he worked as a journalist for the BBC and Radio Free Europe, which was supported by the CIA. Markov's criticisms of the Bulgarian dictatorship were broadcast to his homeland, where they fanned social unrest. Angry, the Communist rulers plotted to silence him.

Enter Russia's secret police, the KGB, and a mysterious laboratory called the Chamber.

Markov was queuing for the bus near the south end of Waterloo Bridge, as he did each workday, when he felt a stinging pain in the back of his right thigh. Turning, he saw a heavyset man bend down to pick up a dropped umbrella. The foreigner apologized in a thick accent, hailed a taxi, and disappeared.

The pain continued as Markov bused to work at the BBC. There, he told his colleagues about the incident, showing one friend a pimple-like bump on his thigh. At home that night, he developed a high fever. By the next day, he was being treated in hospital for a mysterious form of blood poisoning.

Before long, he was vomiting blood, and soon his kidneys and heartbeat crashed.

Markov died on September 11.

If not for Markov's reputation, his illness might have been put down to natural causes. Instead, his body underwent a forensic autopsy. From his thigh, pathologists recovered a tiny metal sphere the size of the head of a pin. The iridium pellet—a jeweler's bearing used in watch making—had been drilled with two minuscule X-shaped bores by a high-tech laser. Stuffed with ricin, a powerful toxin derived from castor bean seeds, the holes were sealed with wax that melted when they came in contact with Markov's warm body.

He was poisoned.

But how?

It wasn't until the fall of the Soviet Union that the facts came to light. Codenamed "Piccadilly," the Waterloo Bridge assassin was an envoy of the Bulgarian secret police. The weapon—created by the Chamber—was an umbrella with a cylinder of compressed air hidden in its stem. A trigger on the handle released the gas, blasting a pellet from the tip of the "barrel" like a gun discharges a bullet.

The means of death in Markov's case was an umbrella gun. With that in mind, Joe stripped away the gold paint from Nick's flesh. He was looking for an entrance wound, some-thing like the pimple on Markov's thigh. Assuming the poison was administered during sex—Gill's theory—Joe needed to determine how and where it was injected into Nick's blood-stream. Curare has no effect when taken orally, so there *had* to be a puncture wound somewhere on Nick's skin.

Working from that theory, Joe examined Nick's back. He focused the magnifying glass from his Murder Bag on every patch of lacquer-stripped skin. When that turned up nothing, he repeatedly parted the dead man's hair to scan his scalp. And so it went, with the Russian checking every nook but coming up empty each time. Then, all at once, a you-don't-suppose insight into a femme fatale's sexuality prompted him to search where the means of death lay hidden.

"Diabolical," he said aloud.

Dialing Robert's cell, the scientist heard a recording that meant the chief was engaged. He abandoned the makeshift morgue for the hall and donned his coat, then stepped outside and locked the door. The quickest route to the El Dorado took him across the backyard and past the corpses still sprawled in the snow. The falling flakes were white on blue, like cotton batting backed by melancholy. Joe was just inside the gate at the far end of the yard, his finger pressing Redial to leave Robert a message, when he walked into the trap.

HOT LOVE

Would there be a knock on the door?

As he placed a mental bet on that question, Zinc ejected the ammo clip from his service pistol and emptied the cartridges into his palm. The trap he'd set for the femme fatale who'd set her own trap for Nick was missing a crucial element: he didn't know *how* Nick had died. Zinc's plan to expose that method would separate him from his gun. If it worked and the femme fatale dashed for his weapon as a fallback, he didn't want to get shot when she pulled the trigger. So he stuffed the bullets into a pocket of his parka and hung the coat in the closet.

Knock, knock …

He'd have to remember to pay himself. He won the bet.

Just in case the attacker had decided to waste no time—greeting him with a hypodermic stab to the neck, for instance—he opened the door at arm's length to give himself space to respond. No need. The vamp who crossed the threshold had her coat draped over one arm and the carryall slung from her opposite shoulder. Zinc could see both hands, and neither grasped a weapon. Her manicured nails held his business card out in front of his nose.

"Is this the party?"

"Yes," he said.

"Invitation only, I hope."

"Uh-huh."

"How many invited?"

"Just you," the Mountie replied.

"Now that's my kind of ball. I don't share toys. It says here on the invite, 'Want a bodyguard to see you through the night?' So let's see your gun."

Zinc raised his ski sweater to flash the nine-mill.

"Tsk-tsk," the sexpot scolded, wagging his card at him. "I thought you Mounties were military men?"

Her finger pointed to his Smith.

"This is my pistol …"

Her finger pointed to his groin.

"This is my gun …"

Her finger returned to the firearm.

"This is for fighting …"

Moving closer so he could whiff her perfume, the vamp danced her hand down his chest and gripped his genitals.

"This is for fun."

The clutch caught the cop by surprise.

"Rifle," Zinc corrected.

"Rifle?" she echoed.

"It's 'This is my *rifle* / This is my gun / This is for fighting / This is for fun.'"

"Smart guy, huh? So whatcha gonna do?" she goaded. "Cry like a baby and arrest me for sex assault? Or stand up like a man and pour me a glass of chilled champagne?"

"Release my gentles and we'll raid the mini bar."

That was the danger of femmes fatales: dumb schmucks let down their guard around them. And what straight male wouldn't play the schmuck with a bombshell like Jessica? The way she tossed her titian mane, the smoldering green gaze, the full red lips that complemented the fire in her hair, the fuzzy emerald sweater that clung to her breasts like moss—all combined to create a siren who turned men into fools.

Including Zinc.

Despite his best intentions.

For it occurred to him that if her nails were poisoned with curare, the next squeeze could lay him out on the slab right next to Nick.

Schmuck, he thought.

Jessica released her grip on what made him a man, then shucked the bag from her shoulder and passed him her coat to hang up. Zinc kept his eye on the carryall, which she retained. Together, they crossed to the mini bar. The vamp dropped her bag on the bed as they passed. Fetching a half bottle of Veuve Clicquot, Zinc popped the cork with a blast that could have put out an eye. He caught the froth in a champagne flute and filled the glass.

"Aren't you gonna join me?" Jessica asked.

"I don't drink," he said. He didn't tell her about being shot in the head in Hong Kong. Or about the pills he took to ward off seizures.

"Good," she said. "The bubbly won't dull you. I have this fantasy I like to play. I'll be Cleopatra, and you'll be my slave. Unless you're the best lover I've ever had, I'll have my eunuchs prepare you to join their ranks."

"That sounds like fun."

"Call it incentive," she teased. "If I let someone make love to me, I want to ensure he performs."

"I get the feeling you *take* what you want."

Jessica drained the champagne flute and wiggled it for more.

Zinc played Jeeves.

"You've heard the Springsteen song 'Red Headed Woman'?" she asked.

"Sure."

"According to the Boss, it takes a red-headed woman to get a dirty job done."

Zinc pretended to mop his brow. "Is it hot in here?"

"That's me," said Jessica, forming a pout. "Did you see the film *Body Heat*?"

"Years ago."

"In it, Kathleen Turner tells William Hurt, 'My temperature runs a couple of degrees high. Around a hundred.' Well, mine, too. Thus the fiery hair."

"You've got me all hot and bothered."

"You know what some president said? 'If you can't stand the heat, get out of the bedroom.'"

"I thought he said 'get out of the kitchen.'"

Jessica put a hand to her brow and swiveled around. "I don't see a kitchen, do you?"

"You want to heat things up?"

"Whatcha got in mind?"

"The sauna's on. Let's sweat."

"DIE ... FRAME ..."

"Chief, something's wrong."

There was deep concern in Rachel Kidd's voice as her words were broadcast through the snowstorm by way of the police radio. Her alert was received by Robert, Jackie, and Dane, but not by Rick. The corporal had turned off his communications equipment for the trudge to the Rover. He didn't want to draw the bad guys to any radio squawks.

"What's your worry?" asked the chief.

"Rick's been gone too long. He should have returned by now."

"Don't go outside."

"I won't. That's why I'm calling you."

"Jackie?"

"Here, Chief."

"Where are you?"

"I'm inching along the highway between Green Lake and Emerald Estates."

"What's your ETA for Gill's chalet?"

"I don't know. It's slow going, and I hear an accident has clogged the road ahead. If I can't worm around, I'll commandeer a vehicle beyond the snarl."

"Dane?"

"I'm doing better, Chief. A plow's pushed through so ambulances can get to the medical center. I'm passing Nita Lake, with Nordic Estates ahead."

"Rachel, send the kids upstairs with the dog. I'll phone Katt on her cell and tell her what to do. Douse all the kerosene lamps and put out the fire in the stove. Complete darkness. Build a furniture redoubt in the hall between the front and rear doors. That way, you'll cover both entrances. What's your firepower?"

"Rick took the shotgun. I have the .308."

"These guys are pros. They may have armor. Aim for the head if you shoot."

"Roger."

"Dane, Jackie, you got all that? Don't burst into the chalet without announcing it's you. Rachel, give Rick a few more minutes, then try vibrating his phone. If he returns, radio me at once. In the meantime, I'll muster the cavalry."

———•—•———

After Katt hung up from talking to Robert, she crouched down by the girl at her coloring book. "Gather up your things," she said. "We're going upstairs. I'll take the colored pencils."

"Why?" Becky asked apprehensively. She'd already endured hell, and she sensed more coming.

"We have to clear the table so we can build a fort. Then you and I will hide upstairs."

"Where's Rick?"

"He's outside, guarding us."

"Are we going to die?"

"No. More Mounties will be here soon."

While Becky stuffed the coloring book into her backpack, wiggled into the straps, and tugged her toque on down to her ears, Katt and Rachel shoved both leather couches across the hardwood floor to build two walls in the hall. The legs gouged the polished planks and bunched the area rugs. Fetching the low table from in front of the hearth, they tipped it sideways to reinforce the couch barricade facing the front door.

"Quick," said Rachel. "Let's get every pan from the kitchen."

The kitchen was divided from the dining room by a counter with cast-iron cookware hanging overhead. Shuttling back and forth, Katt and Rachel lined the backs of the couches with an impregnable layer of pots and pans.

"I'll do the rest," the sergeant said. "You two get upstairs."

Lit from below by the flames of the wood-burning stove, Katt led Becky up the staircase to the landing that overlooked the hearth. As they climbed, their shadows stalked them across the smooth-hewn logs. With the crossbow and a fistful of arrows, Katt did look like William Tell. At the top, they turned toward the bedroom in the dormer on the creek side of the roof.

The floor creaked as they walked.

Below them, Rachel opened the door of the stove and tossed in a pot full of water. As the fire went out, so did half the shadows besieging the kids. Rachel held her breath until they entered the room, then blew out the lamp and took up her position in the redoubt.

Outside, the Icemen closed in.

———•••———

Robert's cell had recorded a message while he and Katt were discussing security measures. He hit the key to retrieve it and cringed from a blood-curdling scream.

"Joseph?" he blurted.

The caller's agony was excruciating. Whatever torture he suffered, it was extreme. Gasping, gurgling, grinding his teeth, Joe struggled to speak. Robert felt sick to his stomach. Even with the manpower shortage, he should never have left Joe on his own.

"Die ..." Joe rasped.

"Ah!" he choked, sucking in air.

Robert was on tenterhooks.

Die what?

"Frame ..." Joe added.

Die? Frame? What did that mean?

"Gate ..." Joe strained.

The recording ended. Robert tried calling back. The phone trilled and trilled until the Russian's recording cut in.

"Hang on," the chief encouraged. "I'm coming."

After he and Joe had puzzled out the trackless double murder, DeClercq had returned to the El Dorado Resort by way of the street. But the shortest route from the morgue to the hotel— where Joe knew Robert was bound—was across the backyard and out through the rear gate. That was most likely the "gate" in his message.

Cold with apprehension over what he would find, the chief rushed back to the morgue by that route.

NAKED PREY

Zinc figured he was on shaky legal ground. So far, the only evidence he had that implicated Jessica in Nick Craven's murder was a Post-it Note in her handwriting stuck to an electronic key for the door to the crime scene. That room, however, had not been registered in the redhead's name, and it was possible that the Post-it Note and the key had stuck together after being pocketed *separately*. Zinc wasn't going to botch the case by showing his cards too soon, so he risked staying undercover until she made a move.

Undercover?

That was another conundrum.

An undercover cop is usually a cop who hides his official status. If a suspect makes an incriminating statement to someone who's undercover, the rules that govern confessions to the police don't apply. This situation was different, though. The suspect knew full well that Zinc was a Mountie, and any confession uttered to a cop under fear of prejudice or hope of advantage was inadmissible. Zinc liked to think that getting bedded by him was the greatest hope of advantage in the whole wide world. Ha, ha. So he had to wait for an attempt on his life before snapping on the cuffs.

"Attempt" was the operative word.

The surest way for Zinc to protect himself was to strip the redhead down. Her coat hung in the closet, so if her weapon was in one of the pockets, he was currently out of harm's way. Her carryall lay on the bed like a ticking bomb, but for the moment, it was out of reach. That left her person. But it was hard to imagine how her tight clothes could conceal anything. And if there was any doubt about that, she put it to rest by taking him up on his suggestion of a steam.

In Zinc's line of work, he got to see a lot of professional strippers clinging to poles. But they all paled in comparison to the teaser toying with him now. Like a rattlesnake shedding its skin, the vamp began to peel off her fuzzy green sweater.

His was tough work, but someone had to do it.

"You think I'm a Barbie doll, don't you?" Jessica asked, once her face emerged from the sheath.

"The thought never crossed my mind."

She folded her sweater and draped it over the back of a nearby chair. After pulling off her boots, she shimmied her ski pants down her hips, her thighs, and her calves. Stepping out, she smoothed them over the same chair. "I had a Barbie once. A Ken doll, too. But they were boring. Want to know why?"

"Why?" Zinc asked.

"Their knees didn't bend."

"That's important?"

"It was to me. My parents had this sex manual in their bookcase. I studied a chart of the various sex positions and tried to mimic them with my dolls. Because their knees didn't bend, Ken and Barbie could only fuck missionary style."

"Did you torture and mutilate her?" Zinc asked.

Jessica frowned. "Barbie?"

"I read about some research done on girls who played with Barbie. Of all products tested, Barbie provoked the most violent emotions. Girls confessed to gleefully maiming their dolls— hacking the hair, twisting off heads, burning, breaking, and microwaving. Is that what happens when you can't live up to body image?"

"Not me."

"So I see."

"Torturing Barbie, I mean."

Jessica turned her back on him, reached around to unhook her bra and shuck it off, then lowered her panties and kicked them up to catch them in mid-air. Looking over her shoulder, she said, "Why torture Barbie when I can torture *you?*"

And with that, without turning around to expose her front to Zinc, Jessica abandoned the bedroom and sashayed like a sex goddess into the sauna next door.

Torture, indeed, thought Zinc.

Was that both a figurative and a literal double entendre?

———·•·———

The steam hit him like a blowtorch. She had splashed a ladle of water onto the burner, so the sauna was as foggy as Jack the Ripper's London. Enveloped in a haze that blurred her features, she lounged on the upper bench, legs crossed and arms folded in front of her chest.

"Where'd the muscles come from?" Jessica asked.

"I was raised on a farm."

"Where?"

"Rosetown, Saskatchewan."

"Making hay while the sun shone, eh?"

"Sort of."

"How'd you get so battered?"

"It comes with the job."

"That scar on your shoulder? What's the story?"

"Two mercenaries tried to kill me in Africa. Y'ever see the movie *Naked Prey*?"

"Nope."

"Well, it was like that. Run through the jungle."

"And the scar on your forehead?"

"A souvenir."

"From where?" asked the vamp.

"Hong Kong."

"You get around. What about that one?" She pointed at his thigh.

"It's a coral cut from a cannibal cave in the South Pacific."

"You're shitting me!"

"I wish I was. It hurt when I got it."

"I'll bet you're wondering if I've got scars, too."

"From what?"

"Implants," Jessica said, spreading her arms to reveal her breasts. "I don't."

"You're shitting *me*," he echoed, genuinely impressed.

"Cop a feel if you want."

The steam had condensed, or evaporated, or whatever it is mist does in a sauna. The cop was beaded with sweat. The vamp was completely naked but for a small gold crucifix around her neck. Sweat ran in rivulets down her skin and trickled like a river through the Grand Canyon between her breasts. An overwhelming urge to lick it seized the Mountie.

Christ, Zinc thought.

Get a grip.

You're playing the schmuck again.

What if that cross around her neck is a plunger, and a poisoned needle is tucked up the stem? "Lick me," she says, and you bury your face between her tits. And that's when she jabs you in your spine.

Femme, as in "woman."

Fatale, as in "You're stone cold dead."

They showered together and lathered each other's skin with soap. He didn't know which was more erotic, his hands on her flesh or hers on his.

Adrenaline was Zinc's drug of choice. He was a danger junky. To feel alive—*really* alive—he had to teeter on the edge of the cliff, with life and death hanging in the balance. This game he was playing offered the added attraction of sex, and Zinc grasped what was going on in his brain.

The human brain is actually three brains in one. The vamp's body language came from her reptilian brain, the R-complex crowning the top of her spinal cord. The cop's reaction to her came from his old mammalian brain, the irrational limbic lobe at the center of his skull. Home to the Four Fs—feeding, fighting, fleeing, and fucking—it had kicked in for sex and survival. The last to evolve, his cerebral cortex, was the center of rational thought. And it was becoming clear that if he didn't keep his wits about him, he'd end up a *dead* schmuck.

Zinc knew he should step back from the brink *right away.* But he was addicted to danger and this was a delicious thrill, so he continued with the perilous game as Jessica toweled him dry, then led him like a stud to slaughter on the bed in the other room.

It's in the bag, he thought.

Whatever she'd used to kill Nick.

This was when he was most alive and knew it most completely. Whatever went on in the murderous mind of the femme fatale was also a mix of sex and death. So if Jessica planned to kill him for a sexual thrill, like the black widow spider, she would do it when she had him in her coital clutches.

"Well, slave?" she said, removing her carryall from the bed and depositing it on the night table. Grabbing the covers, she stripped the bed to its sheet. So voluptuous was this creature stretched out on the altar that the horned beast in Zinc hoped the cop was wrong so he would be free to have her.

"What's my name?" she asked.

"Cleopatra."

"What's your role, slave?"

"To satisfy you or else, mistress."

"One way or another, I want your balls. So crawl on top of me and let's see you perform."

Like a panther after its prey, Zinc closed in on hands and knees from the foot of the bed. But now the thrill of the hunt trumped the thrill of sex in the Mountie, and his cerebral cortex—his new mammalian brain—took control.

"We need a condom," Jessica said, reaching for her bag.

Zinc's heart beat faster, his nerves tingled, and his muscles tensed for action.

Now, he thought.

"Why did you write the note that invited Nick Craven up to room 807?"

Jessica froze with her hand at the mouth of her carryall. "Hey, what is this?" she asked.

"We found the note stuck to the key. I compared the handwriting with yours."

Judging by the scowl on her face, it had dawned on the vamp that she was caught in a honey trap.

"You bastard!" she snarled, baring her teeth as her hand sank into the bag.

JAWS

The gush of arterial blood had spread so wide that red snow extended beyond the perimeter of the flashlight beam. The Mountie stood just inside the gate to the back of the trauma center, shivering as he looked down at the corpse of his friend. Joseph lay sprawled at the center of the pool of light. The snow around him had been churned up as he'd thrashed in agony, trying to claw himself free of the leg-hold trap. Buried under the snow at the mouth of the gate, the deadly device had been positioned so anyone leaving the yard would step on the pressure plate and set off the trap.

Snap ...

Crack ...

Splinter ...

Like the jaws of a monstrous Venus flytrap, the large steel frame had slammed shut on Joe's leg, smashing bones, severing arteries, and hurling him into shock. In his imagination, Robert saw the blood spurting from his friend's leg as he struggled to choke out his cryptic dying message. It would have been obvious to a forensic scientist steeped in the pathology of fatal wounds that he wouldn't crawl away from this trap.

"Die ..."

"Ah!"

"Frame ..."

"Gate ..."

What had Joe been trying to say with his last gasps?

The Mountie was shaken to his core. Never had he felt as trapped as he did now, not even in the darkest hours of the Headhunter nightmare. Mephisto had him caught in a trap as deadly as the one locked on Joe's leg.

Twice in the past, the chief had played a chess game like this with the psycho killer. Both times he had failed to grasp what motivated him. Mephisto seemed to have deluded himself into thinking that causing doomsday would give him a place in history. And Grof's Frankenvirus might be just what he needed to bring on Armageddon.

Was it possible that Mephisto was the buyer of the Soviet scientist's bio weapon? What if he'd bought Grof's super-virus and had had it on the boat with him when he tried to escape from Ebbtide Island? A Coast Guard cutter had sliced the boat in half. Did that send the virus to the bottom of the sea? Joe said no one knew why the bio weapon had never been used. Maybe it took Mephisto all these years to recover it. Is that why he returned to the island for his Fountain of Age plot? To search where the scotched boat sank?

If so, Mephisto had created the perfect opportunity to use the Frankenvirus. Whistler was cut off from help. No one could get in or out. The murders of Nick, Jenna, and the two skiers had triggered the herd instinct in the hundreds of Olympic hopefuls, who were now congregating at the El Dorado Resort, looking for protection in numbers. It would be an easy thing, Robert realized, for Mephisto to infect them, and each infected person would then scatter to his or her own corner of the globe. Then, it was only a matter of time until the incubation period ran out and the Frankenvirus exploded.

By striking now instead of in February, Mephisto had taken crippling aim at Whistler's Achilles heel: its lack of pre-Olympic security. The bridge explosions and ensuing avalanches had sucked every available cop out to the highway or up the mountain slopes. And with Safesite tests taking place in Vancouver, both VISU and the Mounties' own biohazard team were out of the picture. Leaving Mephisto free to set his supervirus loose.

This was about revenge as much as megalomania.

Getting even.

Settling the score.

By snuffing Nick, Jenna, Becky, and Gill, Mephisto would both avenge himself on those who had escaped his clutches and eliminate everyone who could identify him. As an added bonus, those deaths would also tear Robert apart emotionally.

Checkmate!

With snow above and snow below and snow eddying around, the chief glowered down at the bloody jaws clamped on his longtime friend. Lost in the blinding curtain of white lay the corpse of his lover, and in the morgue beyond her lay his poisoned corporal. For all he knew, Zinc was dead in the hotel behind him, and Katt and Becky had fallen prey to professional mercenaries at Gill's isolated chalet.

Tick ... tock ...

Time was running out.

VENOM

The instant the redhead's hand plunged into her carryall, Zinc responded by closing the mouth of the bag around her forearm like the cuff of a boxing mitt. Jessica's yelp of pain was disproportionate to the pressure of the Mountie's squeeze, and suddenly she stopped reacting to his accusation.

Her arm went limp.

She appeared to be in a drugged stupor.

Moments later, she began hyperventilating.

Zinc had no idea what was happening. The redhead had seemed perfectly healthy until she'd put her hand into the bag. Now, her entire body was slick with perspiration, but the skin touching his wasn't feverish.

His free hand felt her pulse.

Her heart wasn't racing.

Whatever malady had seized her, it didn't affect circulation. Instead, her limbs slackened from their tips toward her torso. They lay like deadwood on the sheet and the night table, while her lungs struggled for breath and she began convulsing. Her gasps were like death rattles. As Jessica slowly asphyxiated, suffocated by her own flesh, the horror in her eyes told Zinc that she was conscious and acutely aware of her fate.

The Mountie tried CPR.

No use.

He couldn't get her breathing.

Once it was clear that her lungs had shut down and she had lost consciousness, he felt her pulse again and found that her heart went on beating … beating … beating.

And then it stopped.

Curare? Zinc wondered. Mixed with tropical snake venom?

Stepping off the bed, the inspector gently pulled the bag from the dead woman's hand. The first thing he noticed was a fresh puncture wound on her palm. Had she jabbed herself with a needle while reaching into the bag?

Zinc confirmed that by emptying the carryall's contents onto the desk. Out cascaded the clutter you'd expect to find in a woman's bag: a box of condoms, a cellphone, and … a hypodermic needle? The protective cap had come off the spike. The plunger was two-thirds depressed, and only a little poison remained. Zinc figured the weapon had been readied for him, but when he'd seized the bag, he had jarred the cap loose and she had inadvertently jabbed herself instead.

It was clear now *how* Nick had died, but not *where* the vamp had stuck the needle. The autopsy would probably reveal that, but Zinc had a kinky inkling from having seen femmes fatales spin their webs in film noirs with Alex. Staring down at the dead vixen, he could picture himself locked between her legs as one hand reached back and spread the cheeks of his ass—ah yes, Whistler girls!—and the other hand jabbed the needle where the sun don't shine.

"Jesus!"

Chances were the puncture would be missed at autopsy. Dissection of the rectum would be traumatic enough to destroy a wound the size of a pinprick.

After Zinc got dressed, he reloaded and holstered his gun. Then he fished his cellphone out of his pocket and called the chief.

"DeClercq," his boss answered.

"The honey trap worked."

"Who is it?"

"Jessica. She picked Nick up in the bar."

"Will she talk?"

"No."

"Dead end?" DeClercq asked.

Zinc eyed the contents of the carryall.

"We may have caught a break."

CONQUISTADOR

El Dorado!

How did that Edgar Allan Poe poem go? Mephisto asked himself.

And, as his strength
Failed him at length,
He met a pilgrim shadow—
"Shadow," said he,
"Where can it be—
This land of Eldorado?"

"Over the Mountains
Of the Moon,
Down the Valley of the Shadow,
Ride, boldly ride,"
The shade replied,—
"If you seek for Eldorado!"

Was that not the prophecy that brought him to this moment? Had his strength not failed him a few years ago, when he'd realized that he was born out of time, doomed to live his life in a claustrophobic nightmare of overpopulation? All the money he had made from selling stolen artifacts and priceless masterpieces on the black market could not buy him a time machine to escape from that.

But then, he'd lucked across the pilgrim shadow of Vladimir Grof, and he came to see that his destiny was to thrive in the interregnum between the fall of Soviet Russia and the rise of Vladimir Putin. Only in that chaos could he have bought the three aerosol cans of the supervirus.

Geneticists calculated that recent outbreaks of Ebola Zaire had wiped out 95 percent of the gorillas and 77 percent of the chimpanzees populating the rainforests.

That's about a quarter of the great apes.

Man's closest relatives.

The mutant virus hidden in the cans sold to Mephisto was in position to virtually annihilate the world's human population. Only seven hundred million survivors! Would that not be El Dorado? Think of all the gold to be mined after the dying wretches bled out.

Ka-ching!

True, the smallpox vaccine was being stockpiled in countries paranoid about terrorist attacks, but there'd be no time to distribute it against a far-flung pandemic like this. So all Mephisto and Scarlett had to do was avoid contact with bodily fluids while the hottest virus known to science burned through the population. With Scarlett immune, he'd have her to fuck while the bleeders depopulated.

Biological weapons were nothing new. In 184 B.C., in what was the first known bio-attack, Hannibal hurled pots of "serpents of every kind" onto enemy ships. During the siege of Kaffa in 1346, the Tartars used catapults to lob plague-infested cadavers over the city walls. That spread the Black Death across Europe, killing twenty-five million people over the next five years.

Hernando Cortez and his small force of conquistadors used smallpox to overcome the Aztecs in 1521. During the French and Indian War, in what's now New York, the British gave smallpox-infected blankets to hostile Indians holding Fort Carleton. Once the epidemic had reduced the tribe, the Redcoats attacked, took the stronghold, and renamed it Fort Ticonderoga.

In the spring of 1918, with the world embroiled in war, a flu virus jumped species from pigs to humans. Spread around the globe by soldiers returning from the First World War, the flu claimed between fifty and a hundred million lives in just over two years.

But that was insignificant compared to the horror Mephisto would unleash.

Pop the cans.

Fsssss ...

He'd go down in history as the *über*-conquistador.

Standing at the window, gazing out at the snowfall, Mephisto saw a monster staring back at him. He was sickened by what the plastic surgeon had done to the features he'd inherited from his father.

As soon as Stopwatch phoned with the news that Katt and Becky were dead, the megalomaniac would unleash his mutant virus on the world.

BLOODHOUND

For cops, cellphones were the greatest invention since DNA fingerprinting. More and more people were carrying their lives in their hands. Calls came in, calls went out, digital phonebooks stored the numbers of every acquaintance, text messages zipped back and forth, and photos were snapped.

How convenient. Especially for the police.

Today, your every action gets stored on your phone's memory chip. The Mounties have gadgets that can suck that record out, downloading your whole life for cyber sleuths to examine. No need for the classic bloodhound tracking a physical trail. Cell wanderings leave a *virtual* trail instead.

"Which one's Mephisto?" the chief asked.

"Damned if I know," replied Zinc, scrolling through the phonebook in Jessica's cell.

"Can we narrow the search?"

"Uh-huh. Assuming Mandy and Corrina are still trolling the bar."

The X men had met up in the lobby of the El Dorado Resort, with Zinc coming down from the room in which Jessica's body lay and Robert hoofing it in from the backyard where Joe's corpse had been found. The snowflakes on the chief's hat had yet to melt.

"What's the plan?" Zinc asked.

"First, listen to this."

The chief played the message the Russian scientist had left on his cell.

"'Die'? 'Frame'? 'Gate'? What does all that mean?" asked Zinc.

"'Gate' told me where to find Joe, so ignore that. But the other two words were crucial enough for Joe to choke them out with his last breath."

"Is someone going to die? Will someone else be framed?"

"How would Joe know that?"

"Beats me," Zinc said with a shrug.

"'Die' must refer to Nick. Joe was in the morgue trying to figure out how he died. Could 'frame' refer to the cause of death?"

"Makes no sense to me."

"Me neither," said the chief. "Perhaps it's Joe's accent. Could we be hearing it wrong?"

"Look, the woman who killed Nick is dead. We know the weapon was a hypodermic syringe. Does it matter anymore what Joe was trying to tell us?"

"I read enough Ellery Queen stories in my youth," said DeClercq, "to know that a dying message *must* be deciphered. Joe was killed trying to reach me."

———•◦•———

When the snowstorm passed and the sun shone down, Whistler would be a winter wonderland, glistening below the soaring summits. From the Peak 2 Peak Gondola, strung across the azure sky like a necklace, riders would gaze down at this snow-smothered highway and across to the glittering fairways of the Whistler golf course. But right now, the mother of all snowstorms had Dane Winter in a stranglehold. At the moment, the sergeant could see fuck-all.

Wait.

Was that it?

Was that the road that led past the golf course to Gill's chalet?

Dane turned, fishtailed, and left the highway.

"Rachel?"

"Here," the radio answered.

"Any sign of Rick?"

"Not a peep. Something's going down."

"Jackie?"

"I'm out of play. What a mess! This route's blocked from pileups in both directions, and I can't find a mobile car on the village side."

"Keep trying."

"I will. But don't hold your breath."

"Rachel?"

No answer.

"Rachel?" Dane repeated.

When the Mountie guarding the girls didn't answer either the radio or her cell, the sergeant called the chief.

———————

Being unable to reach Rick Scarlett was a cause for concern. Being unable to reach Rachel Kidd increased the tension. But when Robert's call to Katt went unanswered, *that* hit the panic button.

As long as he was physically able, Zinc would answer the call of the wild. It meant he would rise no higher in the ranks of the RCMP, but then, administration work didn't thrill him. Most cops nowadays were mired in the gutters of urban streets, but the Mounties were still the guardians of a northwest frontier. That's what had drawn Zinc to the red serge. The Horsemen's uniform had spurs on the boots.

He swung into action.

"Follow me," he said, dispensing with rank.

He and Robert had to push their way through the crowd in the Gilded Man. From what they heard as they passed, Joe wasn't the only one who'd fallen prey to a bear trap. Others had also been crushed in strong metal jaws.

Jittery barflies were afraid to go outside.

Mandy and Corrina were seated at the same table as before and had hooked a pair of Olympic hopefuls: trim, buff Swiss skiers.

"Ladies, we need your help," Zinc said, interrupting. "Gentlemen, save their seats."

"Who's he?" Corrina asked, nodding at Robert.

"Chief Superintendent DeClercq," replied Zinc, leaving the senior officer to wrangle the sex kittens while he pressed on to the bar.

"What happened?" Karen asked, mixing a cocktail. "You get stood up?"

"In a way," said Zinc.

"Hopefully that leaves room for me?"

"I haven't forgotten. But right now, I need two favors: use of a backroom, and that microphone turned on."

"You're going to sing?" Karen exclaimed.

"No, make an announcement."

"Just flick the switch."

A bandstand was wedged in one corner of the pub, beside the bar. Zinc took the stage and amplified his voice. "Testing

one, two, three," he said, to quell the hubbub. "Will the owner
of the snowmobile parked outside please come forward and
identify himself to me."

A worried man with a drinker's nose approached. "What's
wrong?" he asked.

"Show me your snowmobile, sir."

"Can't you tell me here?"

"I need to establish it's yours."

"Shit, it's locked in the back of my truck. Did someone try
to steal it?"

"Let's go see," said Zinc.

As they passed the chief en route to the parking lot door, the
inspector gave him the cell he'd seized from Jessica's carryall.

"My gamble paid off," Zinc whispered. "I'm heading to
Gill's chalet. Karen, the barkeep, will find you an interview
room."

Outside, the man with the mottled nose led the Mountie
across the lot to his truck.

"Hey, my snowmobile's still there," he said with relief.
"I was worried it had been stolen."

"Not stolen," replied the inspector, flashing his regimental
badge. "Commandeered."

SHATTERED GLASS

The Icemen closed in around the chalet like a noose cinching tight around the neck of a condemned man. Though each hailed from a different European nation—Sweden, Finland, Norway, Austria, and Russia—all had been drilled in sub-zero tactics. And Stopwatch had spared no expense to equip them with black market hardware. The Swede and the Finn had crept on snowshoes around to the back door. The Norwegian crouched by the window on the side away from the frozen creek. The Austrian and the Siberian peered in through the windows flanking the front door. Both doors had tiny limpet mines near their locks.

The chalet was completely dark, but that didn't matter. Stopwatch had armed all five killers with night-vision goggles. The men peeping into the chalet from their crossfire positions could clearly see Rachel in her hallway redoubt.

Blinded by the stygian darkness, she couldn't see them.

"Ready?" Ice Ax whispered into the headset mike hidden in his hood.

"One."

"Two."

"Three."

"Four."

Each man counted himself off to report his readiness.

The goggles strapped across the eye slits of the white bala-clavas were like the inch-thick lenses of jewelers' loupes. They jutted from the blank faces, transforming the cold-blooded mercenaries into bug-eyed monsters besieging a lonely ski chalet in a horror movie.

"Go," Ice Ax ordered.

———————

"Are you scared?" Becky whispered in the darkness.

"No," said Katt.

"Why not?"

"We've got the best dog there is protecting us."

"Him?" said Becky.

"Uh-huh."

"Napoleon's too friendly."

"Don't let him fool you. This dog's a killer. He'll tear apart anyone who tries to hurt us."

"How do you know?"

"Because the Mounties trained him. And because I know he loves me, and he'll obey my command."

Crouched beneath a cracked dormer window, the girls sat facing the door to the hall. Napoleon was on the floor in front of Becky, careful not to block Katt's view. The teen had a clear trajectory and was ready to nail the first person through the door with her improvised arrow.

"What's your last name?"

"Bond."

"That's why Napoleon will protect you, too. Guess what Mounties call their dog-training program."

"Bonding?" Becky said.

"BOND," Katt replied. "B-O-N-D."

"What's that?"

"It's an acronym. B stands for Believe in the dog. You *believe* in Napoleon, don't you, Becky?"

"If you do."

"O is for Observe the dog. You've *seen* how much Napoleon likes you, right?"

"He licked my hand."

"Well, there you go. Give him a pat on the head."

Becky reached out in the darkness and ruffled Napoleon's fur.

"N is for Nurture—that means educate—the dog. The Mounted Police have a dog school at Innisfail, Alberta. Only purebred German shepherds get in. The Mounties train them from when they're pups to protect their handlers, to protect themselves, and to attack on command. You've heard of King of the Royal Mounted, haven't you?"

"No," said Becky.

"Sergeant Preston of the Yukon's dog? He's only the most famous police dog in the history of the world."

"Oh," said the girl.

Actually, Katt was fudging things a little bit. Instead of being dogmatic—ha, ha—she was being creative. King *was* the name of Sergeant Preston's fictitious hound, but *King of the Royal Mounted* was a 1930s comic strip and a series of films, with fictitious Corporal King played by Alan "Rocky" Lane, later the voice of TV's talking horse, Mr. Ed.

"The truth," said Katt, "is that Napoleon got better marks in everything at dog school than King did."

"Wow!" said Becky, impressed.

"Shhhh," Katt shushed. "Remember to whisper."

"What does D stand for?"

"D is for Depend on each other. Have you still got your hand on Napoleon's head?"

"Yes," said Becky, stroking the crown of the German shepherd's brindled face.

"You know what Senator George Graham Vest of Missouri said about dogs, don't you?"

"No."

"'If fortune drives the master forth an outcast in the world,'" quoted the teen, "'friendless and homeless, the faithful dog asks no higher privilege than that of accompanying him, to guard against danger, to fight against his enemies.' Ain't it so, Napoleon?"

"He nodded," Becky whispered.

"He's telling you not to be afraid," said Katt, smiling to herself for having trained her dog to nod at the command "ain't." "He'll kill anyone who tries to hurt you, just like he killed a guy named Corkscrew when he tried to hurt my—"

And that's when it happened.

———•••———

Rachel had the Winchester aimed at the front door when the limpet mine blew in the back, spraying splinters down the hall. As she blindly spun in that direction to meet the threat, her cellphone buzzed with Dane's call and the front entrance exploded. Like a pendulum, she swung back and forth, caught by an attack that could come from either direction, or both at once.

In the noise created by the blasts, she missed the crunch of glass as Ice Ax smashed his climbing hammer through the double-glazed window beside the front door. The mercenaries were armed with silencer-equipped pistols, but there was no need for those now. The explosions had already made a racket, and the overall plan was to scare as many people as possible into gathering at the El Dorado Resort.

Eschewing the pistol, Ice Ax stuck the snout of his Uzi through the jagged hole in the window, aimed it at Rachel, and let it rip. To ensure he didn't hit one of the other Icemen, he kept the gun pointed toward the far corner of the chalet, between the back door and the window at the side. Through his night-vision goggles, Ice Ax saw the Mountie jerking like a puppet on a palsied hand.

Torn and tattered by the bullets, Rachel dropped the Winchester.

"Take her!" the mercenary snapped into his mike.

Having shucked their snowshoes, the four killers at the front and back stormed in through the blown-open doors as the Norwegian trudged around from the side to watch the drive-way. The first Iceman to reach Rachel, sprawled motionless on the floor of her redoubt, let her have an Uzi burst to the face to guarantee she'd be no problem.

"Let's get the heads," Ice Ax said, "and get out of here."

The soldiers of fortune split up to search the chalet. Two roamed around the lower level, while the Austrian and Ice Ax clomped up the stairs to find and butcher the kids.

SKELETON

The Winter Games include three sledding sports: bobsled, luge, and skeleton. In bobsled, which dates back to a nineteenth-century Swiss gentlemen's pursuit, the driver and brakeman carom down the course in a bullet-like vehicle. In luge—that's French for "sled"—the athlete lies face up on a flat platform and zips feet-first downhill. The sport originated in sixteenth-century Russia, but the first sleds were hollowed logs used in ancient Scandinavia. The skeleton driver, no bones about it, is into speed. On a streamlined sled like a large cafeteria tray, he zooms headfirst at eighty miles an hour around some of the sharpest and iciest curves in the history of sport.

If the girls were to escape, skeleton was their sport.

Napoleon sprang to his paws the moment the back door blew. Katt placed the crossbow on the floor beside her flash-light, pencil arrows, and cellphone. Scrambling to her feet, she shoved the unlatched dormer window open. Robert had told her during their last conversation to crack the window, giving them a means of escape if someone burst into the chalet.

The floor shook when the second blast demolished the front door, making Napoleon growl.

"You can do it, Becky."

Machine-gun fire boomed below.

"Pretend you're on a toboggan plowing downhill."

The window opening gave them barely enough room to crawl out headfirst, so there'd be no swinging out feet forward like a luger going for the gold.

Another machine gun went rat-a-tat-tat.

"Go, Becky. *Go!*"

Katt grabbed the child by the seat of her snowpants and literally tossed her like a sack of potatoes out the hole.

Boots stomped up the stairs.

"Jump, Napoleon!"

The police dog obeyed the command, springing out the opening and bounding down the roof.

By touch, Katt clamped the trigger lock onto the firing mechanism of the cocked crossbow. If the bowstring released by mistake, she wasn't strong enough to tug it back in place.

Footsteps on the landing turned her way.

The arms of the bow bounced back from the window frame.

Please let it fit, Katt prayed.

The clomping reached the bedroom door.

By tilting the bow, Katt managed to maneuver it through the window. The door to the hall was locked, but it wouldn't withstand much stress. With one hand gripping the bow, Katt stooped to retrieve her accessories from near her feet. The jiggling door handle made her jump, and she whapped the flashlight like a hockey stick, hurling her pencil arrows and phone across the floor.

Bam!

Crack!

The wood fractured as a shoulder hit the door.

Losing the backup arrows was no catastrophe—since Katt couldn't rearm the bow, she could only fire the pencil currently in the slot. But losing her phone—her only link to her potential rescuers—was devastating. Still, there wasn't time for a scramble to retrieve what she had lost. At least she still had the crossbow. A bird in the hand is worth two in the bush, the proverb teaches.

Bam!

Crack! Crack!

There wasn't a moment to spare.

Katt was half outside the dormer when a spray of bullets tore the door's lock to scrap metal. Wriggling her tail end like a fish, she jackknifed through the opening. As one arm crooked the crossbow back over her shoulder, she arched her other across the crown of her head. In that posture, she plowed down the A-frame's steep roof.

"Downstairs!" Ice Ax snapped behind her.

———•—•———

The earliest Mounties swung up into the saddles on their steeds. That's what had put the "mounted" in the Mounted Police. Later Horsemen climbed onto the runners of their dogsleds. But the last dog patrol had made the rounds in 1969. These days, Mounties like Zinc got to straddle the seat of a Ski-Doo instead.

Fortunately, this snowmobile was fit for conquering all wilderness trails, from tight and twisty to rough and tumble. Like an army halftrack, it was propelled by a studded tread at the rear. The studs dug into ice like cleats on a muddy sports field. The skis in front were wide so the vehicle would "float" high over snow. With his glove on the throttle, his heart in his throat, and the track churning up a powder wake, Zinc aimed the Ski-Doo for Gill's chalet.

Yee-ha!

The route was mostly ice coming through Whistler Village, but on the far side of the highway, the golf course had wide-open fairways of deep, freshly fallen snow. The Ski-Doo had regulators and foam padding to dampen its sound, but in this eerie stillness, you could hear Zinc coming from miles away.

Vroom!

Wind chewed at his face and bit into his bones. Needles of ice struck his goggles and cut his skin. Even with the earflaps of his fur cap pulled down and tied under his chin, he couldn't stop shivering. The black Ski-Doo had turned white from snow. Leaning into turns to keep from flipping, Zinc wondered if he'd be found frozen in his tracks, man and machine fused together as a weird ice statue.

The eaves of the A-frame weren't the end of the slide. Wind blowing across the ice of the frozen creek had piled a massive drift on both the bank and the side of the house. Katt's ride continued until she landed in a billow on the solid waterway.

"Becky?" she whispered.

"Here," replied a voice in the darkness.

"Where's Napoleon?"

"He's with me."

"Good. Hold out your hand."

Katt was reluctant to switch on the flashlight, for fear of attracting a machine-gun blast from the dormer window above. So she swept the blackness before her with the back of her palm until it brushed Becky.

"Grab my arm, hold tight, and I'll pull you behind me. How deep is the snow?"

"It's up to my waist."

"Napoleon," Katt commanded, "follow me."

A woof acknowledged.

Overhead, she heard the stomp of boots exiting the chalet.

Here they come, thought Katt.

———·+·———

By the time Ice Ax and the Austrian had descended the stairs from the upper floor, the Swede and the Finn were outside the back door, strapping on their snowshoes again.

"Angle upstream," the Siberian ordered them. "If you shoot the kids, don't damage their heads."

He and the Austrian stepped out front to put on their snowshoes. With his back to the house and his Uzi pointed down the driveway, the Norwegian stood guard by the front door. Through his blinder-like night-vision goggles, he'd failed to notice the girls' escape to his right.

"Down to the creek," Ice Ax commanded his companions. "Track their footprints. They may go downstream."

"Look," said the Norwegian, pointing dead ahead.

A vehicle creeping along the road at the bottom of the wooded lot had turned up the driveway.

PLAYER ON THE OTHER SIDE

While Zinc was off commandeering the Ski-Doo and mounting up in the lot, Robert ushered the reluctant snow bunnies into the stockroom he'd been directed to by Karen and locked the door. Cases of booze were stacked up to the ceiling along all four walls, encircling the cramped business area where paperwork was done.

"Do I need a lawyer?" Mandy asked, arms folded across her chest for a stance of authority.

"No," said Robert. "I need your help."

"Help how?" Corrina asked, arching an eyebrow.

"Jessica's cellphone"—he held it up—"has a list of contacts. Tell me everything you know about each name."

"No," said Mandy, firmly.

"No?"

"I'm no snitch."

"How'd you get her phone?" Corrina asked suspiciously.

"Time is tight. That doesn't matter."

"It matters to me," said the Raven.

"The psycho responsible for all that's going on here could be listed in this phone," said Robert, exasperation in his voice. "If so, *you two* could be next."

"You're bluffing," scoffed Mandy.

DeClercq snorted. What a world! It used to be that only the punks gave you attitude, but now every Joe Cool on the block thought that was the proper way to behave. Pulling his regimental badge from his pocket, he held it up beside his face and telescoped in until his angry eyes were a foot from the Blonde's.

"If you don't help me and someone dies as a result, I will see to it—so help me God—that you waste your precious youth in prison." The chief had spent enough years in harness to know the smell of fear. "Do I have to call *your* bluff?" he asked.

He plunked a chair down at one of the tables.

"Sit," he ordered.

Mandy sat.

"Here," he said, slapping a pen and a pad of order forms down before her.

Swinging another chair into place, he set it down at a second table so the seats were back to back.

"Sit," he said again.

Corrina sat. She also got pen and paper.

"Exam time, ladies. No cheating. As I call out each name, scribble down what it means to you. No holding back, understand? This is life or death. When we're done, I'll compare what you wrote. I expect the info to jibe. If it doesn't, you'll explain why. There isn't a moment to waste, so let's work fast. Help me catch this killer and you'll be heroes. Try to hoodwink me and ..."

The chief left the sentence unfinished.

He called up the contact list and read the first name.

After the list was whittled down to its most suspicious members, the chief thanked the snow bunnies and left the Gilded Man. He followed the most trampled path he could find to the Special X outpost in Whistler Village, to avoid the fate Joe had suffered. The detachment was deserted when he stomped snow from his boots and swung open the door.

Everyone was off dealing with the chaos.

Ghost Keeper answered his call to Vancouver HQ.

"Any luck finding information on the company that booked the room where Nick was killed?" asked the chief.

"Negative. Ecuador Exploration is a shell within a shell. We can't pierce the corporate veil."

"I'm going to download the contents of a henchwoman's cellphone. I'll send it shortly. I've trimmed the contacts down to the most likely suspects. See what you can glean from calls in and out, text messages, photos, and browsing history. Anything that could link a number to Mephisto."

"What's your strategy?" asked the Cree.

"A long shot," said the chief.

———•—•———

The only move Robert had left was the chanciest of gambits. If Ghost Keeper could unmask Mephisto from the contacts in Jessica's phone, the service provider would cough up a billing address. And if the address was in Whistler, Robert would kick in the door.

Should that fail, there was also the phone itself.

An activated cellphone emits a signal. Robert could call every suspect in Jessica's contact list and use a handheld gadget to triangulate the location of those who responded. Or if he had some inkling of where Mephisto would be tonight, he could track which phone was at that location.

Did he have that inkling?

The trick in chess was to anticipate the next moves of the player on the other side. If Mephisto planned to spread his supervirus, he would need to release it in a crowd of globetrotters who would disperse before it took effect.

Mephisto would know about the 1966 U.S. military experiment to test America's vulnerability to biological weaponry. A man took harmless bacteria down into New York's subway system, stood at the edge of the crowded platform, and waited for the next train. When the doors opened, he dropped a light bulb full of bio-agents onto the tracks below. The bulb burst, the doors shut, and the train pulled away. Thirty minutes later, detectors picked up bacterial traces ten blocks across town. The test proved a crowd on the move could disperse biological weapons.

Was there such a crowd here tonight?

Mephisto's reign of terror had frightened Olympians into huddling together for safety.

Where would they gather until they could burst free?

The El Dorado Resort and the Gilded Man were clues. The names evoked Spanish conquistadors seeking gold. Ecuador Exploration—the company that booked the ambush room—and the gilding of Nick's corpse were also clues. Every move Mephisto made was part of the overall game, and he was taunting DeClercq by hinting at where he would strike, just as a chess player warns his opponent by calling "Check!" before he attacks.

"Going for the Gold!"

"Checkmate!"

The chief packed Jessica's phone and the triangulation device into his briefcase. As he bundled up for yet another trudge through the storm to the El Dorado Resort, he turned on the police radio for an update from Dane and Zinc.

What he heard was the cry most dreaded by officers of the Mounted Police.

"A member is down!"

DOGS OF WAR

"Made it," Dane said into his police radio. "I'm turning up the driveway to Gill's chalet."

Blind from the headlight beams reflecting off the dazzling snow, Dane depended on ruts in the groundcover to show him the way, just as he had throughout the harrowing drive in from the highway. With the defroster on full blast and the radio squawking in his ear, he hadn't heard the machine guns firing minutes ago.

Risky though it was to plow straight up the driveway, the cop couldn't see without the headlamps. His compromise was to climb no farther than the parking alcove, which, he noticed as he approached, was occupied by Zinc's Rover. Then he saw Rick Scarlett's body crumpled in the bloody snow.

"A member is down!" Dane warned the others. Nothing more was required to convey the image of one of their own on the ground.

"It's Rick," he added.

Shifting into neutral and yanking on the emergency brake, the cop reached with one hand for the Winchester in the foot well of the passenger's seat while the other released the seatbelt and swung open the driver's door. As Dane's upper body emerged from the four-wheel drive, a sputter of machine-gun fire drilled a row of spider-webbed holes across the windshield.

Bam! A bullet struck the rifle and wrenched it out of Dane's hand, spraining his wrist.

Before he could dive for cover ...

Bam! The driver's-side window fractured into splinters. A second bullet slammed against his heart so hard that the wind was knocked from his lungs. Luckily, his Kevlar vest stopped most of the dagger-like shards, and the rifle plate protecting his chest flattened the slug.

His left arm wasn't as lucky.

Bam! The third slug tore through his biceps and sprayed the snow behind him as red as that around Rick.

"A second member is down!" he gasped as he hit the drift close to Rick's body.

"Me," he added.

———•———

The dogs of war had swung into action on several fronts. Though trained by different national armies, they'd been whipped into a team by Stopwatch's precision timing. He'd set them tasks to complete with the promise of cash for every soldier of fortune who made the cut. After that, he'd had them perfect each task by timing them with the stopwatch strung from his neck.

Now, as the Austrian and the Norwegian descended the driveway to exterminate any survivors in the bullet-riddled four-wheel drive, Ice Ax followed the skid marks gouged by the kids during their ride down the roof to the frozen creek. Maneuvering down the bank, he picked up their trail as they struggled to escape upstream.

"They're coming your way," he radioed to the Swede and the Finn out back of the chalet.

"If someone breaks in," Robert had told Katt during their last talk, "escape through the dormer window and slide down the roof. The snow heaped against the wall will carry you onto the creek. Do you remember the treehouse?"

"Yes," Katt had replied.

"Hide there so the backup team will know where to find you when it arrives."

So here they were, Katt, Becky, and Napoleon, struggling through the two feet of snow smothering the frozen creek. The world around them was nothing but cold and blackness. The wind infiltrated the gaps in their clothes and bit at their skin. Both girls had to wipe the backs of their mittens across their teary eyes to keep their eyelashes from icing together when they blinked. Unable to see a thing, they inched ahead by feel. As long as the snow was flat, they knew they were on the creek. Both banks were thick with underbrush.

Finally, Katt figured they were far enough upstream. Memory told her the treehouse was near.

As a girl growing up in Barbados, Gill had dreamed of lazing away the torrid summer heat up in the cool branches of a leafy tree. As a woman with buckets of money, she'd indulged that childhood whim by building a nifty treehouse behind her chalet.

Summertime ...

And the living is easy ...

It wasn't summertime now, and living hung in the balance, so Katt hoped she had the distance right. Huffing and puffing from the exertion of hauling Becky behind her, she strained to scale the tangled bank to the invisible trees. Her first step caused the rime to crack and swallow her leg to the thigh. When she planted her other boot, that leg sank as well. It seemed to Katt as if the forest was booby-trapped. With every step she took, bushes beneath the snow tripped her up.

"Ouch!" Becky yelped.

"What's wrong?" Katt whispered.

"Brambles," said the child.

"Shush," Katt silenced her. "I think we're there. In a minute, we'll take a peek."

In the woods out back of the chalet, the Swede and the Finn stood as still as ice statues among the trees, listening to the silence between the gunfire out front. The mercenaries caught Becky's yelp as thorns tore her flesh.

The kids were close …

Off to the left …

This side of the frozen creek …

Downstream, Ice Ax heard Becky's yelp, too.

WINTER WARFARE

The Norwegian moved forward as point man, and the Austrian backed him up. If the cops in the car had survived, surely they'd have returned fire. But the Norwegian couldn't know for certain without checking. The headlights were too bright for the night-vision goggles strapped to his mask. He'd be like a stage actor caught in a spotlight if he snowshoed down to the car in this glare. So—*Brrrddt! Brrrddt!*—he aimed two bursts of gunfire at the gleaming eyes.

The headlamps exploded like dying stars. As the night plunged back into darkness and the volleys echoed away, a new sound pierced the vacuum like a dentist's drill. From off in the direction of the golf course, a snowmobile was roaring in fast along the frozen creek.

----·•·----

As near as Dane could tell, his upper arm bone wasn't broken. Though it bled profusely, the blood didn't squirt, meaning the gunshot wound had missed the artery. The casualty report from his other arm wasn't as good. It throbbed so bad that he feared his wrist was cracked. The pain was excruciating as he fumbled to raise the hem of his parka to gain access to his sidearm.

On his belly, the sergeant had crawled away from the gunfire ripping at his vehicle. By the glow of the headlamps, he could see Rick Scarlett sprawled near the front of Zinc's car. A sidearm was no match for the firepower blasting down from above, so Dane knew his survival depended on finding the shotgun Rick had with him.

Brrrddt!

Glass smashing …

Brrrddt!

Glass smashing …

Both headlamps extinguished.

Lack of sight jolted Dane's other senses to alertness. He felt his heart pounding against the snow and shivered from the chill seeping up into his chest. He heard the *crunch, crunch, crunch* of snowshoes cracking the brittle ice crust, and he knew the shooter was coming to finish him off.

Coup de grâce.

Suddenly, Dane was lightheaded, and he feared he might pass out. Was it the agony of fumbling for his gun? Was he bleeding to death from the wound to his arm? Parched, he licked a scoopful of snow, and the freeze that stabbed him behind his eyes jerked him awake.

Again, the machine gun erupted, but this was a longer burst. Slugs drilled into the vehicle Dane had abandoned and around to the other car, causing a *thump, thump, thump* above his head. Then something tumbled off the hood and struck Dane's skull.

Katt weighed the pros and cons and decided to chance it. The unnerving eruptions of machine-gun fire told her the action was taking place out front of the chalet. She could hear a snowmobile roaring in fast from the other direction, heading downstream from the golf course to this forest behind the house. If the gunmen trudged around back to ambush the rescuer—Katt was certain it was Zinc zooming for the treehouse—she didn't want to get caught in the open and gunned down.

She flicked on the flashlight.

Eureka! There it was! The treehouse, behind a tattered curtain of fluffy white flakes.

"Come on," Katt whispered to Becky. "Up you go. The Mounties will be here soon."

Then, as she placed the crossbow down at the foot of the tree, Katt saw what had somehow slipped her mind as she'd made her way up the creek and thrashed through the blanket of snow to here.

The crossbow was still cocked.

But the pencil—her only missile—was missing from the trough on top of the stock.

———·•·———

"Found them," Ice Ax heard the Swede report quietly through the plug in his ear.

"See it?" added the Finn.

"Yes," the Siberian answered. His night-vision goggles had picked up the glow of the flashlight beam as his snowshoes topped the bank of the creek. Beneath the webbing of his footwear were the boot holes the kids had left behind.

"Orders?" asked the Swede.

"Wait for my command. As soon as the snowmobile passes, rush them."

———·•·———

The shotgun literally fell into Dane Winter's hands.

For a second, he thought he'd been clubbed on the head, taken from above by some stalking assailant as Rick had clearly been. On reflex, his arm went up to protect his brain from the next blow, and that's when his palm hit the barrel of the shotgun. Rick had either set it down or dropped it on the hood of Zinc's car, and the hammering of the bullets had jarred it loose from its perch.

Dane didn't wait to see the whites of the gunman's eyes. He knew roughly where his attacker was from the crunch of his footsteps. Gritting his teeth against the pain shooting up both limbs, he swung the muzzle in that direction and somehow hooked the trigger with his broken hand.

Bwam!

Bwam!

Bwam!

He pumped three blasts in rapid succession across the driveway up to Gill's chalet.

———•·•———

For a split second, both lenses of the Norwegian's goggles registered the muzzle flash. Then just one. The shotgun pellets had all but torn away the other half of his head.

The force of the scattershot whirled the Iceman around on one foot like a figure skater executing a spin. The jerking of his trigger finger let loose a final spray that ripped into the trees along the driveway and brought several branches crashing down.

Had the Austrian not ducked as soon as he heard the shotgun, he'd have fallen victim to friendly fire. Flat on his belly in the middle of the driveway, he arched his head and raised his

Uzi, using his arms for a tripod, then blew a full magazine of slugs at the shotgun's position.

Brrrdddddddddddddddddddt!

Katt was boosting Becky up the ladder to the treehouse when the snowmobile roared by on the frozen creek. The rungs were slippery with snow and ice, so the child's boots released a chunky cloud on Katt's head.

The booms of the shotgun mixed with the snarls from the machine gun and echoed upstream. Shivering, she watched as Becky was swallowed by the trapdoor above, and she was about to scramble up herself when the red beam of a laser hit the trunk near her face.

As Katt turned to face death, a longer machine-gun blast echoed back from the battle out front.

Zinc heard the noise of the shotgun through the radio plug in his ear. His attention was focused on what he could glimpse in the lights of the Ski-Doo. The beam of Katt's torch was smothered by the snowfall as he whipped by.

"Dane, it's Zinc," he broadcast. "Are you still on the driveway leading up to Gill's place?"

"Yes," replied the sergeant.

"I can't see where I am. I'm relying on you. Shout when the sound of the snowmobile goes by."

"Now," said Dane before the words had died away.

Angling the skis to the left, the inspector cranked the throttle. The snowmobile left the frozen creek for the slope up to Gill's property. As the tread churned up the grade, Zinc leaned his weight into the hill to keep from flipping over. Squinting into the light, he searched for the spot where a bridge spanned the creek, and when he spied the gap in the trees, he aimed the Ski-Doo for it. Another rev of the engine and he was up on the road below Gill's chalet, where the driveway climbed her property.

The next machine-gun blast stuttered in stereo. Zinc's earplug relayed the noise captured by Dane's mike, while the sound in his other ear came directly from the Uzi.

The Icemen were closing in from three directions. With her back against the tree and the laser dot sinking with her heart, Katt slithered down until the roots stopped her.

"One in my sights," said the Swede. "Permission to fire?"

"A pistol shot?"

"Yes."

"Where's the beam?"

"Bull's eye on her heart."

"Permission to kill, but don't mangle the head."

The Swede had his finger on the trigger, ready to squeeze, when naked fangs filled his field of vision and he was knocked off his feet by a hundred-pound leaping beast.

KING OF THE ROYAL MOUNTED

When the Swede was a boy, his father had taken him to hear Prokofiev's *Peter and the Wolf*. Composed to cultivate musical tastes in children, the symphony was performed with a narrator, and each character got its own instrument and theme.

An oboe for the duck, a clarinet for the cat, a bassoon for Grandpa, strings for Peter ...

And three French horns for the wolf.

Grandpa scolds Peter for leaving the yard and venturing off to the meadow. "Suppose a wolf came out of the forest?" he chides. Later, that happens, and when the duck waddles out of the pond, the wolf gulps it down.

Eventually, Peter captures the wolf and leads it to the zoo in a victory parade. The symphony ends with the narrator telling kids, "If you listen carefully, you can hear the duck quacking in the wolf's belly, because it was swallowed alive."

To this day, the sound of a French horn reminded the Swede of a wolf. And now here he was, like Peter's duck, being *eaten alive* by this beast.

"*Fan ta dig!*" he cursed.

In addition to the laser sight, the Iceman's handgun had a tactical light. Accidentally, the light got switched on. As the "wolf" shook the killer's wrist to make him drop the weapon, the beam jerked back and forth like a *Star*

Wars lightsaber in a drunk's fist. To make it easier to see, the soldier of fortune shoved the parka hood off his head, baring the balaclava.

Hidden in the Swede's boot was a combat knife. As the beast tussled with his arm for possession of the gun, the mercenary reached for the blade. Pulling it free, he pushed away the jaws to get at the "wolf's" belly. Then he drew back his hand to sink the steel into the animal's gut.

———————

Bullets buzzed around Dane's head like hornets at a nest. Slugs peppered the abandoned vehicle to his right, made Swiss cheese of the Rover above him, and thudded into Rick's body. After firing the shotgun, the sergeant had rolled behind the corpse for cover.

"I'm at the bottom of the driveway," Dane heard Zinc say through the plug in his ear. "There was only one gun in the last volley. Blow into the mike if you agree."

Dane blew.

Talking would expose his position.

"When I say 'Now,' do something to draw the gunner's fire. Show me where he is."

———————

The Finn could see the teen huddled at the base of the tree. It was a reaction common to those facing death. The doomed curled up in a fetal ball, leaving life in the same position they'd occupied in the womb.

Like the Swede, the Finn was currently armed with his pistol. The dog's attack had knocked the Swede from his lead position, and while he dealt with the hound, the Finn had rushed Katt.

He could see Ice Ax at the edge of his vision, with that pointed hammer raised to strike.

"Light her up," the Siberian ordered, "and shoot her through the heart. Then hold your fire and cover me while I find the brat. She can't be far away."

The Finn liked to see the fright in the eyes of those about to die, so he pushed back his hood and goggles to peel away the night-vision glow, and switched on the pistol's tactical light to illuminate his quarry.

The teen blinked.

A deer caught in the headlights, thought the Finn.

———•·•———

You can't teach an old dog new tricks.

The dog masters at the RCMP Police Dog Service Training Centre had taught Napoleon well. As top of his class in the apprehension of dangerous suspects and the protection of his handlers, he performed his duty by biting the hand that threatened Katt, without thought for himself. That's why he overlooked the knife peril to his gut, and why he was in danger of joining other K-9 heroes on the National Police Dog Monument.

You can't teach an old dog new tricks.

Years ago, Napoleon had been in this same situation. A hit man by the name of Corkscrew was about to kill DeClercq. Leaping, the dog had smashed through glass to take out the punk, but he got knifed in the abdomen in the process. With the German shepherd bleeding in his arms, Robert had staggered through driving rain to the nearest road to flag down help. Luckily, the driver who screeched to a halt was the son of a nearby doctor. Napoleon's life was saved on the kitchen table of the doc's home.

Now, as the dog shook the hand back and forth to free the weapon, the light beam hit the blade. The sight of the shiny steel brought it all back—the pain, the rain, the long recovery—and Napoleon reacted. Man's so-called best friend has no sense of fair play. At heart, he's an opportunistic predator. A wolf.

Napoleon went for the throat.

Turning his head and yawning as wide as both jaws would stretch, he gulped up the Swede's neck and bit down as hard as he could. His fangs sank into the soft flesh of the Iceman's jugular vein, and when the dog tore with all his might, the Swede's throat came with him.

Vertebrae peeked through the gaping hole in the mercenary's now-red balaclava.

BLACK ICE

Katt wasn't blinking from the sudden glare of the tactical light. What the Finn mistook for her being blinded by the beam was actually Katt squinting to take aim without the aid of the scope on the crossbow.

Take aim?

In sliding down the tree trunk, his prey wasn't curling up in a fetal ball as he'd thought. Instead, Katt had been reaching for the crossbow nestled in the drift beside her. During the seconds the Finn was shoving his hood and night-vision goggles away from his face, she had lifted the crossbow to firing height. The arms of the bow were still cocked to shoot.

Shoot what?

True, the colored pencil was missing from the trough on top of the stock. Necessity, however, is the mother of invention. Winter had strung not only the eaves of Gill's chalet but also the rungs of the ladder to the treehouse with icicles. In boosting Becky up the tree, Katt had been hit by a chunky cloud.

That's how she'd got the idea.

As she'd turned to face the threat behind the laser beam, the teen had snapped an icicle off the rung closest to her. By slotting it into the trough, she'd rearmed the crossbow with black ice. A flick of her thumb released the safety catch on the bowstring, and when the Finn paused to enjoy the look of fright on her face, she pulled the trigger and let the icicle fly.

Shew!

The missile struck the Finn in the eye and snapped back his head. It cracked through the bone of the socket and sank into his brain. Before he even hit the ground, the warmth of his gray matter had begun to melt the ice.

———•••———

With the lights out, Zinc was flying blind. Sometimes you had to rely on instinct and the lay of the land. The slope down from the chalet was mottled with trees. Back when Gill was building, a bulldozer had cracked a rock, releasing an underground stream. The water filled a hollow to create a pond, the overflow from which was channeled into the creek. A path arced down the far side of the property to link the chalet with the pond. Zinc chose that route up the hill.

Vroom!

His camouflage couldn't be better. The journey so far had caked both man and machine in white. Only by constantly wiping his ski goggles was he able to maintain his sight. Now, in the dark, camouflage would be his best defense if the gunner surveying the landscape had night-vision lenses.

Veering to the right carried the Mountie off the driveway and onto the pond. Again, Zinc was using flatness to guide the way. How thankful he was for that pooled water. Land could slope—and here it did—but the pond could not. The trick was to sense where the path branched away.

Here, he guessed ... and was right.

Vroom!

Like a racecar speeding around a track, the Ski-Doo circled toward the far property line and then curved back. It was a miracle Zinc didn't slam into a tree. In seconds, his trajectory would take him across the driveway. The man with the machine gun was somewhere ahead. Dane was downhill with the shotgun. Undoubtedly, the machine-gunner had heard the Ski-Doo churning toward him. With pistol in hand, Zinc zoomed in at a right angle to the driveway.

This was it!

Do or die!

"Now!" he barked into his mike.

The Remington shotgun held four shells. Dane had already pumped three shots up the driveway. Had Rick fired, Rachel would not have been perplexed about what had happened to him. So that meant a single shell remained.

Too many slugs had missed Dane for his luck to hold out. Only in action movies did the good guys never get killed.

When Zinc shouted "Now!" through the plug in Dane's ear, the cop shot to live, not to kill. His orders were to provoke the gunner's fire so the inspector could home in on his position. To that end, Dane clenched his teeth against the pain and used all his wounded strength to heave the barrel of the shotgun straight up in the air.

Bwam!

When the muzzle flared at that height, it made it look as if Dane was standing up. The shooter evidently thought so, for the Uzi erupted once more, and the sergeant hunkered down behind Rick's body to weather the barrage.

———•••———

The shotgun boomed, and the Uzi stuttered in response.

Through the haze of snow and darkness, Zinc saw the machine gun spit light. Multiple muzzle flashes streaked across the night. A slight jog of the skis and he was on a collision course with the gunman. Flicking a switch pooled the Ski-Doo's headlight beams around him. The Iceman reacted to the blinding glare by craning his head toward it. A white balaclava in a white hood faced Zinc. To someone looking through night-vision goggles, the glare of the beams would rival the searing of the sun.

The Uzi swiveled.

Before the Austrian could fire, Zinc hurled himself off the saddle. He was still in the air when his Smith began ejecting casings. Holes reddened the pale mask like smallpox. The Ski-Doo's momentum plowed it across the gunner. No reaction. The Uzi nuzzled into the snow and lay as still as the man.

———•••———

How foolish to underestimate the daughter of a cop.

Ice Ax felt nothing but contempt as he watched the Finn go down. That was the trouble with using sadists on military missions: they broke stride to savor the thrill of the kill.

Idiot!

Seconds count.

Professional that he was, Ice Ax sharpened his focus. Gunfire from the driveway told him that battle raged on. The dog was still in the throes of a knife fight with the Swede, and he wouldn't be able to get from there to here before Ice

Ax cleaved Katt's skull. Time was too short and the distance too long.

Lacking the strength needed to cock the bow a second time, the teen discarded the weapon and tried to scale the tree. Her only escape was up.

Like the Finn, Ice Ax had swept back the hood of his parka. But he'd kept on his night-vision goggles, and they exposed the teen as starkly as high noon.

Ice Ax grabbed Katt's leg before she could climb out of reach. Her boots slipped off the ladder rungs, and she fell to the ground at the mercenary's feet in a cloud of snow. With the hammer raised to strike, he tore the toque off her head and aimed for the part in her hair. Before he could slam down the weapon, however, the blades of a double guillotine got the drop on him.

Up in the treehouse, Becky had removed her razor-sharp ice skates from her bag. Wearing them on her fists like boxing gloves, she stood so her legs straddled the trapdoor. As Ice Ax hovered over Katt, ready to strike, Becky jumped into the opening and rode her skates down like guillotine blades slicing into the neck of a French king.

Thud, thud.

The blades shaved both sides of Ice Ax's skull and sheared off his ears. They sundered the strap of the night-vision goggles, releasing them from his face. Sinking into his shoulders, they severed arteries and veins, which spewed like a fireboat welcoming an ocean liner to its harbor.

With a quick, sharp gasp, Ice Ax buckled to his knees. Just before he lost consciousness, the soldier of fortune saw Becky somersault off his head.

How foolish to underestimate the daughter of a cop.

GOING FOR THE GOLD

Robert rarely packed a gun, but he was packing now. The chief had returned to the El Dorado Resort to find the doors of the Gilded Man locked. The barkeeps had moved over to the ballroom to mix drinks at the "Going for the Gold" event. Niles Hawksworth darted in and out, fretting over every detail as a long line of jumpy patrons inched forward to clear the improvised security detail at the ballroom doors. With luck, that would unearth either Mephisto or the device he intended to use to disperse his supervirus. But Robert was doubtful. This megalomaniac was far too devious to leave anything to chance, and the security detail—a pair of hotel employees— was more for show than safety.

So where was the superbug hidden?

The chief was about to jump the queue by flashing his regimental badge when a call buzzed his phone. For privacy, he retreated to a corner of the lobby and pressed Talk.

"Got something," Ghost Keeper said. "One of the names from Jessica's contact list is a man who stood trial for extortion."

"Who was he extorting?"

"A pharmaceutical giant got threatened with product tampering. A payment was made, and this guy was picked up during the exchange, but he slipped through a legal loophole."

"How much was the payoff?"

"Half a million dollars."

"Where?"

"New York City."

"What's he doing in Whistler?"

"No idea. Skiing?"

"Extortion fits Mephisto's psychology. That's not a lot of money, but smaller amounts are more likely to be paid."

"Here's the mug shot."

A face appeared on the screen of the chief's cellphone. It occurred to him that this was the ideal situation for a virtual lineup. In his palm was a digital witness with the suspect's face in its memory. And there at the ballroom doors stood a lineup of possible matches. If he could spot the suspect without the suspect knowing he'd been spotted, they'd have a chance to stop him before he could do what he planned to do.

The journey back was easier than the journey coming. The snowfall was lighter, so Zinc could actually see. With Becky sandwiched between him and Katt, he followed his earlier tracks back along the creek from Gill's chalet and through the golf course to the highway. Dane was left behind—with Napoleon as backup—to wait for Jackie, who had finally managed to commandeer a car, and an ambulance.

The inspector kept the chief informed of their progress through the plug in Robert's ear.

Mephisto fingered his facial scars as he watched DeClercq. If Gill and Nick had provided an accurate description of the man who'd held them captive on Ebbtide Island, the chief would never connect that face with *this*.

Slowly, the lineup was moving through security and into the ballroom beyond. As soon as the room was full, Mephisto would release his plague and plunge the world into a new dark age. No matter how hard they tried, the Horsemen would not be able to stuff that viral genie back in its bottle.

———··———

The Mountie walked to the front of the line and flashed his badge as if to jump the queue into the ballroom. Then, for all lined up to see, he pretended to answer his cell. The phantom caller must have made the chief change his mind, for he turned and walked along the line, as if heading for the lobby. The suspect's mug shot was stored in his mind for comparison, but you'd never guess it from how he nonchalantly scanned the queue.

It wasn't hard to spot him.

The scar on his lip matched that in the photo.

Got you, Robert thought.

———··———

DeClercq seized Hawksworth by the arm as he rushed through the lobby.

"I need your help."

"Good Lord, man. Can't you see I'm trying to put on a memorable event? I have no time to waste."

Prat, thought the chief. "Are you going to force me to shut you down?" he asked. "I will if you push me."

Hawksworth sighed. "What now?"

"See that man lined up ten people back from the ballroom doors? Sporting a leather jacket?"

"Yes."

"Tell your security people to note *everything* he's carrying. I want an immediate report."

"Why?"

"Just do it. And be discreet."

———•·•———

After the suspect entered the ballroom, the chief strode to the front of the line and questioned one of the security men.

"Well?" he asked.

"Nothing but his wallet, his keys, and some coins."

Stepping inside "Going for the Gold," Robert assessed the venue. The device must already be in place, he realized. If I were Mephisto, what would I do?

It irked him to see the Olympic spirit so poisoned by politics. If it wasn't Hitler using the games to showcase his theory of Aryan superiority, it was two medalists giving a black power salute on the podium in 1968. If it wasn't more than sixty nations boycotting the 1980 Moscow games to protest Russia's invasion of Afghanistan, it was fourteen socialist countries boycotting the 1984 Los Angeles games in a Cold War *quid pro quo*.

Capitalism versus Communism.

Ah yes, the Olympic spirit.

Germany was banned for ten years after the First World War. The Japanese and the Germans were *personae non gratae* in London in 1948 because of the Second World War. Apartheid saw South Africa shunned from 1960 to 1988, and thirty-odd African nations left the Montreal games in 1976 because New Zealand's rugby team had toured South Africa. China boycotted the Melbourne games in 1956 because Taiwan was recognized by the International Olympic Committee.

The worst political act, of course, was 1972's massacre of eleven Israeli athletes by Palestinian terrorists at the Munich games. And now, Mephisto was out to trump even that through the most horrific political atrocity of all.

But *how*? wondered DeClercq.

"We'll be there in minutes," Zinc reported through the plug in the chief's ear.

As he gazed around the ballroom, now about three-quarters full, he tried to pick out the athletes. Most were easy to recognize from their strut and swagger. Somewhere, he'd read that athletes are hard-wired to show pride—by puffing out their chests, tilting back their heads, and throwing their arms in the air. If you have success, others must know. "Look at me," the body gloats. "I'm powerful."

Was this not the perfect arena for the megalomaniacal Mephisto?

Cower in awe, jocks.

Look at *me*!

I'm the god who sits atop Mount Olympus!

The bar stretched along the wall opposite the doors. It was dominated by a pyramid built from cans of Coke, one of the sponsors of the games. The suspect and the chief joined parallel queues.

With so many bartenders, the lines moved fast. Robert glimpsed Karen shaking a martini. Even Niles Hawksworth was serving the thirsty. His self-appointed job was to transfer cans of Coke from the pyramid to the barkeeps.

"We're outside," Zinc reported through Robert's earplug.

Jesus Christ!

The answer came to him like a clock striking the hour.

Mephisto was the *player* on the other side.

Of all the symbols recognized around the world, the Mounties' scarlet tunic was number two.

It beat the Golden Arches, but it couldn't trump number one.

Coca-Cola!

Coke versus the Mounties.

If *that* didn't appeal to Mephisto's warped psychology, what would? The irony was that Coke itself had provided the clue that told the chief where the contagion lurked.

The suspect in the leather jacket had reached the bar. Because he was in the last line along that flank, he could charge past the serving counter, grab the can of Coke, pop the pull tab, and release the supervirus—*Fssssst*—into the room before anyone even knew what had happened.

"What'll you have to drink, sir?" Hawksworth asked. Like a jack-of-all-trades, the hospitality manager was now doubling as a barkeep.

"Rum and Coke," said the suspect.

"It's on the house, thanks to Coke," said Hawksworth.

Robert's hand closed on his gun. "You!" snapped the Mountie.

The suspect turned. "Me?"

"Yes. Freeze where you are."

The suspect frowned.

Out of the corner of his eye, Robert saw the hospitality manager reach for the Coke can.

What the … ?

His thought was broken by the sound of Becky's voice.

"That's him!" said the girl, pointing. "That's Mephisto!"

MORPH

The mutant Frankenvirus had come out of the Soviet Vektor lab during the Cold War. With Communism and capitalism engaged in worldwide struggle, it must have seemed deliciously ironic to Russian warmongers to export death in the Trojan horse of recycled Coke cans, the universal symbol of American capitalism.

When Mephisto's first battle with DeClercq had sent his boat to the bottom of the sea around the San Juan Islands, the watertight case containing the trio of deadly Coke cans went with it. But during the years it had lain submerged in Davy Jones's locker, Coca-Cola had designed a *new* Coke can.

Rebranding was common in commercial markets.

Mephisto's original plot must have been to stash the tampered cans in a pyramid of *identical* Cokes. Each can popped would have been another spin of the roulette wheel, and as the pyramid shrank, the odds of drawing the "dead man's hand" would have increased.

When Coke supplied "the real thing" for tonight's event, though, the glitch became evident. The mismatched cans scotched plan A but spawned plan B. Now, the plague-infected can could be plucked from the pyramid at a moment's notice by the psycho himself.

And that's what Mephisto was doing.

Standing in the queue next to the suspect, Robert had noticed the anomaly in the pyramid of cans. No way would a sophisticated company like Coca-Cola make an error like that at a sponsorship event. And that's when it had hit him. What better means of transporting an airborne contagion than an aerosol can?

But Robert was still focused on the suspect with the harelip from Jessica's contact list. His fear was that his quarry would lunge to the pyramid and pluck one of the incongruous Cokes. Only when he saw Hawksworth reach for the tampered can— Why *that* can when it wasn't the nearest at hand?—did he catch his mistake.

"That's him!" said Becky, pointing. "That's Mephisto!"

Zinc and Katt had entered the ballroom with Becky hidden safely behind them. Approaching the bar, they'd parted so she could step into the gap and point out the man whose voice she recognized from her ordeal on his San Juan island.

Robert swung his pistol to follow her finger.

Hawksworth had the tampered Coke in one hand. Before he could move to pop the pull tab, he found himself staring down the muzzle of the Mountie's gun.

"Move a muscle," Robert warned, "and I'll fire."

———————

Careful not to get between the muzzle and Mephisto, Zinc moved swiftly to remove the deadly can from Niles Hawksworth's hand before he cuffed him, cautioned him, and hauled him away. Robert took custody of the Coke from the inspector and pulled the other two suspect cans from the dwindling mountain of the real thing.

The chief commandeered the hospitality manager's office for his interrogation. As he paused at the threshold, he studied the man sitting on the chair facing the desk, his wrists locked together around the stiff wooden back. It was disconcerting how this chameleon had sucked him in.

The chief had often wondered what this face-off would be like. If Jack the Ripper had been caught, would he hold the same fascination he does today? No. Unmasking a monster cuts him down to size. And Mephisto had always seemed a bit like an overblown villain in a superhero comic. When he was captured, the chief had expected him to be nondescript, a psychotic with delusions of grandeur.

But he wasn't.

From the moment they'd first engaged, Hawksworth had been in the chief's face. How clever to have had Jessica telephone his office and demand to speak to *him,* making his assistant a witness to the suggestion that he call Special X. By the time the chief had arrived, the hospitality manager was in a fit. All he could talk about was his precious event and how it *had* to go ahead.

Every element of the plot revolved around this hotel. Its pub was the beheaded snowboarder's favorite watering hole. That fact was certain to draw Nick to Jessica, who then had only to entice him upstairs to set Mephisto's plan in motion. They must have somehow gleaned from Nick that Becky was coming to Whistler, which explained the attack at Alpha Lake. And of course, Hawksworth had been present for Robert's call to Gill and, under the guise of supplying a medical man, had provided the man who killed her.

But Hawksworth had no more substance than skin sloughed off a snake. Already, Mephisto was morphing into another self. It was as if the lights had gone down on the closing night of a play, and the star was already rehearsing his next role.

Robert repressed an urge to beat the madman to a pulp. He approached and positioned another chair facing his. Sitting down, he told Mephisto his rights. Then he asked, "Have you anything to say?"

"You must be gloating."

"Over what?"

"The mess you made of my face. I used to be handsome. Now I'm nothing but scars."

"Scars?"

"You're mocking me. It's because of *you* that a plastic surgeon carved me up. I no longer recognize myself when I look in a mirror."

"Do you have anything else to say?"

"Yes. This won't be over till I have my pound of flesh."

"It's over now."

"Not till I *eat* your heart."

At first, it seemed odd to DeClercq that a megalomaniac would be obsessed with facial scars that weren't, in fact, there. Then it began to dawn on him what had happened. According to the psych profile, Mephisto suffered from narcissistic personality disorder. An overwhelming trauma in his boyhood had induced an inferiority complex so severe that it had turned him into a hollow man, destroying his sense of self-worth. Then his mind had overcompensated by creating an all-powerful personality to take the place of the one that had been erased.

Mephisto.

You can't get more powerful than that.

Not unless you're God.

From chronic inferiority to overblown superego, Mephisto had morphed from one extreme to another. His sense of self-importance, his preoccupation with fantasies of limitless power, his lack of empathy—all were symptoms of malignant narcissism.

But of course, this was a *false* front, just as the seemingly solid rock face looming above the Sea to Sky Highway masks the fractured bedrock behind. And with a strong enough quake, all false fronts will crumble.

In Mephisto's case, that quake was plastic surgery.

In the past, Mephisto had assumed various roles and inhabited them completely. The delusions morphed, but the face at the center did not. His mistake was in changing his physical appearance to fool those who could identify him.

Nick.

Gill.

And Becky.

Now, when he looked in the mirror, he didn't see *himself.* Instead, some scarred interloper glared back from the glass. No matter how good it was, this new face had to be flawed, since it had replaced his *perfect* one.

Mephisto was plagued by body dysmorphic disorder, an obsessive preoccupation with imagined, or minor, defects in one's physical features. The chief knew enough about it to pick up the signs. The illness shared symptoms with eating disorders caused by body-image distortion. Mephisto was like those young women who starve themselves into looking like death-camp inmates because they think they're fat. There's a puzzling disparity between the inner and the outer selves.

Whatever Mephisto saw in the mirror, it wasn't the face DeClercq saw before him. When he viewed his reflection, his psychological scars came to the surface. He could function normally for a while, but eventually, his disorder compelled him to glance in a mirror, a window, or a glass door to see if the monster in his mind was on the loose.

And it always was.

Perhaps Mephisto would go to prison, but more likely, he'd go to a forensic mental institution. In either place, he would spend the rest of his life like Narcissus, staring at himself in the black water of the River Styx.

ENDGAME

"It's over now."

"Not till I eat your heart."

Haven't you already done that? Robert thought. Gill, Joe, Nick, Jenna, Rachel, and Rick were all dead. Katt, Becky, Dane, and Zinc had come close to joining them. If only Mephisto had tried to pull the tab on top of the can, the chief could have put him down like the mad dog he was.

If only.

With so much left to do, Robert couldn't succumb to grief. Instead, he took a brief break to count his blessings. On exiting the office, where he'd left Mephisto in the custody of two officers who'd come down from rescuing skiers buried by the avalanches, he met Zinc in the lobby.

"Well?" he asked the inspector.

"Ghost Keeper says the cavalry will reach us by morning. They're going to put a Bailey bridge across the stream to reestablish the road link to Vancouver."

"And the weather?"

"It should improve by dawn."

"Knowing Mephisto, he'll have a backup plan. If we move him to Vancouver by the highway, we'll be running a gauntlet along one of our most treacherous roads. Who knows what other traps could be waiting."

"So what's our plan?"

"Leave that to me. I want you to get some sleep. You've had more than enough for one day. If you push yourself further, that could bring on a fit."

The scar in Zinc's brain, a souvenir of the Cutthroat Case, required him to take several antiepileptic pills a day. Overtiredness was like playing with dynamite. He knew the chief was right. And besides, he had a promise to keep.

The Mounties parted ways in a lobby full of milling people, one of whom was Stopwatch. The mercenary had remained in the village while the Icemen laid siege to Gill's chalet. Now, his contract unfinished, he watched DeClercq approach the locked door to the Gilded Man and Chandler head for the ballroom.

———•—•———

The bar had stopped serving drinks the moment DeClercq pulled his pistol. Without a reason to be there, the crowd was trickling out. As the chaos around the village came under relative control, individual members of Whistler's skeleton security crew returned. No sooner did each arrive than he or she was corralled into locking down the hotel. Once the ballroom had been cleared, the doors would be sealed until an Ident team could process the scene. Zinc reached the entrance just as Karen exited.

"I knew you wouldn't stand me up," the barkeep said. "Be careful not to step on any ducks."

"What?"

"Have you got a pair of handcuffs?"

"Sure," said Zinc.

"Show me how they work."

Puzzled, the Mountie removed his cuffs and opened the bracelets. "You snap them on each arm."

"Like this?" Karen asked, cinching one of the cuffs around her left wrist.

Only now that he was free to think about sex did Zinc grasp how *very* attractive the barkeep was. Unlike the Blonde, the Redhead, and the Raven, she lacked artificiality. Her brunette hair was mussed, as it would be in bed, though no doubt teased like that with brush and comb. Her eyes were dark and her lips ruby red, and what Zinc spied down her deep neckline would make any man mortgage his house.

Yep, no doubt about it. The inspector hoped to bed her.

"Three men die in an accident and go to heaven," she said. "When they get there, St. Peter says, 'We have only one rule here: Don't step on the ducks.'

"The newcomers enter the Pearly Gates, and sure enough, they see ducks all over the place. With clouds underfoot, it's nearly impossible *not* to breach the rule. They haven't been there an hour before one man steps on a duck. *Quack!*

"On hearing that, St. Peter rushes over with the ugliest woman the man has ever seen and handcuffs her to him. 'Your penance for stepping on a duck is to spend eternity chained to this woman,' St. Peter tells the offender.

"The next day—*Quack!*—one of the others accidentally steps on a duck. St. Peter handcuffs an even uglier woman to him. 'Your penance for stepping on a duck is to spend eternity chained to this woman,' he repeats.

"The third man—Zinc by name—doesn't want to spend eternity chained to an ugly woman, so he is *very* careful not to step on any ducks. Days go by and nothing happens. Eventually,

St. Peter strolls over with the most gorgeous woman Zinc has ever seen—her name is Karen—and, without a word, chains them together."

Karen snapped the other cuff onto Zinc's wrist.

Then she waited.

"Okay," Zinc said, "what did I do to deserve being chained to you for eternity?"

Karen winked. "I don't know about you," she said, "but I stepped on a duck."

———•·•———

The door to the Gilded Man was guarded by an armed cop. Until he was confident Whistler Village was safe, the chief intended to keep the girls locked away in the stockroom at the back of the bar. Inside, Katt sat on one of the tables, while Becky was asleep with her head in the teen's lap.

Easing out from under the girl, Katt used her ski jacket as a pillow. She followed Robert to a far corner of the stockroom.

"I'm proud of you," the chief whispered. "Improvising with the icicle was using your brain."

"So was Becky's use of the skates. She saved my life."

"Still want to join the Mounted?"

"Hell, yes," Katt replied. "In fact, I've been thinking about making some changes. Let's face it, the last thing my mom needs while she's enjoying a new love affair is me hanging around. Would it be okay if I lived here instead?"

"Your room's waiting. Napoleon and Catnip will be pleased."

"You forgot Waif."

"So I did. The last waif I took in turned out well. So yes, Waif can stay."

"Do me a favor, Dad?"

"Anything you want," he said, choking down emotion. It suddenly struck him how very close he'd come to losing her.

The teenager nodded toward the sleeping girl. "Can we find room for another waif?"

———•—•———

Karen's room in the El Dorado Resort had a hot tub instead of a sauna. Naked, the two of them bubbled away like cartoon missionaries in a cannibal's pot.

"How'd you get all the scars?" she asked. That's what they always asked. Zinc satisfied her curiosity by describing his day, while the hot water relaxed his tension.

"Sounds exhausting," Karen said.

"Yes," he agreed. "I came up here planning to seduce you, but I'll probably sleep instead."

"You don't get off that easily. *I'm* seducing *you*. And anyway, I can't let this opportunity slip away. It sounds like your odds of survival decrease with each passing day. When your number inevitably comes up, I want to be able to say, 'I fucked him, you know.'"

"I don't think I have the energy."

"I'll do all the work."

Karen stood up in the hot tub, water running down her curves, and loomed above him. "Going once ... going twice ..." she said, stringing it out. "Going ... going ..."

"Sold!" said the Mountie.

———•—•———

This deadly game DeClercq was playing with Mephisto had been an uneven contest from the start. It was a steady onslaught, not the balanced match most rivals wage. Robert could not afford to lose the last move.

Moving Mephisto out.

He would spend the rest of the night setting it up. There would be no run down the Killer Highway. Better odds were to be had by playing the shell game. Beneath the El Dorado Resort was an underground parking lot. The chief gathered every available police car there, then had the security cameras disabled and the lot sealed from sight.

He found every field where a helicopter could land and assigned a police car to each one. In the hour before dawn, he and a few carefully chosen officers would stash Mephisto, in a straitjacket and leg shackles, in one of the cars. All the vehicles would leave the subterranean lot together and drive to the scattered fields. A helicopter would land at each field, and any would-be rescuer would have no idea which shell hid the pea.

The cops who actually had Mephisto would shove him into the chopper and off he'd go.

A tracking device was the only potential glitch. So before the psycho was taken to the car, he would be scanned with a debugging gizmo that would catch any radio signals emitted by a GPS.

Skin ...

Teeth ...

The works.

TEETH

Karen entered the bathroom and faced Scarlett in the mirror. Blindsiding Zinc had been easy.

Boomer's death was certain to lure a Mountie to the Gilded Man, and Scarlett—as Karen—had been waiting for the bait to walk in. Since Mephisto was the hospitality manager, it was simple to get Scarlett a job at the pub. And as barmaid, part of her job was to clean up after the trio of vamps, who often left unused assignation notes on the table. That's how she got hold of the Post-it Note she later stuck to the keycard and slipped into Nick's pocket.

It was Scarlett whom Nick met in room 807, not Jessica. And while there, she'd overheard the call from Jenna Bond that told Mephisto Becky was coming to Whistler. That set up the attack at Alpha Lake. And of course, Nick's murder was sure to bring another Mountie to the bar, and once again Scarlett had been waiting.

She'd watched Zinc remove three business cards from his wallet and jot a note on the back of one. When he distributed his cards, Scarlett knew the assignation went to Jessica. Once again, it was easy work to slip the hypodermic needle with its loose cap into the bag on the back of Jessica's chair. The next time the redhead plunged her hand into that bag, she spiked her palm on the needle and was poisoned.

With Nick's supposed killer dead, Zinc had lowered his guard. He was currently stretched out on the bed in the other room, about to fall prey to the same trap that had caught Nick.

Scarlett shivered.

Killing men with an ice pick was an orgasmic experience. It was like fucking them with a steel cock and watching them die in your arms. But the device Mephisto had created was even better.

His inspiration for the *vagina dentata*, or "toothed vagina," was the anti-rape condom. Inserted with an applicator, like a tampon, it was a latex sheath embedded with rows of sharp barbs. When a rapist stuck in his penis, he got a painful surprise. And because the barbs were like fishhooks, the device pulled out with him and could only be removed by a doctor.

In Mephisto's version, the barbs inside an impenetrable sheath were brittle needles filled with curare that snapped off as the penis slipped in. The barbs were made of a compound that dissolved after half an hour, leaving no trace but tiny pinpricks in the folds of the non-erect penis. By gilding Nick, Mephisto and Scarlett had lacquered over the holes. It would take one hell of a forensic scientist to figure out the means of death. Macbeth and the Russian were both dead. So that was that.

Now, having carefully inserted a second poisoned condom, Scarlett opened the door.

Want to play motorboat, Hake? she thought.

———•◆•———

"My God," said Zinc. "You have a stunning figure."

"Would you believe I used to be a showgirl in Vegas?"

"What brought you to Whistler?"

"It's a long story," Scarlett said, climbing onto the bed. "Lie back and let me do all the work."

"Actually, my energy is coming back," said Zinc.

"So I see," said Scarlett. "That's what I call a second wind. If you had your shorts on, the sail would billow." She grabbed hold of his cock. "Let's skip foreplay. I want you *now!*"

Zinc was up for that. Tension still rippled his body from the action at Gill's chalet, and he could think of no better way to work it out than to enjoy a roll in the hay with this woman.

Karen had a condom in her other hand. She tore the square packet open with her teeth, removed the ultra-thin sheath, and rolled it down his penis. Then she swung a long leg over his hips and straddled his groin.

From the smile she flashed, you'd think she was Eve handing Adam that apple. Gripping the snake in her palm, she poised his cock under her vagina.

"That condom looks *awfully* thin," Zinc said, running his eyes down her body to her crotch. "Aren't you afraid it will break?"

"Don't worry. There's backup. I have a diaphragm."

Die ...

Ah!

Frame ...

Holy shit!

That's what Joe had been trying to say through his pain and his accent. What he and DeClercq had thought was a gasp was actually a syllable. What Joe was trying to blurt out was "Diaphragm!" Whatever had killed Nick was inside his killer's vagina!

What banged these thoughts together like boxcars in a shunting yard was the mark Zinc saw on the inside of Karen's thigh. Nobody her age had a vaccination scar.

Not unless they'd been immunized by Mephisto!

Zinc grabbed Karen by the waist to stop her from sinking his cock into her body.

Reacting, Scarlett punched the cop in the nose, drawing blood. She never let go of his penis.

The Mountie's palms flew wide from her waist, seeming to release her so she was free to plunge, before slamming together like cymbals on both sides of her head.

Scarlett screamed like a banshee as her eardrums blew, baring her teeth in a twisted snarl that brought to mind every female monster buried in the male psyche: Lamia, vampire, succubus, fury, harpy, Gorgon, and the like.

She released his cock …

Grabbed it again …

And this time, sank in her claws.

His left hand grabbed the back of Karen's skull, locking it in his grip. Then he slammed his right palm against her chin with every fiber of his strength. Her spine didn't stand a chance. Scarlett's neck snapped like a breadstick as Zinc hurled her out of bed.

———•·•———

At dawn next morning, the snow clouds over Whistler parted, allowing three helicopters the visibility to land. They set down on the scattered fields, just as the chief had planned.

The two cops who'd won the lottery to transport Mephisto hauled him out in the straitjacket and leg shackles. As they led him toward the chopper, both thought he was clenching his teeth in anger. What they didn't know was that one of his molars hid a spring-driven GPS bug. When his jaw was slack—as it was when the Mounties had searched his body with the scanner—it emitted no radio signals. Once he was in the trunk he'd bitten down, activating the tracker so Stopwatch could follow.

Because the *über*-mercenary knew which shell hid the pea, he'd had time to crawl into range with his high-powered sniper's rifle. The whirlybird in the crosshairs was a Eurocopter. Stopwatch could fly it. As a planner who allowed for all that might go wrong, Mephisto had mapped out an intricate escape plan.

Just in case ...

The door to the chopper opened. Its solitary occupant stuck out his head. Having a single pilot was part of the low-key blind.

The telescopic sight zeroed in on the pilot's bare head.

Stopwatch pulled the trigger.

Bam!

Bam!

Bam!

AUTHOR'S NOTE

This is a work of fiction. The plot and the characters are a product of the author's imagination. Where real persons, places, incidents, institutions, and such are incorporated to create the illusion of authenticity, they are used fictitiously. Inspiration was drawn from the following non-fiction sources:

Beaudry, Michel. *Whistler: Against All Odds*. Boulder, Colorado: Mountain Sports Press, 2002.

Browne, Douglas G., and Tom Tullett. *Bernard Spilsbury: His Life and Cases*. New York: Dorset, 1989.

Davis, Wade. *The Lost Amazon: The Photographic Journey of Richard Evans Schultes*. Vancouver: Douglas and McIntyre, 2004.

Descola, Philippe. *The Spears of Twilight: Life and Death in the Amazon Jungle*. Translated by Janet Lloyd. New York: The New Press, 1996.

Evans, Colin. *The Father of Forensics: How Sir Bernard Spilsbury Invented Modern CSI*. London: Icon, 2009.

Fawcett, Percy Harrison. *Expedition Fawcett*. London: Phoenix Press, 2001.

Gaute, J. H. H., and Robin Odell. *The New Murderer's Who's Who*. London: Harrap, 1996.

Grann, David. *The Lost City of Z: A Tale of Deadly Obsession in the Amazon*. New York: Doubleday, 2009.

Harner, Michael J. *The Jivaro: People of the Sacred Waterfalls*. Berkeley, California: University of California Press, 1984.

Hemming, John. *The Search for El Dorado*. London: Michael Joseph, 1978.

Hitching, Francis. *The World Atlas of Mysteries*. London: Pan, 1978.

Lloyd, Tanya. *Whistler*. Vancouver: Whitecap Books, 1998.

Naipaul, V. S. *The Loss of El Dorado: A Colonial History*. New York: Random House, 2003.

Owen, David. *Hidden Evidence: Forty True Crimes and How Forensic Science Helped Solve Them*. Willowdale, Ontario: Firefly, 2000.

Silverberg, Robert. *The Golden Dream: Seekers of El Dorado*. Athens, Ohio: Ohio University Press, 1996.

Time-Life Books. *The Search for El Dorado*. Alexandria, Virginia: Time-Life Books, 1994.

Up de Graff, Fritz W. *Head Hunters of the Amazon: Seven Years of Exploration and Adventure*. New York: Garden City, 1925.